THE FIGHT IN THE DOG

Book Nine of Underdogs

Geonn Cannon

Supposed Crimes LLC • Matthews, North Carolina

Published in the United States.

ISBN: 978-1-952150-06-7

www.supposedcrimes.com

This book is typeset in Goudy Old Style.

PROLOGUE

ARIADNE WILLOW'S nature as a *canidae* meant she was more comfortable naked than clothed. She generally preferred blank tees under button-down shirts, hoodies, jeans, the type of clothes that could easily be pulled off and discarded if a transformation became necessary. Today was an aberration. Today, the collar of her blouse kept threatening to choke her, so she constantly brought her hand up to tug on it only to remember she was wearing a tie. Every time she shrugged in an effort to loosen the tension in her shoulders, she felt the suspenders pulling her down.

"Stop fidgeting."

Ari glared at the open door of her office. "You can't even see me," she called back.

"I can hear you fidgeting," Dale replied, still out of sight at her own desk. "Just relax."

"You're not the one wearing a tie."

"You wear that leather collar every day, and suddenly a tie is too much?"

Ari grunted. "It's different."

Dale sighed. "Well, no one told you to wear a tie."

Ari pushed back from her desk and got up. She waited until she was at the door before she responded. "I just want to make sure

I do this right. I've never done this sort of thing before. I want to take it seriously."

"Sure. I get it." Dale looked Ari up and down. "Would it help with your anxiety if I said you look really sexy in that get-up?"

"Yeah?" Ari looked down at herself. The tie was black, and the shirt was a light brown. Not too Businesswoman Chic, but still professional. She supposed the suspenders did look good... even if she didn't like the constant feeling that she was wearing a backpack.

Dale turned to face her fully. "Oh yeah. Slick your hair back and you'd look like the bad guy in an eighties movie."

"Is that a good thing?"

"Well." She tilted her head to the side, narrowing her eyes. "It's not a *bad* thing."

Ari grinned, once again reminded of how lucky she was to have Dale in her life. They went through a small rough patch after Dale freed herself from being brainwashed by a book of anti-*canidae* essays. She felt like she was herself again and was horrified by the things she'd said while under the book's influence, but she confided to Ari that she was worried there might be some hidden subconscious triggers waiting for her to trip over them when she let her guard down. So she stayed with Diana and Lucy for a few weeks just to err on the side of caution.

They talked on the phone, continued working together, and met up for dinners, so Ari never actually believed they might lose what they'd had, but the separation had made her much more aware of just how precious the relationship was.

"You know~"

Ari was interrupted by a knock on the door. She straightened her posture, smoothed down her tie, and reached up to tug on the collar of her shirt.

"Stop it," Dale said under her breath. Louder, she said, "Come on in!"

The door opened, and Shae Segura stepped into the office. Dale started to greet her but, instead, laughed and put a hand over her mouth as she waved the other in apology.

Ari's former cellmate froze. "Uh. Sorry..."

"No, no, I'm sorry," Dale said. "I'm not laughing at you. You look amazing."

Segura reached up and tugged at the knot in her tie. "Yeah... Melissa's idea. Her clothes, too. She said if I was going on a job interview, I needed to dress appropriately. Even if it was with a friend. I wanted to be sure I did it right, so..." She finally seemed to notice Ari was also dressed up. Her posture became a little more relaxed. "Looks like we had the same idea."

"I've never interviewed anyone for a job before." Ari cleared her throat. "For the record, after today, no ties required for the job."

"Music to my ears," Segura said.

Ari gestured into the office. "Well, let's... let's, um, get this started."

Segura smiled at Dale as she walked past the desk. "Good seeing you, D."

"You too," Dale said. "Sorry for laughing."

The first time they met, at a dinner to celebrate Segura being released from prison, Dale immediately stood up and wrapped Segura in a tight hug. "I respect if you're not a hugger," Dale had said without letting her go, "but you kept Ari alive in jail. You watched over her when I couldn't. You saved her. So for that, you get one hug. That's just the way it is." Segura had accepted that argument, and the hug, and the two had become fast friends.

Segura followed Ari into the office and shut the door. She took a moment to look around the room before she sat down.

"So this is where you do all your detective stuff."

"Most of it," Ari said. "I get out on the street from time to time, of course. That's going to be part of your responsibilities. Sitting around, watching cars and windows, waiting outside of people's work. The boring stuff I can't be bothered to do."

Segura laughed. "I'll be happy to be bored as long as I'm outside getting some fresh air."

"Are you doing okay since getting out?"

"Yeah. It's weird, but a good weird. Luckily I have Melissa to help me."

Ari had fond memories of Melissa Vogel, Segura's girlfriend and a guard at the prison where they'd shared a cell. At first she'd been skeptical about the power dynamic of a guard and an inmate engaging in a physical relationship, but she was eventually won over by how much they clearly cared for each other. Melissa offered a place to stay when Segura was released before she'd worked up the courage to ask.

As for their interview, part of Segura's parole required gainful employment. Working for a private investigator would be a little tricky since she was supposed to avoid criminals and illegal activity, but Ari felt like she could assign her to things that kept her from crossing the line. If a case required trailing a criminal, Segura could stay at the office doing paperwork.

"I know you need a certain number of hours, so we'll make sure you get what you need to make your parole officer happy. Even if it's just coming in here to dust or wash the windows."

"Hell, you need someone to pick up your laundry, I'm here for you."

Ari snapped her fingers and wrote down a reminder. "Actually, that's not a bad idea. We don't have the time to maintain my stashes around the city or find places to leave new ones. That could fill up a few hours if we don't have anything else for you to do."

"Stashes?"

"Bags of stuff hidden around Seattle. Clothes, money, shoes. Things that will come in handy if the wolf takes me out at night and leaves me naked in the middle of a park."

Segura said, "Ah, okay. Well, sure. I'll bury you some treasures."

"Excellent. You and Dale already talked about the salary, right? We can't offer you a whole lot..."

"Hey, like I said. Just happy to be here, and happy to keep my parole officer happy. Hopefully I won't be your problem for very long. I'm going to be looking for something more permanent when I'm not on the clock."

Ari nodded. "Well, as long as it takes, we'll be happy to have you." She stood up and extended her hand across the desk. "It's probably not the most professional job interview, but I think it's good enough. We're pretty casual here."

Segura shook her hand. "So I'm hired?"

"You're hired," Ari said with a smile. "Welcome to Bitches Investigations."

CHAPTER ONE

ARI WAS one strike away from giving up on their latest potential client. Strike one was being forced to dress up again. She wore a white turtleneck and tan slacks, her hair pinned up in a style that made her feel like a schoolmarm, and her feet were constricted inside a pair of flats. The turtleneck spared her the indignity of a tie, but now she felt like she was being choked by a pillow. She wasn't fidgeting, though. She took a little bit of pride in that. She did like that she was able to stand in the lobby of this building with her head held high and her shoulders back, looking like someone who belonged.

Strike two was where the meeting was taking place: a law firm. Meeting with lawyers meant money was involved, and she hated clients with money. Rich meant entitled. The Burroughs family turned out nice enough. But in general, she really hated dealing with rich people. She wanted to be the defender of the little guy, not a tool used by the wealthiest people in the city.

"We take plenty of little-guy cases," Dale told her after scheduling the meeting. "And we are very lax about making them pay the full amount when the case is resolved."

"Right," Ari said. "But~"

"And Seattle is a rich city. And rich people have a lot of problems."

Ari nodded. "I know. Believe me, I–"

"Plus we just took on a new employee, and we're going to need to keep the coffers full if we want to pay her. Otherwise her parole officer might not consider this a real job."

Ari glared at her. "Nobody likes you when you're like this."

Dale only smiled and added the meeting to the schedule.

So she was at the meeting, in a law firm. She was dressed nicely. But if there was a third strike between now and when she reached the conference room, she was ready to walk away with no regrets.

She signed in at the desk and received a visitor pass which would allow her onto the elevator. She rode to the fifth floor, to the offices of Abraham Daggett and Ryman, where a receptionist pointed her to a conference room at the end of the hall. The room was empty when she arrived but there was a plate of ube crinkle cookies on the table. Ari picked up one of the peculiar purple cookies and took a bite as she walked to the window. The taste alone was almost enough to make her remove one of the strikes, and it was all she could do not to stuff her pockets with the rest of the plate.

"Rich people and lawyers," she muttered as a reminder to herself. "Never a good combo."

"The cookies are good, though."

She turned and saw a woman standing in the doorway, smiling shyly. "Sorry. Didn't mean to eavesdrop." She cupped a hand by her mouth. "I tend to agree with you on the sentiment, by the way."

Ari said, "Well, I agree with you about the cookies. So we're off to a good start."

The woman smiled. It lit up her entire face, narrowing her eyes and revealing deep dimples. She was tall, lanky without being awkward, redheaded, and dressed just casually enough that Ari knew she wasn't a lawyer. Her voice had a seductive rasp to it, making her seem older than she was. When she stepped forward, she rolled her shoulders in a manner so casual that it told Ari she was the sort of person who could feel at home no matter where she was.

Ari finished the cookie and wiped her hand on her hip before extending it to the other woman. "I'm Ariadne Willow."

"Yes, I assumed." She took Ari's hand, giving it a solid squeeze before letting go. "I apologize for having the meeting here, but it was the best choice among limited options. I promise, though, it's just going to be you and me, no lawyers. I just wanted neutral ground to have our first meeting before I decided if I can trust you."

"I understand," Ari said as they moved to sit at the table.

Ari chose a seat at random, and the woman started to sit next to her before stretching out to pull the plate of cookies closer. She smiled and gave Ari a conspiratorial wink.

"They put them out, right? Might as well."

"If only there was milk."

The woman said, "The cookies are free. You have to pay for the milk. That's how they get you."

"Lawyers, am I right?"

The woman laughed and took a bite of her cookie. Ari mentally groaned and took off one of the strikes. She liked this woman, even if she did turn out to be rich.

"So," the woman said after she finished chewing, "my name is Dierdre Macrae. But that's not the name most people know me by."

"Are you Banksy?"

Dierdre laughed, a short and sharp sound. "No! God. That would be amazing. No." She turned her right wrist over and unsnapped the leather band encircling it. She stretched her arm across the table so Ari could see the tattoo inked just below the heel of her palm. It was a large A drawn inside the curve of an S. The letters were an elegantly carved monogram, and vaguely familiar to Ari.

"A-S?" she guessed. She finally realized where she'd seen the logo before. "Oh, S-A? Like..."

Her voice caught in her throat and she looked at Dierdre again. Her blue eyes were sparkling, and she was holding back a laugh.

"No."

"What?" Dierdre said, her withheld laughter only making her voice deeper and rougher. Ari immediately knew what that voice would sound like with backup singers and musical accompaniment. She also knew without a doubt the identity of the woman sitting across from her, but she couldn't bring herself to say it out loud in case she was wrong. She would look so stupid if she was wrong. But if she was right...

"You're Saint Artemis."

Dierdre finally let out her laughter. She withdrew her hand, replaced the leather strap, and nodded.

"Guilty as charged."

Ari fell back in her chair and stared. Saint Artemis was a pop star and performance artist. She never appeared out of costume, never allowed photographs of her face without a mask or enough makeup to render her unrecognizable. Television interviews were done through proxies; she famously once held a press conference where every answer came from a puppet held by one of her assistants. It was rumored that only a handful of people had ever actually heard her speak in person, not counting concerts, and the internet was full of conspiracies about her true identity and why it was such a closely-guarded secret.

"Wow. I really thought you were Dash Warren. Faked her death, started a new career without all the baggage..."

"That is such a popular theory," Dierdre sighed. "I take it as a huge compliment if people think I sound like her. But she would have to be in her sixties if she was really still alive now."

"With the amount of makeup and costumes you wear on-stage, you can understand why people might be confused."

Dierdre shrugged and nodded. "Sure. Sure."

"How do you even know who I am?"

"Tyler Dubov and I have a mutual friend. When I asked about hiring a private investigator, he said Dubov sang your praises to anyone who would listen. He said you found out he was bisexual and you kept it a secret. I felt that meant I could trust you with mine."

"Absolutely," Ari said. "There are two people I work with, but we don't have to tell them who you really are if it doesn't have bearing on the case."

Dierdre sighed heavily and rolled her eyes. "Oh, it has a bearing on the case. I wouldn't mind you telling them anyway, as long as you trust them."

"With my life," Ari said without hesitation.

"Okay, then."

She folded her hands on the table in front of her and stared at her fingers. Ari recognized the posture of someone trying to figure out how to put a difficult thought into words, so she took another cookie and waited.

"I've been getting threatening messages."

"Death threats?"

Dierdre wrinkled her nose. "I hate that phrase. My manager

calls them that, but I don't think they're as bad as that. It's not like 'I'm going to cut your head off' or that sort of thing. The last few weeks, I've gotten quite a few messages in my private email that my manager thinks are from the same person." She took her phone from her pocket, poked the screen, and slid it across the table to Ari. "That's the latest one."

Ari picked up the phone. "U CAN WEAR ALL THE MASKS U WANT, U NO WHAT U REALLY R. WHO U REALLY R. U CAN'T HIDE FROM URSELF OR N-E-1 ELSE." She raised an eyebrow and handed the phone back. "Seems pretty threatening to me."

"Yeah, but they're not saying they'll kill me."

"Thin line."

Dierdre shrugged and turned her phone face-down on the table. "Stuff like this comes in all the time. Twitter, mostly. I have people who go through and block or report the worst ones before I see them. But about a month ago, these messages are coming to my personal email account, which no one but my closest friends and family should have. Even then I was willing to just ignore it as spam because it was just emails, you know?"

Ari said, "So what made you decide it was worth coming to me?"

"Last week, a note was left in the mailbox at the place I'm staying while I'm in Seattle. An actual note, in the real mailbox. That's scary enough, but there was no postmark, which meant it was hand-delivered. After that, I couldn't really talk my manager out of calling in extra help. I didn't really want to take her out of it, to be honest. That was really frightening."

"You want me to find out who is sending them?"

"Partially. But my manager wants me to hire security. I don't want five giant ex-football players surrounding me everywhere I go. I don't want to hide behind a bunch of guys, no matter what they look like. Dubov told me you kicked a lot of ass back when the two of you knew each other. So I thought in addition to being trustworthy, maybe you'd be able to hold your own as my bodyguard."

Ari said, "Your bodyguard."

"I know it's asking a lot. You'd have to follow me wherever I go, keep an eye out for threats. It would take up a ton of your time. You'd be paid appropriately, I promise. With hazard pay if anyone, you know, actually tries to hurt me."

"Sure," Ari said.

Dierdre started to say something, stopped herself, and looked down at her hands. "The truth is, I'm not scared. Yet. Right now it's a nuisance. I've trained myself to ignore the worst of the worst, you know, so it's all just white noise. But if more stuff shows up at my house, I'm going to get scared. And if I have a whole team of bodyguards looming over me every waking hour, that's going to make me scared, too. But one woman, who sounds pretty awesome from everything I've heard... I think I can handle that. I think that would keep me feeling safe."

Ari looked down at the table as she considered it. She wanted to help the little guy, not the people who could just throw money at any problem they might have. But having money didn't always mean someone was invulnerable. Saint Artemis had enough money to borrow a law firm's conference room for a private meeting. She could probably have rented out an entire office if she'd wanted to.

Dierdre Macrae was a different story. She risked exposure of her identity and the loss of a carefully-cultivated privacy. She was taking a risk just by showing up at this meeting. If Dierdre wasn't the sort of person Ari wanted as a client, who was?

"I think we can help you."

CHAPTER TWO

"YOU'RE MY *hope, you're my heart-ache*," Saint Artemis sang against a driving backbeat. "*You're my grail, and my biggest mis-take.*"

The video on YouTube wasn't the best quality, but whoever was recording held the camera steady enough for Ari to get a good idea of how the concert was staged. Saint Artemis - Ari couldn't bring herself to think of the performer as Dierdre - marched from one side of the stage to the other as she sang. She also occasionally detoured down a long catwalk which led her out into the audience, prompting hands to rise out of the darkness for her to brush their palms with her fingers. She played guitar on some songs, and a keyboard on others, but usually relied on the seven or eight backing members of her band to provide the music.

For this concert, she wore a low-cut white jumpsuit revealing her cleavage and a good portion of her stomach. Every inch of exposed skin was painted a pearlescent white that sparkled when the lights hit her at the right angle. Her hair was also colored white and slicked back against her skull. Her eyes were concealed by a pair of goggles, but Ari could tell it was the same woman she'd met that afternoon. She'd actually confirmed it with the first video she watched, an official and slickly-produced music video where she was also disguised, but the shape of her face and the sound of her voice fit too well for there to be any doubt in Ari's mind.

Dale came into the office. In one hand, she held Ari's iPod. In the other, she had one of the ube cookies Dierdre had insisted Ari take with her when the meeting adjourned. Ari moved the headphones down around her neck and took the phone.

"All of her albums are on there now."

"Thanks. The cookies are great, right?"

Dale sat down and gave an indifferent shrug. "Not quite good enough for me to forgive the fact you met a huge megastar and didn't get her autograph for me..."

"I stopped at the store and got you milk for them."

Dale stared at her, put her feet up on the desk, and took another bite.

"I actually went to two stores because the first one didn't have almond milk." When Dale continued to stare, Ari hung her head and began to softly whimper.

"Oh, no," Dale said. "You can't do pitiful puppy noises when you're an actual puppy. That's not fair."

Ari widened her eyes and pushed her bottom lip out.

"You don't play fair," Dale said. "Okay. Fine. You're forgiven."

Ari grinned and sat up straighter. "What did you find out about Saint Artemis while you were loading me up?"

"Pretty much just what's on her website. She started out in clubs, always with her face obscured, never giving her real name. She got a reputation and started getting invited to perform at burlesque clubs, which introduced her to people in the music industry..."

"Wait, how did she do all of this with only a handful of people knowing her real identity?"

"I assume some of them figured it out or had to be told," Dale said. "She had a manager even back then, but I'm sure plenty of mucky-mucks demanded an introduction. But they're apparently willing to keep the secret. The mystery probably helps record sales. Her first album came out six years ago, and she's never shown a hint of revealing herself. Everyone has a conspiracy theory about who she really is, how much of her backstory is real, if she's a celebrity in disguise..."

"The Dash Warren theory."

Dale nodded. "Anything that gets buzz going is probably considered a good thing in that industry. Everyone loves a gimmick."

Ari looked at the computer screen, where pyrotechnics had gone off behind Saint Artemis and turned her into a dark silhouette. She held her arms out to either side and spun in a circle while her band continued to play. She could hear the tinny reverb of the music through the speakers around her neck.

"Someone who knows the secret wants to hurt her. Either someone she told at the beginning of her career or someone who has figured it out since then."

"I put the list she gave you on the computer. Segura and I will start tracking them down this afternoon. Hopefully only one or two will be here in Seattle."

"That would certainly make our job easier."

The list she'd given Dale was the name and contact information of everyone who knew Saint Artemis was actually Dierdre Macrae. It was mostly managers, handlers, wardrobe and makeup people, band members. The list was much smaller than Ari would have guessed, but it was still a lot of potential suspects. And that was assuming the stalker wasn't someone who had just connected the dots.

"While we're doing that, what exactly is your job going to be?"

"Basically, I'm going to be a shadow." Ari picked up the schedule Dierdre had given her. "She's staying here for two months preparing for a trio of shows at the Callahan Concert Hall. When she isn't prepping or rehearsing for the shows, she's going to be working on a new album. So I'll be hanging out with her while she's at home, working at a home studio, and following her around the venue to make sure no one is lurking in the dressing room."

"What if the person doesn't show their face before she leaves town?"

Ari said, "Then I think the threat goes away. The alarming notes only started arriving when she got to Seattle. The note being hand-delivered implies it's a local. Whoever is sending them is going to strike when she's here."

Dale shrugged. "Makes sense. I do like the idea of having Segura lending a hand. And if you're going to be away more than usual, it'll be nice to have company around the office."

"No gossiping about the boss."

"You are literally the only thing we're going to be talking about. Non-stop." She got up and went back to her desk. "All your juiciest secrets laid bare."

Ari called after her, "You better have saved me some of those cookies."

"They're long-gone, puppy," Dale said.

Ari pouted and put her headphones back on, rewinding the video back to the point where she'd stopped paying attention.

Dale actually did put aside a few cookies for Ari, wrapping the plate in cellophane and putting them in the minifridge behind her desk. She felt like faking anger and play-fighting was the right response to the situation. It was how she would have reacted if things were normal. Scratch that. Things *were* normal, and she wanted to keep it that way. Her instinct was to let Ari have all the cookies. She wanted to wake up early to make her breakfast, and rub her feet, and whatever other act of contrition she could think of.

It was all because of Isaac Hayden and that damn book. She couldn't stop thinking about what she'd done, the things she'd said, what she'd almost become. She remembered everything. Not with the haze of a drunk waking up after a blackout, but with perfect clarity. She heard herself calling Ari a mutt. She remembered her skin crawling at the thought of touching or being touched by "an animal."

She'd spent the weeks at Lucy and Diana's coming to terms with what happened. Yes, everyone was in agreement that the book was to blame. And yes, when the moment of truth arrived, Dale's true nature won out and she snapped back to herself. But those feelings had to come from somewhere, right? She knew that during the early days of their relationship, a part of her was anxious about the fact Ari was technically a different species.

Of course in the years since, she'd come to the conclusion that Ari was still human, no matter what blood she might have. But what if there was a part of her, a small subconscious part, that still had an issue? Maybe it was a primal remnant that feared anything different, a part of her lizard brain recoiling from the unfamiliar. She was herself again, but what if that little seed was just waiting to be triggered in a year or a decade? What if the next time, she wasn't able to stop herself?

She wiped a hand over her face and decided to stop thinking about it. Things were fine for the time being. She wasn't going to pick at a scab that was almost healed. Work was the answer. Settling the case would help focus her mind. She pulled her keyboard closer and focused on the easier mystery.

A storm rolled in late that afternoon, darkening the sky so quickly that Dale twisted in her seat to look outside just as thick raindrops began splattering against the window. Ari came out of her office and watched as the random drops turned into a full downpour. "Damn it," she said, hands on her hips. "I was hoping to do a really long run tonight. I'm going to be on-call with Dierdre for the next few weeks so I don't know when I'll be able to get out again."

"This is Seattle," Dale pointed out. "You've gone running in the rain lots of times."

"That doesn't mean I enjoy it. And at some point, I'm going to transform back into a naked human lady, and I'll have to deal with one of my stashes to find clothes and money to call you..." She sighed. "Oh well. Hopefully there will be a few days off from the case."

Dale shook her head. "Do you really think the wolf will be satisfied with that?"

"She's going to have to be."

"What if I go on the run with you?"

"What if... what?"

Dale shrugged. "You transform and head out, I wait for you at a prearranged destination. That way, when you change back, you don't have to worry about finding a stash or calling me for a ride."

Ari considered the offer. "I can't promise the wolf will stick to a particular route or that she'll end the run where we decide."

"Then I follow you. She usually takes you somewhere near a stash, so if I lose track of you at least I'll have some idea of where you're going." She could see Ari was close to accepting the offer, so she redoubled her efforts. "It's just one night. You need to get it out of your system before you take on this big job. I'm happy to do it. I'm always happy to help with your runs."

Ari chewed her bottom lip and stared at Dale, then came closer and lowered her voice. "Dale, if you're doing this as some kind of penance for what happened with the book..."

"Maybe I am," Dale said. "After everything I put you through~"

"You didn't put me through anything. Honestly, Dale. It's like if you got sick and I took care of you. You don't owe me anything for that."

"But it's not the same. When I get the flu, I don't yell slurs at you and think horrible thoughts about you and your family." She stood up and came around the desk. She cupped Ari's face in her hands and kissed her. "Let me do this, puppy. I know it's not something I have to do in order to win back your trust, but it's something I want to do to prove to myself that I'm... myself again."

Ari nodded and put her hands on Dale's wrists. "Okay. But after this, we're back to normal. No more putting yourself out just because you feel guilty."

"Deal. For the record, I'm not putting myself out. If what you did was like taking care of me when I'm sick, then this is just... I don't know, giving you a ride to the airport. It's just something I do for you."

"Okay." She reached for Dale's hand. "We also need to start thinking about that proposal we've been neglecting."

Dale smiled and rested her head against Ari's. "I haven't forgotten. We're going to figure something out. And it's going to be perfect."

"I have no doubt."

They kissed again before Ari stepped back. "I'll wrap things up in there and we can head out for dinner. It's your choice tonight."

"Mean Sandwich?"

Ari grunted from the other room. "I don't want to go all the way out to Ballard. Veto."

"Katsu Burger?"

"Now you're talking."

Dale went back to her computer to shut everything down for the night, then paused. There was something else she could do, something very important and symbolic, not to mention necessary. She chewed her lip and narrowed her eyes, briefly trying to talk herself out of it because once she put things in motion, there would be no easy retreat. After a moment she went to her email and typed out a message.

Ari came out of the office and turned off the light just as Dale hit send. "You ready?" Ari asked, tugging on her jacket.

"Ready." Dale shut off the computer and got up to join Ari. She didn't know if what she'd done was a great idea or a disaster waiting to happen. The only thing she knew for sure was that she wasn't going to get the wasabi mayo on her burger. Everything else would sort itself out in due time.

CHAPTER THREE

THEY STOPPED at the apartment after dinner so Ari could transform without being seen. Dale went to get some towels for the ride home and went back into the living room in time to see the end of Ari's change. She watched the skin of her partner's back ripple and widen as her ribs reshaped, heard the pop as her shoulders repositioned themselves. Ari hung her head and rocked it back and forth, her quiet grunting turning into breathy huffs. Her hands, now paws, drummed on the carpet before she arched her back and stood up straight. She looked at the door, then swung her head around to see Dale.

"Hey there, puppy." She never knew how much of Ari's human side lingered when she let the wolf take control. Sometimes it was like Ariadne Willow had just slipped into a fur coat to run around the woods. Other times, she might as well have been any wolf in the wild. Despite that, the wolf always seemed to know who Dale was.

She approached cautiously and crouched down. She looked into the wolf's eyes. "Ari? Who's running the show in there...?" The wolf only stared. "Okay. Just in case you went all-animal, you know the plan, right? You're going to run like normal, but I'm going to follow you. That way I can pick her up when the run is finished."

The wolf leaned in and licked Dale's face. Dale squeezed her eyes shut and rubbed the scruff of Ari's neck.

"I'll take that as an 'I understand, let's get this show on the road' lick."

She stood and went to the door. The wolf hesitated when she saw the rain but didn't require much prodding to run out into it. Dale looked back when she reached the car. She expected the wolf to still be in the yard, but she was nowhere to be seen. She tossed the towels onto the passenger seat and pulled out of the driveway. At the first stop sign she squinted through the downpour until she spotted a flash of movement on the next street over. The wolf burst out of a hedge, cut north, and then weaved into the shadow next to a house.

"There you are," Dale muttered as she turned left to begin her pursuit.

The rain didn't let up, and the wolf didn't make it easy for her. Dale pulled over twice and leaned over the steering wheel to scan the area for signs of Ari, only moving forward thanks to fleeting glimpses of a tail or the flicker as Ari passed in front of landscape lighting. Eventually the wolf got enough of a lead that Dale knew she wasn't going to catch up. She pulled into a parking lot and opened a map on her phone.

Even when the wolf seemed to be completely in control, Dale knew that wasn't the case. The soul and mind was always Ari's, and she always worked toward her best interest. That meant that the wolf didn't transform back into a human until it was near a stash site. Dale chewed her bottom lip as she examined the route she'd already taken. Pretty much a straight shot north with only a few westerly deviations.

Occasionally the wolf ran to the outskirts of the city, but she didn't think that would be the case in the rain. Ari had three stashes nearby: Alder Creek, Volunteer, and Interlaken. If she was aiming for Volunteer, she would have been angling east. Interlaken would have been a straight northerly line. West meant Alder Creek. Dale put her phone away and drove to the park, finding a spot near where the stash was hidden. She parked in front of a large brown building with the headlights aimed into the wilderness.

If she guessed wrong, Ari could find a phone and call her for a pick-up from wherever she was. Ten minutes passed. She worried about someone in the building seeing her, calling the cops, a loitering charge... but she didn't want to drive aimlessly around the city like a Lyft waiting for a customer. She drummed her hands on the steering wheel and looked out the rain-streaked windows. Ten minutes turned into half an hour.

At forty-five minutes, she was starting to wonder if she'd misjudged the wolf's stamina. Maybe she'd gone past Interlaken to Roanoke. Did they still have a stash in Roanoke? Maybe the wolf had misunderstood the situation and circled back, taken herself home. Surely Ari would call her if that happened. Maybe the wolf had—

She was mid-speculation when she spotted movement in the headlight beams. The wolf emerged from the undergrowth and lifted her head, staring at the car. Dale flashed the lights on and off, grinning at her success. The wolf faced her fully and began walking toward her. She was mid-step when she began to change. Her gait became different, her paws pushing her upright as they reformed into hands. Fur receded to reveal pale skin that was immediately soaked by the downpour. One shoulder jerked, then the other, and Ari pushed her hair out of her now-human face. She swayed a little on unsteady legs, but she was smiling even as she blinked the rain out of her eyes.

Dale's smile had faded as she watched. When they were just friends, and at the beginning of their relationship, Dale had gone out of her way to avoid witnessing the transformations. That was back when they caused Ari immeasurable pain, so that was one reason she didn't want to see it, but she also had to admit she thought it was wrong and unnatural. It didn't take long before she was more comfortable with seeing it, before it became as natural as seeing someone change clothes. But seeing it like this, like some kind of fairy tale magic caught by the lights, in the rain...

Ari opened the passenger side door and threw herself into the car. One towel was already spread across the seat, and Ari retrieved the other and began wiping off her face.

"The wolf took it as a challenge." Her voice was muffled by the thick terrycloth. "She thought you wanted to chase me, so she was hiding." She laughed and dried her hair, then dropped the towel to look at Dale. She smiled, looking almost as giddy as she sounded. "But you found me. Just like you always do."

Dale tried to think of something to say. Instead, she cupped the back of Ari's head and pulled her forward. Ari was obviously surprised by the kiss but welcomed it eagerly, gripping a handful of Dale's shirt to keep her from pulling away. Dale heard the growl in

Ari's moan and felt her body's reaction to it. She broke the kiss and moved her lips to Ari's neck to suck a spot just above the leather strap of her collar. Ari squirmed into a better position on the seat, one hand sliding down to cup Dale's breast through her shirt while the other squeezed her thigh.

"Take me home," Ari muttered against Dale's cheek.

"No..."

"No?"

"Here." Dale unfastened her seatbelt and crossed over onto Ari's lap.

Ari settled her hands on Dale's hips. She barely had time to say, "Oh, okay," before Dale's lips were on hers again. Ari's skin was slick under Dale's fingers and her muscles were still twitching slightly from the transformation. Dale pressed down harder when she felt those tremors, remembering those long-ago days when a run would be followed by a completely platonic massage. All those days and nights rubbing out the tension in Ari's weary muscles... now she cupped Ari's small breasts and ran her thumbs over the nipples. They were already hard from the cold rain, but she felt them grow harder at her touch.

She was so distracted by her own explorations and ruminations that she barely noticed Ari had unbuttoned her shirt until she felt kisses on her chest. She leaned back and then gasped as Ari's tongue moved across her bra. She moved her hands up into Ari's hair and held tight as Ari's licking turned into gentle bites. Ari brushed the back of her hand over Dale's stomach down to the waistband of her pants.

"Couldn't have worn a skirt?" Ari whispered.

"Didn't plan this," Dale said. "Sorry."

"Don't be. That makes it better."

Dale smiled and reached down to help Ari with the belt. When it came free, she wrapped her arm around Ari's shoulders and arched her back, pressing into Ari. Ari rested her cheek against Dale's chest and eased one hand into her pants, repositioning until Dale gasped and tensed. She flattened her hand against the back of Ari's neck and closed her eyes, rolling her hips. She pressed her knees into the seat. Ari dragged her tongue from the lace of Dale's bra up to her throat, where she began to suck and lick gently. Dale turned her head and smelled Ari's hair. It smelled like her, but also of earth and ozone from the rain.

"I love you, Ariadne," she whispered.

Ari grunted and bit Dale's earlobe. "When you say my name..."

"Ariadne," Dale said again, and she felt Ari shiver.

"I'm going to make you come," Ari said, "and then I'm going to do it again. But I'm going to torture you first. Make you wait..."

"No," Dale whined.

"I'm going to make you wait," Ari repeated, "so I can treat you right at home. Not through the clothes, not giving each other cramps." She kissed a triangle on Dale's neck and filled it in with a sweep of her tongue. Dale's body twitched involuntarily. "You're going to be comfortable. Naked. And I'm going to take as long as it takes to make you melt."

Dale pulled back until she found Ari's lips. "You're evil," she whispered. She flickered her tongue against Ari's mouth, and Ari captured it. When she was able to speak again, she said again, "I love you, Ariadne."

"I love you, Dale," Ari replied, and then her fingers curled and the heel of her hand rubbed and Dale's spine stiffened as her eyes rolled back and her grip on Ari tightened. "That's it, that's my girl," Ari said barely louder than a sigh. She put her head down on Dale's shoulder and kept stroking with her fingers until Dale stopped quaking.

Dale sagged forward against Ari to catch her breath. Ari freed her hand but kept it under Dale's shirt, stroking the small of her back where she knew Dale was sensitive. Dale could see the windows were fogged up, smiled at the cliché, and sat up to look into Ari's eyes. She put her hand on Ari's cheek and extended her thumb to brush it across her lips. Ari didn't break their gaze but parted her lips and closed her teeth around the pad of Dale's thumb.

"I think I'm still a little wolf-brained," Ari said. "I'm a little fuzzy on what started that."

"I didn't exactly consult you." Dale kissed Ari's forehead. "I just saw you change, and I was... I was overcome. I couldn't stop myself."

"Good. Never stop yourself, if that's what it leads to. Goodness, woman."

Dale grinned. "I'm going to have to move eventually. There's a building back there." She gestured with her chin. "I didn't see any lights on, but someone might be inside. They could come out to see what we're doing here."

Ari raised an eyebrow. "So you're saying we might get caught."

"Don't make it kinky."

"Someone could catch us at any second."

"Puppy," Dale scolded.

Ari said, "I think someone's about to knock on the window..."

Dale grunted and lifted herself off Ari's lap, returning awkwardly to the driver's seat. "You're a pain, you know that?"

Ari laughed and looked in the backseat. "Did you bring me anything to wear?"

"Shit," Dale said. "I only thought about the towels..."

"So you get me all riled up and then expect me to ride home completely naked?"

Dale grinned and winked at her. "What were you saying about torture...?"

Ari grabbed one of the towels and wrapped it around her shoulders like a shawl. Dale reached over and squeezed her thigh.

"I'll make it up to you when we get home, puppy."

"You'd better."

Dale pulled out of the parking spot and drove back to the main road, earning a glare from Ari when she started humming Jackson Browne's 'The Naked Ride Home.'

CHAPTER FOUR

WHEN ARI woke the next morning, Dale was already sitting up on the other side of the bed, hunched over her phone. The night before, when they'd gotten home, Ari had been sitting in that same position when she saw Dale's phone light up with an incoming call. She'd stroked Dale's hair back and looked down at her.

"Who's calling you at twelve-thirty?"

Dale had lifted her head and looked toward the phone. "Oh, it's... nothing," she said, and bowed her head to go back to what she'd been doing.

Ari closed her eyes, briefly distracted by what Dale's tongue was doing. "It... m-might be Segura. Or a client. Dierdre..."

"Stop saying other women's names while I'm doing this."

Ari knew that work calls were forwarded to her phone, not Dale's, so it probably wasn't a client, and she was able to ignore the call and focus on what was happening. Afterward she'd fallen asleep before she remembered to ask Dale about it.

Now, she reached over and dragged the back of her hand over Dale's hip. Dale squirmed appreciatively and reached and to give Ari's fingers a squeeze before she went back to typing.

"Everything okay?"

Dale nodded. "Everything's fine. Just an email I have to send." She put the phone back on the nightstand, twisted, and stretched out to kiss Ari's lips. "Good morning."

"Morning." Ari brushed the hair out of Dale's face. "You sure everything's okay? You have... you look..." She narrowed her eyes and tried to quantify the emotion in Dale's eyes. "Nervous."

"I'm fine." She looked away and plucked at the material of Ari's T-shirt. "Look, um. I know after everything that happened, you have a right to be suspicious of me when I keep secrets."

"I'm not suspicious."

Dale spoke over her. "After everything I did, and almost running off with Isaac Hayden~"

"I trust you."

"I need to earn back the right to~"

"I put a loaded gun in your hand, Dale," Ari said. "Then I pressed the barrel against my stomach. I didn't even have to cross my fingers. You went down a dark path, but you came back. I don't need to know what you're emailing about or who or why. As long as you promise me that everything's okay."

"Everything's okay."

"Is it about Mom or Milo?"

Dale shook her head. "No."

Ari sat up and kissed Dale's lips. "Then okay. I don't need to know."

"I promise, when the time is right, I'll tell you."

"Okay."

Dale kissed her. "I'm going to take a shower."

"Okay," Ari said again.

She dropped back down onto her pillow and grabbed her phone as Dale went into the bathroom. When she heard the water start, Ari glanced at the other nightstand where Dale had left her phone. The detective in her wanted to just take a quick peek and see if she recognized the number. It had nothing to do with trust; it was just a mystery with a very simple path to a resolution.

Ari looked back at her own phone, scrolling through the news to see what had happened overnight. Solving this mystery wouldn't be worth it. She'd proven her trust in Dale, and Dale deserved to have that same trust in her. Whatever the call was, whoever she was emailing, she didn't have to know. She focused on her phone and on the fact that in a little over an hour, she would begin working for Saint Artemis. She needed to go over the singer's itinerary for the day. She also needed breakfast. And it would be nice to get a workout in, since she didn't count letting the wolf run as exercise for her human anatomy. Counting the time she would need to actually get to where Dierdre was staying, time was incredibly short. If there was any way to shave a few seconds off the morning routine...

She kicked away the blankets and tossed her phone onto the pillow, stripping off her sleep shirt as she went to join Dale in the shower.

The rental in Denny-Blaine was the type of home Ari had heard called "urban farmhouse." Rustic exterior, surrounded by thick vegetation that concealed it from prying eyes while creating the illusion it was out in the middle of nowhere instead of fifteen minutes from downtown Seattle. The street was barely wider than an alley, a comparison made even clearer by tall fences on every nearby property. Every house was blocked in by walls, overgrown vegetation, and trees, preventing casual passersby from seeing past the sidewalk. Ari felt like she was entering the world's largest and most expensive maze as she followed the directions Dierdre's manager had sent her.

She parked in the driveway, nudging up against the ivy-covered garage door. A flight of stairs led up to a second-floor landing. Before announcing her presence, Ari walked to the street to examine the sturdy brick structure that enclosed the mailbox. The front had a slot wide enough for most envelopes to fit through, and mail was retrieved through a locked access hatch in the back. Ari looked up and down the street. More high fences and thick foliage around the properties provided privacy, sure, but it also provided a lot of concealment for someone to sneak up or lurk unseen.

Ari went back to the house and ascended the stairs. She had almost reached the top when Dierdre came out through a sliding glass door dressed in a gray hoodie halfway zipped over a white T-shirt and red shorts. She was holding a tall glass of orange juice and raised it in a toast.

"Private eyes," she sang, and then hummed the next line of the song. "Glad you found the place. I swear this neighborhood is like an experiment where a mouse has to find the cheese."

"I thought of the maze thing, too," Ari said, "The people who live here can afford to protect their privacy."

"And they overcompensate." Dierdre's voice was rougher in the morning, deep and husky. "Ten-foot cement walls and I swear I saw a hedge maze around the corner. Unbelievable. Come on in." She started back inside but twisted so she wouldn't turn her back on Ari. "Have you had breakfast?"

"Yeah, I ate."

The rustic aesthetic was completely abandoned with the interior. Everything was white, black, or chrome, and polished to a high shine. The room reminded Ari of an airport lounge: a seating area to the left, a glass dinner table to the right, and a kitchen directly ahead next to the stairs leading up to what Ari assumed were bedrooms. The room smelled of bacon and coffee, and despite having breakfast with Dale, Ari's stomach growled in anticipation.

Dierdre was barefoot and made quiet patting noises as she crossed the tile floor to the kitchen counter. "Sure you don't want anything?"

"I'll take some coffee." She went to the door behind the dinner table and looked out at a patio with a large jacuzzi. "I was hoping I could meet some of your team this morning."

"You will. I sent her out to get breakfast so we could have a little more time alone together." She brought Ari a mug of coffee. "We're going to be attached at the hip for the next little bit. I thought it was only fair if I got to know you a little better before I opened my whole life to you."

"I suppose that makes sense."

Dierdre smiled. "Excellent."

They sat together at the table. Ari wrapped her hands around the mug, and Dierdre leaned forward on her elbows.

"I'm not expecting every dirty detail of your private life, you understand," she said.

Ari nodded. "I know what you're looking for. I get the feeling I'm already farther into your inner circle than a lot of people get. And despite that, I'm still a near-stranger to you. I wouldn't feel comfortable in your situation, either. So what do you need?"

Dierdre shrugged. "Whatever you want to share."

"Broad strokes." She tapped her fingers on the mug. "I was raised by my mother, never really knew my dad. When I was a teenager, mom and I had a falling out because she'd done... something unforgiveable to me. It's really too complicated to go into, but it was enough for me to cut all ties and live on the street instead of staying in her house. I lived there for a while, then I met a woman named Glory Bennett who ran a detective agency. She gave me a job. Trained me. When she left town, she gave me her office and I started my own agency."

"Bitches Investigations."

"Right."

Dierdre smiled. "My manager hates that name. She refuses to say it."

Ari shrugged. "We find it repels a certain kind of client."

"I'm sure it does. Married?"

"Girlfriend. Uh, partner. Engaged. Not officially engaged, but we're..." She stopped herself fro going down that rabbit hole. "We don't really give ourselves titles. We're just together."

Dierdre nodded. "Excellent. Sounds good to me. I did some research on you last night. It seems like you do good work for good people."

"I try."

"Drugs? Alcohol?"

Ari said, "I drink from time to time. I won't have an issue abstaining while I'm working for you."

"You don't have to do that."

"If I'm on-call, I want to be sure I have a clear head." Dierdre shrugged and nodded. Ari continued, "I used to smoke pot to help with some pain issues, but they went away so I stopped."

Dierdre said, "So you won't take offense if I smoke weed sometimes?"

"Nah."

"Very cool." She checked her phone, obviously referring to a list of questions she'd written earlier. "Oh. Prison. The article I read mentioned you were in jail for a little while."

"Cleared of all charges," Ari said. "But if that's going to be an issue, you should know my former cellmate is a recent employee of the agency. She did the crime she was accused of, but she's also making an effort to live clean. I'm not exaggerating when I say I trust her with my life. But given the level of secrecy we're dealing with, I would understand if you're not comfortable with her being part of the investigation."

Dierdre leaned back in her chair and chewed her bottom lip. "With your life...?"

Ari nodded. "Someone was trying to kill me. Shae stepped in when it would have been easier to look the other way. I might not even be here if it wasn't for her."

"The fact you brought her up without being asked, and that

you vouch for her is enough for me. We should talk about–" Her gaze drifted past Ari to the front door, and she rolled her eyes at what she saw there. "Crap. Okay, I guess we do this part now."

Ari turned as a woman swept into the house with a plastic to-go bag of food. She wore a white pantsuit over a black blouse, and a Bluetooth device was clipped over one ear. She hadn't bothered to take off her sunglasses so Ari could see herself and Dierdre reflected in the large black lenses.

"Ariadne Willow," Dierdre said, "meet Nellie Bain, the bane of my existence."

"It's her favorite joke, and not nearly as original as she thinks it is. I'm her manager." She took off her sunglasses and examined Ari. "You're the private investigator?"

"That's right."

"You're nothing. You're a twig. Stand up."

Ari complied, taking the opportunity to examine Nellie. The woman was probably in her early fifties, full of a manic energy that didn't come from coffee or drugs. This was the kind of person who woke up buzzing and probably didn't stop until she'd been asleep for fifteen minutes. She was statuesque and held herself with the bearing of someone who probably had strangers step aside to make a path for her when she walked down the street.

"Well, you're tall," Nellie said. "I suppose that's something."

Nellie telegraphed her next move by twisting her wrist, so Ari wasn't totally surprised when she suddenly threw the to-go bag at her. Ari knocked it out of the air with one hand, pivoted on her left foot, and struck out with her right into the side of Nellie's leg. Her knee went out and she dropped. Ari grabbed Nellie's arm, twisted, and put her other hand on the back of Nellie's neck to keep her from straightening up. The entire thing took less than ten seconds, and Dierdre had barely risen from her chair by the time Ari released Nellie and stepped back. She held out her hand to help Nellie up.

"What the hell!" Dierdre snapped.

"Impressive," Nellie said, accepting Ari's hand. "But next time it will probably be something a little more dangerous than a plastic bag."

"I'll be ready," Ari promised.

Dierdre glared. "This is why I made you swear you'd be out at breakfast when I met with her."

"I went out to breakfast." Nellie pointed at the bag, which had landed near the couch. "I never said I would eat it at the restaurant."

"That's not funny," Dierdre said. "I asked for an hour. You couldn't even give me that."

"You don't know this woman, and you're inviting her into your house. I'm not going to let you be alone for that."

Dierdre stormed off toward the kitchen. Since it was the same room, it wasn't much of an escape. She turned back and waved a hand at Nellie.

"She thinks the definition of manager is ruler of my entire life, if you hadn't figured out by now."

"I kind of got that impression."

Nellie smoothed down the front of her suit jacket. "I'm only concerned with your safety, Dierdre. Whether it's protecting you from stalkers or predatory contracts or people who want to take advantage of you, it's my job to watch out for you whether you like it or not."

"Well, now it's Ariadne's job to do that, so you can back off." She looked at Ari. "Oh. You're hired, by the way. I had other questions, but they don't really matter after seeing how you knocked Nellie on her ass."

Nellie twisted her lips. "Do I get a say in this?"

"Nope," Dierdre said without hesitation. "She's going to be following me. I'm the one who is going to be spending most of the day with her. So I get the final say. It's her or nobody."

"Well, then I suppose that settles it." She turned to Ari with an insincere smile. "Welcome aboard, Miss Willow."

"Ariadne is fine. Or just Ari."

Dierdre had crossed back into the living room area. She scooped up the fallen bag and held it out to Nellie.

"Go eat in your car."

Nellie glared at her. "You can't be serious."

"I asked for a fucking hour." Dierdre returned the glare without wavering.

The two women stared at each other. Ari felt as if she'd become part of the furniture and did nothing that might draw either woman's ire. Finally, Nellie grabbed the bag and turned her back to leave the house. She didn't slam the door but she did close it firmly behind her, leaving no doubt to her mood. Dierdre stared after her until she disappeared down the stairs, then she pushed her hands through her hair and exhaled sharply.

"Sorry about that. You're probably going to see a lot of

headbutting while you're working for me. Nellie and I don't exactly see eye-to-eye very often, and we're both stubborn. So… that sort of thing happens. Just try not to get caught in the crossfire."

"I'll do my best," Ari said. "She seems pretty invested for a manager."

Dierdre grunted. "She was my music teacher. She's the one who first realized I had talent. First she had to protect me from my mother, who just wanted to live vicariously through me and steal any money I might make. Then she had to protect me from evil record labels who just wanted to get rich off me. I think now she's just in permanent protector mode."

Ari said, "That can happen." She mentally added Nellie to the suspect list. People could get addicted to being a protector. If there was no threat to be found, sometimes they created a new one.

"I need to get out some of this nervous energy," Dierdre said. "Come on. I'll take you on a tour of the place and we can talk about the schedule."

"Lead the way."

Dierdre started for the stairs and turned to look at Ari over her shoulder. "I'm really glad you're here. And please don't take this the wrong way, but I really hope you turn out to be completely unnecessary."

Ari smiled. "You and me both. Nothing would make me happier than to close this case as a waste of time."

Dierdre laughed. She headed upstairs to begin the tour, and Ari followed.

CHAPTER FIVE

DALE'S MORNING was occupied figuring out the realities of working with a second person in her space. There wasn't room for another desk, and the idea of sharing hers was just too awkward. Segura offered a temporary solution by sitting in one of the chairs reserved for clients with her own laptop, borrowed from her girlfriend. She was scouting potential new locations for Ari's stashes using maps of the city and a guide Dale sent to her of the existing stashes. Looking over it reminded her of how long it had been since they rotated any of them. There might be stashes with clothes covered in mildew, or they might have been found and emptied out by homeless people.

"I really appreciate you taking care of this," Dale said. "It's not technically agency work..."

"Sure it is," Segura said. "Ariadne might need to use one while she's working a case. My main concern is what I'll tell my parole officer when he asks what my duties involve."

Dale shrugged. "Just tell her the truth. Your boss is *canidae*, commonly called a werewolf, and sometimes she ends up naked in the middle of the city and needs clothes and supplies to get home."

"And then I get to take a super-fun drug test."

Dale laughed. "Filing is a good catch-all. Balancing the books. Following up with outstanding payments from past clients. There are lots of things you can do without convincing your parole officer that werewolves exist."

Segura said, "Can I ask you a dumb question?"

"Is it about vampires?"

"Yeah."

Dale shrugged. "We've never met one, but I can't say for sure. We have met a mermaid, and a succubus. There are other shifters, too. Cats, mostly. Also one person who can change gender."

Segura said, "Whoa. I can't decide if that would be handy or inconvenient."

"Probably depends on the day."

"Probably." She looked at the computer screen. "It... it really, um... what Ari's doing for me... and wh-what she did for me, finding out what happened to my sister... It really means a lot to me."

Dale said, "Ari wouldn't have survived prison without you. You took her under your wing. When the time came, you jumped into action. As far as I'm concerned, that's a debt that can't be repaid. So keep that in mind if you ever feel like you're taking advantage of us. If you didn't have a girlfriend to take you in, we probably would have demanded you take our couch."

Segura smiled. "Good thing I have Mel, then. I've never been good on couches."

After that, they went back to their respective tasks. Dale had been forwarded all of the threatening messages sent to Dierdre Macrae's private email. They were all written in the same all-caps text speak - U instead of "you" - so she took the time to translate each message for her own ease of reading. When she was finished she examined them to see if there was any kind of pattern.

"*Hiding your face means shame, fear, hiding. You're a coward who sings lies of strength.*"

"*Do all your little followers know what a coward you really are?*"

"*You can wear all the masks you want, you know what you really are. Who you really are. You can't hide from yourself or anyone else.*"

"*Do you ever think that if the people who scream and shout for you knew what you really were, they would be calling for your head? I bet they would. I bet they would hunt you down no matter how many masks you wore.*"

There were more, but she'd read enough of them to know why Dierdre's manager thought they were from the same person. And

Dierdre was right, they weren't really death threats. Whoever was sending them never actually threatened to harm her. But they were, without a doubt, threatening. The overall theme was identity, not just who Dierdre was but what she was allegedly hiding. That could be useful to identifying a suspect.

She closed the file and opened the page with the names and contact information for everyone who knew Dierdre was Saint Artemis. It was a surprisingly skimpy list of twenty-seven names, along with a note from the manager which said everyone on the list signed a non-disclosure agreement to keep her identity secret. That was no real guarantee that they kept her confidence, however. Assuming everyone on the list told two people, that was eighty-one potential suspects.

First, she made a list of professional acquaintances. There was a very small team of people she worked with regularly who had been entrusted with the name Dierdre Macrae. Band members, her manager, people who worked for the label, roadies, wardrobe, and makeup. One of the names was a fourteen year old girl who asked Make-A-Wish for a meeting with Saint Artemis, who not only agreed but unmasked when she was alone with the girl. Dale vaguely remembered reading about that on Twitter. "Saint Artemis felt Rebecca deserved to meet a person, not a persona," Nellie Bain had been quoted as saying.

"Hm..."

"Everything okay?"

Dale looked over the top of her laptop at Segura. "Oh. Sorry. I'm not used to having someone in the office with me. Sometimes I make little noises or talk to myself about something I'm reading."

"Oh. I can ignore it."

"No, no. You're here. It'll be good to have someone to bounce ideas off. One of the people who knows Dierdre's identity is a cancer patient who would be sixteen now. My knee-jerk reaction is to eliminate the teen cancer survivor."

"Fair."

"But Dierdre revealed her identity because she wanted to meet the girl as a person, not a persona. These threatening messages have the same theme. Wearing a mask, hiding who you really are. I don't think we can rule her out as a suspect, even if it makes us feel pretty skeevy to think of her like that."

Segura said, "Yeah, but you'll look stupid if she does turn out to be the one."

"Local Detective Harasses Teenage Cancer Patient..."

"People with cancer can be a-holes, too."

Dale shrugged and made a note next to the girl's name - Rebecca Albright, "person, not persona" - and glanced at the clock.

"I usually stop for lunch around twelve, twelve-thirty. If you want to go grab something a little earlier, feel free."

"I'm fine." She smiled, almost bashful. "Mel cooked me a big breakfast for my first day."

Dale grinned. "Oh, she's one of *those* girlfriends."

"She is, yeah. I think she's still just really stoked that she won't see me in a cell when she goes in to work. She likes it a lot better this way."

"I'll bet. Just let me know when you get hungry. We aren't too strict here as long as you don't go nuts with the breaks."

"Gotcha."

Dale looked at the computer screen and ran her eyes down the remaining names. "There aren't many personal connections on this list." She counted. "Four people listed as friends, one as family. That seems really low."

"How many people would you list?" Segura asked.

"Well... Ari, Ari's mother, Milo, Lucy, and Diana. My father, I guess."

"I only have Mel and an uncle. Most people only have a really small group of close friends. There are acquaintances, like you and me, but with someone like Saint Artemis, I'm not surprised she keeps the tally low."

Dale nodded as she considered that. Normally she would have to go through these logic puzzles on her own. It was a relief to have someone to go back and forth with.

"I think I'm going to like having you around, Segura."

"I do come in handy from time to time."

Dale chuckled and focused on the list.

It was an observation Ari had made before, and probably would make again in the future, that some of the most expensive homes had the least amount of actual living space. People paid for views and locations, ending up with cramped living rooms and crowded bedrooms stuck haphazardly on a second level. In this case, all the effort to retain privacy meant it didn't have much of a view, either. The tour of Dierdre's temporary house didn't take any time at all because Ari didn't even have to leave the hallway to see into all the second-floor bedrooms. She followed Dierdre back downstairs and out the back door to a small recording studio.

"This is where I'm going to be making my music," Dierdre said.

"The house you're renting just happens to have a recording studio in the back yard?"

"Of course not," Dierdre said. "We looked all over town for a place with the right privacy and a studio on-site. You don't really think that's just a coincidence, do you?"

Ari shook her head. "No. Just pointing out that if the note-sender knew you were coming to Seattle, they might have been able to deduce where you might stay based on available rentals and property specs. I was wondering if someone on the inside leaked your address, but now I think someone just paid close attention to what was on the market."

"Oh. I don't know if that's more reassuring than having a mole on my staff or not."

"I think it's a wash."

The backyard was fully enclosed by an eight-foot fence, which was dwarfed by a wall of blackberry plants. It was cramped, but Ari couldn't see how anyone might get through the fence without causing themselves a lot of grief on the thorny branches. Still, she wanted to make sure the gate was secure before she felt comfortable with Dierdre spending much time out here alone.

Dierdre had unlocked the French doors to the studio and left them standing open as she went inside. Ari followed and watched her toy with the soundboard in the control booth.

"This might seem like an odd question from someone who is only here because you have a stalker," Ari said, "but why do you wear a mask? Why be Saint Artemis rather than Dierdre Macrae?"

"Because then this would be the mask," Dierdre said, gesturing at her face. "This face, my name, it would belong to everyone. I would have to cover it up if I wanted to go out and, like, get sushi. If I wear a mask on-stage, if I make my public self a character, then I get a private life. I've waited at the airport next to girls wearing my name on their shirts. I've been in the grocery store and heard my voice coming out of someone's headphones. I hide onstage so I don't have to hide every second of every other day."

Ari said, "That makes a lot of sense."

"The hard part is that I really love and appreciate my fans. I'd love to thank them face-to-face, but they don't know who the heck I am. You have to pick and choose what you're willing to sacrifice." She sighed and spun her chair to look at Ari. "So what's the plan?"

"I have Dale looking into the list you gave me. We're going to see who was close enough to have left the note in your mailbox and focus on them. In the meantime, I'll make sure no one is lurking around to leave another note. I'll be here when you're working in the studio and if you venture out into the city, I'll be there with you."

"What about at night? Are you going to be staying here?"

That was where things got tricky. The truth was that Ari would prefer to spend the first night scouting the neighborhood as the wolf to pick up any suspicious scents. But she couldn't exactly tell Dierdre that part.

"I think it would be best to spend the first few nights away. I'll be keeping an eye on the place, but we don't want to stalker to notice too much disruption to your schedule."

Dierdre said, "Sure we do. If we scare him away, the problem is solved."

Ari shook her head. "If we scare him away, he hides until I leave. Then he just comes back. It's better if I keep my distance at first."

"I suppose that makes sense," Dierdre said, shifting in the chair. "It's a shame. I was already feeling a little better having you around."

"I'll still be around most of the day. And don't mention this to many people, but I'll still be close by even if you can't see me."

"Ooo, mysterious," Dierdre said, using one foot to push her chair back and forth. "But I like it. So what's going to happen next?"

Ari nodded at the soundboard. "Now you go about your day like normal. Do whatever it is you were going to do otherwise. I can be in here with you, or I can go in the house to look over the threats if you want some privacy. I'll also take a closer look at the property to see if I can find any vulnerable areas. No matter what, I should be close enough to hear if you shout."

Dierdre said, "Well, I feel better already. I think I want you in the house for now."

"Works for me. Call if you need anything."

Dierdre saluted and Ari walked across the yard and went back into the house. Nellie was sitting at the kitchen counter with her phone. She only gave the briefest glance when Ari came in.

"I'm going to need to look at the threatening notes. I have

copies of everything that was sent electronically, but–"

Nellie pushed a manila envelope across the counter. "The one that came to the house."

Ari went to the counter and examined the envelope. No return address, Dierdre's name spelled out in big blocky capital letters with a black marker. She opened the flap and pulled out the note which seemed to be written in the same unidentifiable style. It also matched the dialect of the online messages.

"U R TERRIFIED OF BEING SEEN. BUT UR BEING SEEN NOW. I HOPE U FEEL MY EYES ON U. MASKS ONLY WORK FOR SO LONG SAINT ARTEMIS. THE TRUTH WILL COME OUT."

"She's right, you know," Ari said. "These aren't death threats. Whoever it is seems to only be threatening her with exposure. That's bad, sure, but I don't think we have to worry about someone trying to physically harm her."

Nellie put her phone face down on the counter and sat up straighter. "I hope you understand that, to Dierdre, exposure is the same as assault. She is extremely protective of her privacy. An unmasking would be the end of her career. The threat is against the life of Saint Artemis."

Ari said, "Protecting your bottom line, huh?"

Nellie grimaced and stood up. "You can think I'm cold. Dierdre certainly does. But this is her dream. It's her passion, and I make sure she can do it the way she wants to. Do you think people are happy about contracts signed with an alias, or entering legal agreements with someone whose face they've never seen? Yes. I am protecting Saint Artemis because she is a shield which Dierdre hides behind. If it goes away, she is exposed and vulnerable. That is what I care about, not the money I'll be losing. There are a hundred acts clawing at the industry's door I could take on if that was all that mattered to me. I believe in Dierdre and her talent enough to let her treat me like shit, to jump through hoops to ensure only two dozen people know her name. So think whatever you want of me, Miss Willow, just be sure to do your job."

Ari could only nod, sufficiently chastised into silence.

Nellie crossed the living room to the front door but paused with her hand on the knob. "The list Dierdre gave you. The names of the people who know who true identity. Was Rudy Paviour on it?"

"Uh…" Ari had the list on her phone, but she was fairly certain she didn't recognize the name. "I can check."

"Don't bother. Dierdre wouldn't have put her on there. Rudy Paviour," she said again, then spelled the surname. "She definitely belongs on the list."

"Who is she?" Ari asked.

Nellie answered as she opened the door and left the house.

"Rudy is the woman who almost destroyed Dierdre Macrae to create Saint Artemis."

CHAPTER SIX

ARI'S FIRST day as Dierdre's bodyguard was much more boring than she would have anticipated, given the job description. "Bodyguard" evoked images of diving in front of bullets and constant vigilance. In reality, it was just watching someone go about their day while remaining aware of their surroundings. When she heard the idling rumble of an engine outside, she peeked through an upstairs window to watch a mailman deliver a handful of envelopes before driving off. She retrieved the envelopes and examined each one carefully; nothing suspicious, mostly junk addressed to Current Occupant.

She walked around the property to look for weak spots, but the fence was incredibly sturdy, the lock was brand-new, and the foliage was thick enough that anyone trying to sneak in would get a plethora of scrapes for their trouble.

Dierdre spent most of the day in her studio with a laptop and her phone. She had large white headphones which she constantly took off only to put the back on a moment later. She bobbed her head to whatever music she was listening to as she scribbled in notebooks. The creative process, Ari assumed. Eventually Dierdre came inside for a session with a personal trainer. She explained that he didn't know what she did for a living, and Ari promised to keep quiet.

After two hours of what looked like a grueling torture session, the trainer left and Dierdre went upstairs for a bath and a nap. Ari assured her she would remain on guard.

Nellie didn't return for the rest of the day. Ari thought about bringing up Rudy Paviour, but she wanted a little more information before she saw Dierdre's reaction to the name. She sent the new information to Dale, who confirmed she would add it to the list.

Dierdre came back downstairs in a fluffy robe, the collar of which bunched on her shoulders to make her look like she didn't have a neck. She took a seat across from Ari who explained that she didn't think the stalker was physically threatening her.

"That's what I said!" Dierdre triumphantly slapped the counter and reached for an orange from a bowl Ari had, until that moment, thought was only decorative. She plunged her thumbnail into the peel and the room immediately filled with a rich, citrus smell. "So at least I don't have to start wearing bulletproof vests. That's a relief."

"For me too," Ari said. "It's nice to know I probably won't be in the line of fire for you. No offense."

"None taken. I would feel horrible if you got shot." She freed a wedge of the orange and put it in her mouth, sucking it until the juices were gone, then spitting out the flesh onto the pile of peel she'd left in front of her. She saw Ari watching. "I eat weird. Nellie says so, too."

"I don't judge."

"So. Okay." She sucked some excess juice off her thumb. "Since I don't have to worry about bad guys breaking in here, why don't you go home for the night? I know we agreed you would be around as much as possible, but you've seen the place. I can lock it down and turn on the alarms. It'll help you and your lady transition to the days when you might not be around as much."

Ari looked at the exits visible from where she was sitting. The backyard was protected, and the alarm system was state-of-the-art. She really doubted the stalker would try to break in.

"You have to put me on speed dial. If you get scared, or even a little anxious, you call me and I'll be here in a flash. It doesn't matter what time it is."

"I can agree to that." She took her phone from the pocket of her robe and turned it around to show she'd added Ari as Rescue Squad. "Now, there might be days when you have to have dinner with me. So before you go, leave me a list of your favorite foods and meals."

"Oh, I'm easy. I can eat anything."

Dierdre leveled an irritated look at her. "That's just what people say when they don't want to be a hassle. Everyone has a favorite meal, and I can afford to order in from literally any restaurant in the city. Also, that's another perk to being famous under a mask. We can go out and eat without causing a riot." She knocked her knuckle on the counter. "Write a list. Aim for the sky. I want to eat well, too, and you know all the best places in town. We both come out as winners."

Ari had to agree with that logic and agreed to write out a list.

She was still reluctant to leave Dierdre alone in the house, but there really wasn't much she could do rather than just sit around and wait for something to go wrong. She waited until dark and made one last circuit of the property to ensure everything was still locked up tight, and headed home with a promise she would be back bright and early in the morning.

She drove to the office with a plan to act like a tough boss, demanding to know what her "employees" had been doing all day while she was out, but the joke died when she approached and heard Dale's voice through the door.

"~about *respect*, okay? You've been here *one day*, okay? You need to learn your place."

"You really cannot be this ignorant," Segura said. "It's *sad*."

Ari threw open the door and stepped in before the violence could escalate. Dale was standing up behind the desk glaring down at Segura, who was sprawled in one of the visitor chairs. Both women snapped their heads around to look at her.

"What's going on in here?" Ari asked, tensing for drama.

Dale said, "Fantastic. A tie-breaker."

"Oh, real fair," Segura said. "The woman you're sleeping with. This will definitely be unbiased."

Dale glared at her, took a deep breath, and then looked at Ari. "Is Seattle on the ocean?"

Ari blinked at her. She looked at Segura, then slowly closed the door. "This is seriously what you're arguing about?"

"It started as an off-hand comment," Dale said, "but now it's a matter of pride."

Segura held up her hand to stop Dale from saying more. "And don't tell her which side you're on. Let her answer."

Ari shook her head. "I clearly need to give you two more work." She went to her office door, stopped, and looked back. "No. It's not."

"It's salt water!" Segura yelled, rising to her feet. "It doesn't matter if someone calls it a sound or a sea, it's still a branch of the ocean! So it's technically part of the ocean!"

Dale held up her hand, raising her middle finger. She pointed at it with her other hand. "This is not my palm!"

"But it *is* part of your hand!"

Dale rolled her eyes and laughed smugly, then faced Ari. "I love you, puppy."

Ari rolled her eyes. "Tomorrow you can work on whether a hot dog is a sandwich or how many holes are in a straw. For now, though, Shae... you are free to go. We'll see you tomorrow at... what... eight?"

"Eight sounds good," Segura grumbled, still annoyed at being outnumbered. She closed her laptop, gathered her things, and faced Ari. "In case I haven't said it, thank you for taking a chance on me. A lot of the women I was inside with have horror stories about what happened when they got out. I didn't know what I was going to do until I met you."

Ari shook Segura's hand. "I'm glad I was able to help."

Segura looked at Dale and scoffed, then said, "Not a sandwich. Two holes."

"Not a sandwich," Dale agreed, "but one long hole."

"Unbelievable." Segura turned away from them. "You two idiots deserve each other..."

When she was gone, Ari put her arm around Dale's shoulder and pulled her close. "She's wrong about that, too. I don't deserve you."

"Well, you're stuck with me." She kissed Ari and smoothed down her collar. "Shake Shack?"

"Yes, please." Dale started shutting down her computer and stood up. When she was ready, she slipped an arm around Ari's waist and let herself be escorted out. "So, sweetie, tell me about your day."

On the way to the restaurant, Ari told Dale about everything she'd done at Dierdre's. By the time they got their food and headed home, the conversation had become about Dale's first day working with Segura.

"She seems to be a hard worker. She spent the day going over the catalogue of stashes and looking for new locations. Tomorrow she's going to scout them, see which ones are viable. I told her we'd give her some cash to buy clothes and whatnot at thrift shops to help refresh any stashes that might need it."

"Excellent. I didn't want to say anything because I know how busy you've been. But some of those bags were getting a little moldy."

Dale rubbed Ari's leg. "Poor puppy."

They took their food home and ate at the dinner table, the laptop on the table between them so they could both watch the same show. When they finished, Dale went to take a bath while Ari stripped down to her underwear and a T-shirt to do a quick workout in the bedroom. She was in the middle of a plank when Dale returned and let out a low whistle.

"Damn, puppy, love them shoulders."

"Can't let the wolf do all the work keeping me lean and mean. You should see Dierdre's workouts, though. That woman flat-out tortures herself."

Ari finished her workout and went to shower. She didn't bother getting dressed again when she went back to bed, pausing to turn off the overhead light before she got into bed. Her heightened sense of smell made Dale's body wash overwhelming, but in a good way. She pressed her thigh against Dale's under the blankets.

"What's a good way to say 'overwhelming'?"

Dale looked up from her phone as she thought. "I don't know. Um, overpowering?"

"Mm." She kissed Dale's shoulder. "You smell overpowering."

"I don't think it works in that context." Dale turned her head and kissed Ari's forehead. "No run tonight?"

Ari shook her head. "I can't be out running around as a wolf if Dierdre needs me."

"Oh, right." She looked at her phone again. "Two days."

"Hm?"

"The secret. The email I got, the whole... I can tell you everything in two days."

Ari said, "Oh. Okay. Is everything still okay?"

"Yeah." Her voice shook a little, hinting at emotion boiling under the surface. "It might blow up in two days, but..."

"I'll be there." She found Dale's hand under the blankets and squeezed it. "Even if I'm at Dierdre's, call me and I'll find a way to be here for you."

"Thank you." She put down her phone and repositioned herself on the pillow so she could hold Ari properly. Ari closed her eyes. "Have you heard from Mom and Milo lately?"

Ari shook her head. "Not since the phone call that said they were heading east. I got the impression they were heading to places without very good cell reception or reliable phones."

"I'm worried about them."

"Me too," Ari admitted. Her mother and Milo had left for Europe a few months earlier to put the book of Magnusson's essays in safe hands. Their trip had become much more complicated than they anticipated. They didn't know who they could trust until they knew exactly how Isaac Hayden found the book in the first place, and following that question apparently sent them down a rabbit hole.

"They're tough," Dale said. "They can take care of themselves."

"I know. I just wish they weren't so far away." She looked at the time and grunted. "I'm not going to lie awake wondering where they are. We can't do anything even if they are in trouble, and I have to be up early in the morning."

Dale set the alarm, turned off the lamp, and they kissed goodnight. "I can't believe I get you for a whole night."

"Believe it, babe," Ari said. "Get ready for some no-holds-barred cuddling."

"Mm, promises, promises."

Ari held Dale and listened to the sound of her breathing, noting when it became shallow and slow. She wasn't scared of Dale, had never actually been afraid even when it looked like she was going to leave with Hayden, but moments like this still felt like a victory. Holding Dale in her arms, feeling her body relax into sleep after someone had tried so hard to brainwash her, was evidence of how strong their love was.

And she knew that if they could get through that, there was nothing in Dale's secret email they couldn't survive.

CHAPTER SEVEN

ARI PLANNED to drop Dale at the office and then drive directly to Dierdre's to begin her shift as early as possible. When they were getting dressed, Dale said, "Oh, I forgot to tell you what I learned about Rudy Paviour. I wasn't able to find anything on her. Nothing contemporary, anyway. She doesn't seem to have a Facebook account or any kind of social media under that name. Today I'm going to start digging in the older records, see if maybe she's dead or just off the grid." Ari promised she would try to get more information out of Nellie if she had the chance.

When she arrived at the house, she wondered if she was supposed to knock or just let herself in. She bypassed the question by taking the opportunity to test the defenses. The front door was locked, the shades on all the windows drawn. She went down the steps and tried the gate. Also locked, with no easy way to scale it. She could pull the trash can over, climb up, and hop over, but she knew from yesterday that doing so would drop her directly into the middle of a blackberry bush. It was better than a mousetrap.

She went back upstairs and knocked. A minute passed before she saw the shade flicker, then heard the locks being thrown. Dierdre threw open the door, already dressed in a red blouse and black slacks. She held up a hand to stop Ari from stepping forward and turned around to close and lock the door behind her.

"Awesome, you're right on time. Do you mind driving?"

"Uh. No, where are we going?"

"We're going to buy some lunch."

Ari looked at her watch as she turned to follow Dierdre back down the stairs. "Isn't it a little early for lunch?"

Dierdre smiled over her shoulder as she practically skipped to the car. "It's not for us. Do you know how to get to Riverview?"

"Yeah," Ari said. "What's in Riverview?"

Dierdre only laughed.

Ari sighed and muttered, "Lord, spare me from redheads keeping secrets..."

The trip took them across Seattle, looping around the south side of downtown and through the Industrial District. Dierdre watched the city roll by out, her knees bouncing with barely contained excitement. At one point while they were idling in traffic, Dierdre took out her wallet and thumbed through the bills. Ari didn't bother trying to count, but every bill was a hundred and there were at least ten of them in the stack.

"Wow. Where exactly are you expecting to get lunch?"

Dierdre only laughed and put the money back in her pocket. They were crossing Harbor Island now, a place Ari had always considered ugly but with a stunning views of West Seattle and Elliott Bay.

"This is my favorite part of touring. I love to see the parts of cities that aren't on TV or in the movies. The real parts."

"Yeah," Ari said, but couldn't think of anything else to say on the subject. She'd lived in Seattle her entire life. She'd seen it from the streets, at night with nowhere to go back to. To her, the city was beautiful and ugly, dangerous and home, all at the same time.

When they got off the bridge, Dierdre used her phone to direct Ari down residential streets. She finally said, "Here we go, this is it," and pointed at an turn-in to the parking lot of an elementary school. Ari found a visitors parking area and followed Dierdre up to the pale brown brick building. Dierdre walked like she knew exactly where she was going, head up with no hesitation, and Ari had no choice but to follow her.

The front office was clearly marked, a glass cube facing a small and neglected water feature. It looked like a place where students were expected to gather and wait for the morning bell. Dierdre swept into the office door and went directly to the tall desk, smiling brightly at the woman on the other side who was currently occupied with a phone call.

They waited. The woman finally hung up and looked at them with exhausted eyes, as if she was already bored with the conversation.

"Welcome to Puget Point Elementary," she said. "How can I help you?"

"Morning!" Dierdre said, much too peppily. "I'm Dee McKay with the Doe & Cypress Foundation. We're a non-profit charity and we're here today to make a donation. I wanted to let you know we were on campus, and would love it if you could point us toward your cafeteria."

"You're who?"

Dierdre produced a business card and handed it over. "Doe & Cypress."

The receptionist examined the card carefully, looked at Dierdre and Ari, then reached under the desk and pulled out a laminated map of the grounds. "You're here," she said, pointing to a spot on the map. "Go out that door, turn left. Take a right through the double-doors and go all the way to the end of the hall. Can't miss it."

"Thank you so much for your help," Dierdre said. "Have a great morning."

Ari waited until they were back in the hall before she spoke. "Doe & Cypress?"

"Nellie set it up for me. It's a real charity, fully legit and everything. Nellie has people who do the research for the cities we go to. Today, they sent me Puget Point."

It was quickly apparent that the map hadn't been necessary. Signs pointed them in the right direction and, once they were in the north hall, they could see the three sets of double-doors that led into an empty cafeteria. Their footsteps echoed off the cavernous space, the sound enhanced by the rows of folding tables and metal chairs. They could see a half dozen workers in white outfits moving around in the kitchen, and Ari could smell cooking meat.

"Hello?" Dierdre called as they approached a window equipped with an old-fashioned cash register. A woman came out of the back, her braided black hair tucked under a hairnet. She wore a white uniform shirt with the school's logo on the chest and took off her plastic gloves as she approached.

"Are you parents?" she asked.

"No, ma'am," Dierdre said. "My name is Dee McKay, and this is… Allison Wilson. We're with the Doe & Cypress Foundation. It's a charity dedicated to helping schools like yours. I'm here today to make a donation. We'd like to pay off the lunch debt."

The woman looked at Ari, then back at Dierdre. "Whose debt?"

"Everyone's. All of it."

"Honey, that's gonna be hundreds of dollars."

Dierdre said, "Our research indicates it could be around two thousand, possibly as much as twenty-five hundred. We can wait if you want to check your records to get an exact amount, but I'm authorized to just round up from your best guess. We just want to make sure every student in this school gets a hot meal today."

The woman looked at them again and then said, "I'm going to go get the records."

"Thank you." When she was gone, Dierdre rested her elbow on the counter and smiled at Ari. "Having fun?"

Ari couldn't help smiling. "Do you do this sort of thing a lot?"

Dierdre shrugged. "At least once in every city I visit. Some celebrities blow this much on a bottle of champagne they won't even bother drinking. Others buy sports cars or houses they can't possibly afford. This is an extremely cheap hobby, relatively speaking, and it gives food to kids who might not get it otherwise. It might be weird…"

"It's not weird," Ari said. "I think it's fantastic."

Dierdre looked past Ari at the windows. "When I was a kid, our school had lunch tickets. You would buy them in the morning, a buck-fifty each or ten bucks for a week. There were some mornings… a lot of mornings… I didn't have it. I always thought, 'what if someone walked in here right now with a big stack of cash and just bought lunch for everyone? Wouldn't that be great?' Well, now I can be that person."

The cafeteria worker returned with a large black book. She placed it on the counter next to the register and opened it to the back.

"Currently, among the student body, there is a lunch debt of one thousand, four hundred ninety-three dollars and fifty cents."

Dierdre smiled and took out her wallet. "What do you say we round that up to an even fifteen hundred?"

Segura stopped by the office to check in and pick up a list of Ari's sizes before she went out to hit some Goodwills and thrift shops. Dale put on Saint Artemis' debut album and let it play as she went into Ari's office to update the bulletin board. Only five people on Dierdre's list were in Seattle or close enough to have hand-delivered the letter, and she'd printed out photos and a page of basic information on all of them so Ari could see it with a glance.

"*Tell me who you are,*" Saint Artemis sang, her voice thick with reverb, "*and I'll show you me, everyone who is sick of being who we're supposed to be.*"

Suspect one, Nellie Bain. It probably wasn't her, but at this point they couldn't rule out anyone with the means of leaving the note. Nellie obviously had access to all of Dierdre's private information and could easily hire someone to have delivered the note or schedule the emails to be sent at times when she had an alibi.

"*Dreams don't come true by playing it safe, baby. Step out into thin air, risk it all on maybe.*"

Suspect two, Rudy Paviour. She still hadn't found anything on the woman, and it was possible she didn't even exist. If Nellie turned out to be their culprit, she might have thrown the name out as a red herring to distract Ari and confuse the investigation. But until she knew more, the name went on the list.

"*Change your face, change your name, I know who you are, your heart looks the same.*"

Suspect three, Lila Brcich, a guitarist who worked on Saint Artemis' debut album. According to Nellie, she'd shown up early to a rehearsal and caught Dierdre unmasked. Dierdre swore her to silence and made her sign an NDA, but Lila didn't seem interested in the mystery. She was quoted as saying, "If you want to stand on your head or wear stilts when you sing, I don't care. I just want to be a part of this album." Dale didn't think she was very likely, either.

"*You don't have to be strong every second, you don't have to hold it all alone. Let me take the weight when you're weary to the bone.*"

Suspect four, Theresa Conrad. A producer who knew Dierdre before the Saint Artemis persona was completely locked in. She'd worked with Dierdre in New York before she became famous, but they were never professionally involved once Dierdre's career took off. According to the internet, Conrad moved to Seattle in 2015 and got a job with Cartography Records.

"*We're an army, you and me, fighting wars no one else can see. Take my hand, take a stand, we're the only weapons we need."*

And finally, the fifth suspect, Renata Morning, was a singer who had pursued Dierdre for years to do a collaboration. Despite repeatedly being told Saint Artemis wasn't interested, every few months she tried again. She sent emails, called Nellie, and basically made herself a pest in the hopes of finally wearing her down. Dale didn't understand that strategy. Why would anyone want to work with a person who had to be pestered into agreeing? Renata seemed more annoying than dangerous, but she was the closest thing the list had to an actual threat, so Dale put her in the middle so she would be more prominent.

She stepped back and examined the names and photos. All five could have done it, but it was equally as likely they were looking for a stranger. It was the age of the internet and constant surveillance. Some total stranger might have found out who Saint Artemis was without Dierdre or Nellie knowing they even existed. Some troll on the internet, some fan whose obsession decayed into Mark David Chapman territory.

That thought made her shudder. If this was some psycho who eventually confronted Dierdre with a gun, Ari would be in the line of fire. The thought took her back to Isaac Hayden's plane, to the weight of a gun in her hand, pressing it against Ari's stomach. A part of her had been screaming to pull the trigger. Ari's trust and love had overwhelmed that urge, but she'd be lying if she said there hadn't been a moment when things might have gone in a very different, very horrible, direction.

The plan she'd set into motion would go a long way to erasing those feelings once and for all. But she refused to think about that. If she opened that door, it would stay open for the next thirty-six hours and drive her absolutely crazy with worry as she scrolled through all the myriad ways it could go wrong.

"Things don't go wrong when Ari's involved," Dale whispered to herself. "She's there to make sure things go right. That's her job."

She nodded, convinced she had convinced herself, and left the board. The plan was to spend the rest of the day digging up whatever she could find on the five suspects.

CHAPTER EIGHT

AFTER LEAVING the school, Dierdre bought them both lunch at Dick's Drive-In. It was "the one place you have to eat when you're in Seattle," Ari had told her, and Dierdre was excited to try it. Spending time together was easy, and Dierdre was fantastic company, but Ari never forgot her presence there was professional. She was there as protection. She spent the drive watching for any cars that followed them for too long. While they waited for their food, she examined all the other patrons who were milling around. No one presented themselves as suspicious, but she remained on her guard.

At one point, after they'd taken their food to one of the outdoor tables, Ari spotted someone wearing a Saint Artemis 2017 Tour shirt. She watched the girl long enough to determine she was just another customer and not someone who had been following them before mentioning her to Dierdre.

"See?" Dierdre grinned. "That's exactly what I'm talking about. If she knew who I was, she would be taking a picture, and that's fine. But then all these people would crowd around, they would text their friends, I'd get all self-conscious about eating, the whole experience would be ruined."

"That's a little egotistical, don't you think? No offense. I know you're famous and everything. But do you really think people would swarm this place just because you showed up?"

"It's a fair question. And at the beginning of my career, it definitely wouldn't have been an issue." She shrugged. "And who knows, maybe the mask adds to the intrigue and no one would care if I was just another singer. But I've seen it with other celebrities, even minor ones. Think about how many pictures you've seen of actresses or singers walking their dog or carrying a shopping bag."

Ari raised an eyebrow. She'd never considered it, but those pictures were definitely ubiquitous.

"I don't know. I just like having the ability to just sit here and have a burger like anybody else."

Ari said, "But isn't the whole fan experience part of being famous?"

"I don't want to be famous. I want to write songs, sing them, and make people happy. Or make them feel something. It's fantastic that I'm able to make a living that way. But I don't want to sacrifice my personhood to achieve it. Like... okay." She took a sip of her drink. "Take Mick Jagger. Do you think he can just walk into a bookstore and browse for an hour? And when he buys the book, do you think he can sit in the park and while away an afternoon reading it?"

"Probably not."

Dierdre looked at the woman in the T-shirt. "When you achieve fame, it's like you give away part of yourself. Dash Warren stopped being a person when she became famous. Paul McCartney, Lana Kent, Adele. Their lives became public domain. There are pages on the internet devoted to biographing their childhood down to the tiniest detail. Avoiding that is worth missing out on interacting with the fans."

If Ari had been in wolf form, her ears would have twitched at that. Dierdre wanted to avoid scrutiny of her childhood. Nellie served as protection against her mother. Maybe the threat was closer to home than she thought. She took out her phone and sent a text to Dale: "Check into DM's mother."

"Get a clue?" Dierdre asked.

"You never know."

"Miss Mysterious," Dierdre sang, then laughed.

Dierdre bussed the table when they'd finished eating and declared the restaurant worthy of a repeat visit before her time in

Seattle came to an end. She apologized on the walk back to the car.

"The rest of your day is probably going to be pretty boring. I'm going to lock myself in the studio and I won't come out until I figure out the end of this song."

"How long will that take?"

"Hours. Days. 'Til the heat death of the universe." She held her hands up, then rapidly tapped her forehead. "I know what I want to say, and it's all up here. I just can't get the shape of it down. It's like trying to translate a poem from one language to another without losing any of its meaning."

Ari said, "Sounds like an impossible task."

"Sometimes it is. That's when you just get as close as you can and hope for the best."

"Well, don't worry about me. Sitting around waiting for something to happen is a big part of being a private investigator. I'm used to it by now."

When they got back home, Dierdre took some water from the fridge along with a family-sized bag of chips and told Ari she could use anything in the house to keep herself occupied. Ari chose the laptop, placing it on the coffee table and searching for Saint Artemis videos on YouTube. She was unsurprised to find dozens of covers, parodies, and remixes, but it was easy enough to find a channel which hosted the official videos. She clicked on one at random, a song called "On Your Knees."

The screen filled with a shot of a woman from behind, head bowed, shoulders straight. Her hair was slicked back and colored neon blue. She seemed to be naked. The music began, and she moved her shoulders to the beat, slowly raising her arms out to either side. She was still facing away from the camera when the lyrics began, but it panned around her in a slow sweep. It eventually revealed most of her face was covered by an artfully-broken porcelain mask. Only her lips were visible under a ragged edge. Her skin was painted an eggshell white color that sparkled when the lights hit it.

"You look at me, you're on your knees, you beg for me, to hear your plea. Your face turned up, you worship, but if you pray to me, who is left to hear me?"

The voice was the same, and she could definitely recognize the shape of Dierdre's jawline, but it was hard for her to reconcile the fact that the woman she'd just spent the day with was the same one kneeling on a white stage covered in body paint.

Ari watched the rest of the video, then switched to another. "Mood" was animated, and Dierdre's identity was concealed by making her face completely abstract. The third video, for a song called "Waking," was her favorite.

The video started at a microphone on an empty stage, then pulled back to begin a long tracking shot. A woman setting up chairs for the performance lip-synced the lyrics until a man passed her and picked up the next line. The camera followed him outside, where he passed the song to someone else. It continued like that, hopping from one person to another, all seemingly in one-shot, until it ended back in the empty performance space. Dierdre, Saint Artemis, stood at the microphone in a flowing red robe, hands behind her back, head bowed. She lifted her head and opened her mouth to sing, and the video cut to black.

Toward the end of the song, Ari's eye drifted to the folder icon at the bottom of the page. Dierdre had given her permission to use the laptop, but that wasn't consent to snoop in her private folders. Then again, Ari's job required her to be a snoop. Dale hadn't had been able to find anything on Rudy Paviour, but maybe there was a lead hidden in the depths of the computer.

She minimized the browser and scanned the desktop folders. Music, lyrics, contracts, "taxes," the normal stuff one might expect. She stared at a folder labeled Chats and let the cursor hover over it for a full minute before she clicked. There had to be a line, a level of privacy she wasn't willing to cross, but she couldn't leave any stones unturned.

A row of files appeared and she clicked one at random.

BOARDCHIK10: Hey.

READY-N-WILLIN: whats up

BOARDCHIK10: depends. what are you ready and willing to do?

READY-N-WILLIN: whatever you've got in mind.

BOARDCHIK10: you a fan of Saint Artemis?

READY-N-WILLIN: hell yes. fucking amazing body

BOARDCHIK10: .tell me what you'd do to her if she walked into the room right now

READY-N-WILLIN: oh shit that would be amazing... I would leave the mask on, but I would tear off whatever she was wearing and throw her on the bed.

BOARDCHIK10: tell me everything you'd do to her...

Ari scrolled far enough to see that the chat went exactly where it seemed to be going, then closed it and opened another. It was more of the same but with a different partner. BoardChik10 seemed to be Dierdre's handle, while the guys were probably people she found on some of the more sundry message boards or chat rooms around the internet. Some of the chats were quote-unquote "romantic," while others got misogynistic, violent, and downright abusive. Dierdre stuck with most of them to the very end unless they hit some particularly vile extreme. But she had still saved those chats, for whatever reason.

She closed out the folder. Maybe she'd let something slip while chatting, maybe one of these fools had tracked her down. She opened the browser and sent herself the transcripts, telling herself she would only read more if it became absolutely necessary, and went back to her snooping.

She searched the computer for anything with Rudy Paviour and variants of the name, but came up empty. Going back to email, she searched for Rudy and came up with almost two dozen results. She found a thread of emails with the subject line "Re: songs for rudy" and it came up a few times in emails with Nellie, but there was no actual correspondence with the woman herself to provide Ari with an email address.

As if summoned by Ari reading her name, the front door opened and Nellie entered. She glanced at Ari as if she was an out-of-place chair and continued into the kitchen.

"Where's your charge?" Nellie asked as she poured herself a cup of coffee.

"Out in the studio."

"Is she aware you're using her personal computer?"

Ari turned it around to reveal the YouTube page she'd returned to. "It's research. I was curious to see how she's managed to keep her face completely concealed all these years."

"Carefully, and with dedication," Nellie said. "From time to time, she uses decoys. She's gone through airport security as a member of her own entourage while someone else was hustled through the VIP check-in. It's a hell of a lot of work. And I can't count the number of people who believe Saint Artemis is actually a half-dozen women with identical voices. Or a puppet for a singer who only performs in studios. I prefer the one that claims her voice is a computer-generated compilation of every famous female singer from the past fifty years, a perfect construct."

"You like that they think she's fake?"

Nellie smiled. "I like that they think she sounds that good, because I know it's her real voice."

"I've seen the conspiracy theories online," Ari said. "Websites that compare the size and shape of her lips and the curve of her jaw."

Nellie nodded and then sighed.

"If it's so much trouble, why do you let her do it?"

"Let her?" Nellie said. "I don't let her do anything. Dierdre refuses to sing unless she's Saint Artemis, and she's too damn good to just drop her. In the beginning, when it was only up to me, putting on the mask and letting her use a stage name was the only way she would sing in public. She was so damn talented that I was willing to agree to anything to support her. And now..." She flipped her hand. "Saint Artemis sells out venues. All of her albums have been huge successes for the label. She dictates the terms and we follow her lead to make sure she's happy."

Ari said, "Did Rudy Paviour stand in the way of making Dierdre happy?"

Nellie made a face as if her coffee had suddenly turned bitter. "You should ask her yourself."

"I would if we could find her. No trace online, no social media at all. It's commendable, but it makes my job a pain in the ass. Maybe if I had a little more information on who she is..."

Nellie looked outside again, her eyes lingering on the closed studio door. Finally she put down her coffee and came into the living room.

"I will tell you more on the condition you don't mention the name in front of Dierdre until you've confirmed her guilt."

"Agreed."

Nellie sat down across from Ari and seemed to sink into the plush cushions of the chair. She rested her hands on the arms, her legs uncrossed and feet flat on the floor. She looked like she had just climbed into a dentist's chair and was bracing for the drill.

"Rudy created Saint Artemis. The name, the first costume, the whole mythology was her idea. It was Lady Gaga to the nth degree. She loved the idea of a musician who never showed her face, whose true name wasn't known. She said it would be like a real-life superhero. To her, it was a game. Just something two friends joked about when they were getting high in their bedroom after school. For Dierdre, it was a way to express herself while avoiding the trappings of celebrity."

"So Dierdre became Saint Artemis, and Rudy…?"

"Rudy was paid for her idea. She was paid very well, both for the intellectual property and the promise she would never reveal the truth for a quick tabloid buck."

Ari narrowed her eyes. "Something tells me it's not that cut and dry."

Nellie pursed her lips and plucked at something on the arm of the chair. Ari waited.

"Rudy had a crush on Dierdre. It was unrequited, and that was fine. But one night, after a show, Dierdre showed up in Rudy's room in full costume. They had sex. In the morning, Dierdre pretended like it never happened. When Rudy finally confronted her, Dierdre said it was Saint Artemis, not her."

"Wait, she thinks Saint Artemis is a separate person?"

Nellie shook her head. "Not anymore. Things were hazier at the beginning. Dierdre was also questioning her sexuality at the time. She believed she was straight, but her new identity gave her an outlet to explore other aspects of herself. Eventually she learned she was bisexual, but by that point Rudy had cut ties and stopped talking to her. Not that it would have mattered. Bi or not, Dierdre wasn't attracted to Rudy."

"You said she almost destroyed Dierdre."

"Saint Artemis was who the crowds wanted. After their night together, Rudy seemed unwilling to go back to being just friends. That friendship was all Dierdre really had. Losing it made her wonder what she had to offer as herself. She refused to drop character even when she was off-stage. When she wasn't wearing a mask, she covered her face with veils, towels, whatever was available. She barely even spoke. I was watching her vanish in front of me and I couldn't think of any way to rescue her."

Ari said, "So what happened?"

"Rudy left. She saw what was happening and knew she was partially to blame. So she removed herself from the equation. And I managed to convince Dierdre that everything she'd gone through to create Saint Artemis was so she could have a personal life. If she was just going to become the fake identity, what was the point of the masks? And then I gave her a purpose."

"The lunch debts."

Nellie said, "Oh, you did that today. Yes. That was what finally broke through. It convinced her there were people in the world who could benefit from knowing Dierdre Macrae. Saint Artemis went back to just being the mask she hid behind, and she was a person again."

Ari said, "And you have reason to believe Rudy is nearby?"

"I don't just believe it. I know she lives in Bellingham."

"How? We couldn't find any evidence of her."

Nellie smiled. "You were starting from scratch. I've been following her from the beginning. Every move, every change-of-address. I wanted to make sure that she wouldn't pop up unexpectedly. I was anxious about spending so much time in Seattle, but Dierdre is adamant about doing these shows. It means a lot to her. So I couldn't exactly deny her without explaining why. Then the letter showed up."

Ari said, "You have her address?"

Nellie said, "I'll text it to you. But tread carefully, Miss Willow, please. Rudy Paviour came very close to killing Dierdre once. I'm terrified that if she pops up again now, it would finish the job."

CHAPTER NINE

DALE DIDN'T expect an answer but she called anyway during her lunch break. The phone buzzed in her ear a few times before she heard a click followed by Gwen Willow's outgoing message. "You've reached Gwyneth Willow. Leave a message."

"Hey, Mom. This is Dale." She spun her chair around to she could look out the window. There had been a brief shower that morning and the trees shading the sidewalk were still dripping the leftover moisture. "I keep worrying your voicemail inbox will be full. I'm just checking in. Ari and I are doing fine, and we hope everything's going okay with you both, wherever you are. We miss having you around."

Someone knocked on the office door. She could see the silhouette of a large man waiting in the hallway.

"I'll leave it at that so I don't fill up your voicemail all on my own. You're missed and we hope you're both okay. Love you both. Bye." She hung up and raised her voice. "Come in."

The man entered, tall and broad-shouldered, black, with closed-cropped hair. He wore a suit but didn't look like any businessman she'd ever seen. The jacket and shirt looked tailor-made to conceal a bulletproof vest. Dale smiled and tried not to feel intimidated, despite the fact this man would probably be a full foot taller than her even if she was standing.

"How can we help you today?"

He gestured at the door, smiling in a way that wasn't entirely unfriendly. "Bitches Investigations. That really what y'all call yourselves?"

"Yes, sir," Dale said.

He stepped forward with a card held between his fingers. "The name's Michael Terrence. I'm Shae Segura's parole officer."

"Oh!" Dale took the card and relaxed her guard. "She said you might be dropping by, but she didn't say it would be today."

He smiled and winked. "That would kind of defeat the purpose." He craned his neck to look into the office. "So is she here...?"

"She checked in this morning, but she's spending the day running errands for us. Getting film developed, picking up checks, that sort of thing. We try to make sure she doesn't interact with people who could be considered criminals."

"I appreciate that, Miss..."

"Frye. Dale Frye. I run the office for Ariadne Willow. She's the detective. She's on a case right now acting as security for a client who has been receiving death threats."

"Mm-hmm. Okay."

"Shae helped me in the office yesterday."

Michael looked around. "Not much room for two people to work in here."

"That's partially why she's doing errands today," Dale said. "This is a real job, even if we're not sitting at a desk for a strict nine-to-five schedule."

"May I sit?"

Dale gestured at one of the chairs. "Of course."

Michael sighed as he lowered himself into it, settling like he'd been on his feet for hours. "I want to be upfront with you, Miss Frye. I like Shae a lot. She's one of the good ones. She has a, um..." He scanned the wall for the right word. "Let's call it a rebellious streak. She's chaotic good."

Dale narrowed her eyes. "Sorry, I played once or twice but I don't really know the alignments."

"She follows her conscience. She's generally a good person, doesn't want to hurt others unless they hurt her first. Laws don't really factor into her ideas of right and wrong. But laws matter, Miss

Frye. And when those laws are broken, amends must be made. I want to make sure Shae stays on the straight and narrow. That girlfriend of hers, Melissa Vogel. She's a good influence. Even if I don't quite believe their story that they only became an item after Shae was released from prison."

Dale raised her eyebrows. "That's the story I heard."

Michael laughed. It was a pleasant, rumbling sound. "Please, we're all grown-ups. I'll take it at face value since the relationship is doing more good than harm. So I don't see any need to dig into it. People like Shae need good influences to keep them from backsliding. Melissa is a good influence. I want to make sure you and Miss Willow are also the kind of people we want Shae spending time with at this crucial juncture in her rehabilitation."

"Oh. What, um... how can we help you determine that?"

He shrugged and looked past her out the window. "A meeting, for one. I'd like to sit down with Miss Willow. Talk to her, get a feel for her. I know she was cleared of all charges against her, but she *was* incarcerated for a time. That runs up a few red flags for people in my profession."

"I'm sure. Ari's current case requires her to spend a lot of hours with the client. Her day starts early and only ends when they're safely tucked away for the night. But I'm sure we could find a time to arrange a meeting."

Michael said, "Any time in the next couple of days would be fantastic. You can just give me a call at the number on the card." He stood up and extended his hand to her. "It was lovely to meet you, Miss Frye."

"You too, Mr. Terrence." She shook his hand.

"I'll be around, Miss Frye. Don't be surprised if I drop in."

Dale said, "You're welcome any time." She kept her smile steady, but she knew what he was really saying. He'd be watching them, observing, trying to decide if they were good influences on Shae. How long would it be before he caught Ari sneaking out of the house after midnight? Or worse, what if he was there when she came home barefoot in dirt-stained thrift store clothes? God, what if he saw her transform?

He took one of the business cards from the stack on the corner of Dale's desk. He ran his finger over the embossed lettering, the image of a white wolf on a field of gold. He chuckled and shook his head.

"Bitches Investigations. My daughter will love that." He tucked the card into an inside pocket of his jacket and turned to leave. "I'll be seeing you around, Miss Frye."

"I'm sure you'll be hard to miss."

Michael smiled over his shoulder at her as he stepped out into the hall. "You might be surprised. Have a lovely day."

The door closed behind him. Dale waited until she was sure he had gotten to the end of the hallway and was outside, safely out of earshot, before she blew out the breath she'd been holding in.

"Well. Shit."

Ari raised a shoulder to pin the phone against her ear as she peeked around the curtain next to the front door. "I expected a parole officer to show up eventually. He'll see that we're a legitimate business and Segura really does work for us, and then he'll move on. He probably has way too many convicts to spend much time staking us out."

The air brakes she'd heard belonged to a FedEx truck which had parked at the end of the driveway. It was wide enough to block the entire street, and the driver hustled up the stairs to leave the package on the porch. Ari opened the front door to greet him. Nellie had left to take care of business elsewhere, and Dierdre was still in the studio.

"That makes sense. I thought it would be good to warn you about him," Dale said.

"It is. You're right." Ari took the package, tucked it under her arm, and scribbled her name on the driver's pad. "Keep an eye out to see if he's watching the office. I really don't expect him to be."

Dale said, "I'll let you know if he lurks."

Ari took the package inside and sat it on the dinner table. "Listen, the thing tomorrow... your secret thing, the thing I'm going to learn all about. Do you want me to be there?"

"Oh. I assumed you would be at Dierdre's all day."

"I can have Segura cover for me if I need to. Besides, I know where to find Rudy Paviour, so if I take the day off I can run over there and have a chat."

"Then yes. It's going to be in the morning. I would love to have you there, puppy."

Ari smiled at the tenderness in Dale's voice. "I'll talk to Dierdre about it when she reappears. I'll see you tonight. Love you."

"I love you."

Ari hung up and examined the package. It was addressed to D.

Macrae, with a return address in Boston of someone named Edith Foss. She used her keys to cut the tape, opened the flap, and lifted the packing material.

A severed head stared back at her.

"Fuck!"

She jumped back a step, the hairs on the back of her neck raising as she brought up both fists in a useless defensive posture. Her brain caught up with her body a second later, and she realized the truth of the situation. One, she would have smelled decomposing skin and blood before she even brought the box inside. Two, there was no blood on any of the packing material. She moved closer and confirmed that the skin was a pale golden color, and the neck ended in a smooth stump.

Closer inspection revealed she even recognized the face as Dierdre. She picked it up by the neck and held it up, turning it one way and then the other, before she put it down on the table to see what else was in the box. Under more packing material, wrapped carefully in bubble wrap, she found a plaster mask that would cover most of Dierdre's face but leave her mouth and chin exposed. The sides extended far enough to cover the ears, and Ari could see room had been left to allow earpieces to be inserted.

A little more digging produced a handwritten note, purple pen with large balloon-y letters. "Dearest Dear," it began, "sorry for the delay but perfection requires it. I can't wait to see what the finished ensemble looks like. Enclosed as always is the mold of your face I used. I can assure you no one saw it, as it was always locked in a cabinet in my private studio. I eagerly await your newest creations. Love, E.F."

Ari put the mask, head, and note back in the box and carried it outside to the studio. She could hear music playing loudly through the door, rattling the windows. The music cut off when she knocked, followed by a muffled curse. The door swung open and Ari was confronted by a red-faced, wet-eyed Dierdre glaring at her with more anger than she'd seen from the woman so far.

"I said no fucking interruptions. What the fuck does that mean to you?"

"You didn't actually say no interruptions," Ari said, unshaken by the anger.

Dierdre looked confused. "Oh. Sorry. I meant... I thought I'd... sorry. I'm sorry." She put both hands in her hair and scratched her scalp. "I'm-I'm..."

"Translating?"

She laughed harshly. "Yeah. I know the song and I know the choreography but I can't write it down. I can't figure it out." She looked at the box. "What's that?"

"It came for you just now. I opened it in case it was another threat."

"My mask." The anger was gone from her voice now, replaced by wonder. She took it from Ari and carried it into the studio. "Come here, I want you to see."

Ari stepped over the threshold. The bag of chips was emptied, discarded on the floor, and a row of empty water bottles lined the floor along the wall.

"I ask her to send me the molds so her other clients won't see it in the studio. I don't think anyone could figure out who I am just from that... oh. Edith Foss should be on the list of people who know who I am. But she lives in Boston. She couldn't have left the note."

"She should still probably be on the list."

Dierdre nodded but was distracted by the mask. She let it rest on her right hand, turning it one way and then the other to let the light catch it at different angles. The base color was lilac, with flames of darker purple, red, and gold extending out from the edges. The inner surface was contoured to match Dierdre's bone structure but the outside was convex. There was no nose, and the cheeks curved in dramatically to give the impression of a very long and narrow face.

"May I model it for you?"

"Sure."

Ari was still trying to find evidence of the enraged woman who answered the door, but the color had faded from her cheeks and she seemed meek now, reverential in the presence of the mask. She put it down and began unbuttoning her shirt.

"Whoa," Ari said. "What's, um..."

"I have a tank top on underneath," Dierdre explained, flashing the shirt open so Ari could see. "It will help me get into character."

"Oh. All right..."

Dierdre shrugged out of the shirt and draped it over her chair. She picked up the mask and turned her back to Ari to put it on. It was designed her hug her face, but Ari assumed they took more extreme measures to ensure it wouldn't fall off mid-show. But for now, her ears would keep it from falling off. She used both hands to position it and, when she'd gotten it settled, she stood up straighter and faced Ari again.

Her hair was parted down the middle and fell on either side of the now-alien face. The hair perfectly concealed the edges of the mask, creating the illusion that her face had actually transformed. Dierdre's blue eyes shining out through eyeholes perfectly shaped to reveal them and little else. Dierdre even seemed to be standing differently, her shoulders back to push her chest forward, her hips cocked at an angle that implied seduction.

Ari nodded, duly impressed. "I can only imagine what it will look like with the rest of the costume."

"Yes, it will be quite a spectacle." Her voice was still husky, but now it was breathier. It was the voice of someone trying to be seductive. "If you don't mind, I have quite a bit of work left to do…"

"Of course. I'll be in the house. Call if you need anything."

Dierdre nodded, and then suddenly looked at Ari again. "I'm sorry, I'm so rude. I forgot to ask your name."

Ari stared at her. "You…" She narrowed her eyes. "Ari. Ariadne Willow."

Dierdre extended her hand. "It's a wonderful thing you're doing for Dierdre, Miss Willow. It's a pleasure to finally meet you."

"Meet…?"

Dierdre smiled beneath the mask. "I'm Saint Artemis."

Ari took her hand, squeezing the fingers, unsure of how else to react. "Oh. Okay. Hello."

Dierdre ended the handshake and turned back to the control panel. Ari looked at her back, trying to figure out what was going on. Nellie had mentioned this when she explained the falling-out between Dierdre and Rudy, but she implied it wasn't an issue anymore. Finally she just left the studio and closed the door behind her. She didn't know if Nellie had lied or if this was a relapse, or something Dierdre was hiding, but it was definitely something she had to consider going forward.

CHAPTER TEN

ARI WENT back to the studio at nine o'clock, relieved to see Dierdre unmasked then the door opened. She was still in her tank top, but the mask had been returned to the box. She smiled sheepishly after she let Ari in.

"I want to apologize for this afternoon. I was frustrated. Roadblock after roadblock. But the mask helped me break through the fog."

"That's okay," Ari said. "Is everything... okay now?"

Dierdre nodded. "Yeah. Oh. What time is it? It's dark outside... you should go home. I'm not going anywhere tonight, so you don't have to stick around. God, you must be starving."

Ari said, "There was some pasta in the cupboard. I made enough for both of us, but I didn't want to disturb you. It's in the fridge."

"Wow! Above and beyond. Thank you so much. Please, go. Go home." Before Ari could think of a way to broach the subject, Dierdre added, "And that whole introduction thing... I started thinking maybe I freaked you out a little with that. I know who I am, even when I'm wearing the mask. You hadn't been in the presence of the persona, so I was being a little cheeky. Sorry."

Ari smiled. "I have to say that's a bit of a relief."

Dierdre shrugged. "Sorry. Would you mind not telling Nellie about it? There was a... thing back when I first started performing as the character. It's over and done with now, but I don't want her to freak out and make more out of it."

"Just between us."

"Thanks. And thank you for everything, for dinner. I'll see you tomorrow?"

"Oh, actually, no. I have some personal business to deal with, and then I'm going to follow up on one of the leads from your list. An associate of mine is going to stay with you. Her name is Shae Segura. I'll email you a photo of her so you'll know it's her. Is there anything else I can do for you tonight?"

"You've done more than enough. Go, go. Oh, is Nellie here?"

"No, she left a few hours ago."

Dierdre inhaled sharply. "Oh, my goodness. Solitude. I won't know what to do with myself." She winked at Ari. "Goodnight, detective."

"Goodnight, Saint Artemis."

She left the studio to the sound of Dierdre chuckling and went back into the house. She checked all the windows and made sure the door was locked behind her. Most of the windows faced the back or sides of the property and were shaded by foliage, and the windows facing the street had blackout curtains. Any random passersby might not even know there was a house there unless they were looking for it. She checked the mailbox one more time before she finally left.

On the way home she stopped and picked up milkshakes. Dale had texted earlier to say she and Segura had dinner together after work. The message prepared Ari for the fact Dale would be in the apartment when she got there, but she was completely surprised to find her vacuuming. Housework wasn't completely alien to either of them, but it was usually a huge weekend undertaking that they did together, sharing the misery of scrubbing and tidying. She stood in the doorway and silently watched as Dale guided the cleaner under the dinner table. Finally Dale saw her and turned off the machine.

"Hi, honey, I'm home."

"Oh hello, dear," Dale said, abandoning the appliance to come get her milkshake. "I'm ever so glad to see you. Tough day at the office?"

They kissed hello. "Brutal. There were spreadsheets, and Joe in accounting is up to his old tricks again."

Dale rolled her eyes. "Ugh. Joe." She licked the top of her shake. "Mm, huckleberry. You're too good to me, puppy."

"I expect you to earn that milkshake, Miss Frye."

"How?"

Ari swirled a finger in the air. "Dance for me." Dale swayed her hips as she went into the kitchen to get some paper towels. Ari took a seat on the couch and put up her feet. "How was your day?"

"Dull. I filled up the bulletin board with a lot of boring stuff about the people on Dierdre's list." She sat down and snuggled against Ari's side. "Your day was more exciting, I bet."

"Maybe not exciting," Ari said, "but I learned a lot." She explained what she'd learned about the mysterious Rudy Paviour and her plans to go out and get her side of the story. "I'll do that after whatever you have planned. I assume that's what the vacuuming is about."

Dale said, "Um. Yeah, uh-huh. And I know it's pretty stupid trying to keep secrets from a detective. You've probably figured out everything~"

"Dale... I'm not thinking about it. I'm not putting together clues or working to solve anything. You said you would tell me when the time is right. I'm not going to investigate you."

"I know." She put her head on Ari's shoulder. "Thank you. For trusting me."

She kissed the top of Dale's head. "Easiest thing in the world." They focused their shakes for a bit before Ari remembered the chats on Dierdre's computer and told Dale about them. "From what I saw, she roleplays as herself with a bunch of different random people on the internet. I can't decide if that's narcissistic or delusional or... just weird."

"Maybe it's weird," Dale said. "I think it's weird. But who knows what kind of personal life she has? It must be hell for her to find someone to date."

Ari said, "She has this huge secret she can't tell anyone unless she trusts them. And if she dates them long enough to gain that trust, how can they trust her knowing she didn't tell them about such an enormous part of her life?"

Dale sat up and looked at Ari. "Like if she could turn into a wolf. I remember how you went through the same thing with the women you dated. Back when I was still just your assistant."

"Yeah." She tucked Dale's hair behind her ear and used the

motion to stroke her cheek. "I'm so lucky I found you."

They kissed and Dale moved her lips to Ari's ear. "That means so much to me... and you're going to be so happy you said it when I reveal the secret tomorrow."

"Yeah?"

"So happy," Dale repeated, and kissed Ari again.

They finished their milkshakes, and Dale slid down to put her head on Ari's lap. Ari closed her eyes and stroked Dale's hair until they were both almost asleep.

"Dale..."

"Mm?"

"You were never *just* my assistant."

Dale squeezed Ari's thigh, and Ari let herself drift off. She knew in a few minutes one of them would startle awake and drag the other's semi-conscious body to the bedroom. For now, though, the couch was plenty comfortable for her.

Dale's phone chimed with an incoming text at 4:16. She was already awake, but Ari twitched and rolled onto her back. "Noises..."

"Go back to sleep, puppy."

Ari rubbed the back of her hand over her eyes. "No I'm up..."

Dale looked over and saw that was a lie, and gently moved Ari's hand down to a more comfortable position. She knew who the text was from; the same person whose arrival was keeping her from getting any sleep. And, sure enough, the text was confirmation. "At the airport now. Landing at SEATAC approx 10am local time. Will cab to you."

She put her phone back on the nightstand. When she put her head back on the pillow, Ari shifted and draped her arm across Dale's stomach. Dale slipped her hand around Ari's shoulders and pulled her closer, giving up on sleep for the rest of the night.

Ari woke up to find Dale staring at her. She craned her neck to kiss Dale's chin. "How much of this is romantic, and how much is stressing over whatever will happen after breakfast?"

"Sixty-forty, with preference toward romance."

"I'll take it." She slipped out of Dale's embrace and sat on the edge of the bed to stretch. "What do you need from me today?"

"You can go pick up breakfast."

Ari nodded and went into the bathroom. She took a quick

shower, brushed her teeth, and went back out to find Dale had fallen asleep. She stretched across the mattress and kissed her lips.

"Hey. Sleepyhead. You want an extra half-hour?"

Dale murmured, "Yes," and Ari kissed her hair.

She left as quietly as she could and texted Segura to make sure she hadn't had any trouble finding Dierdre's place. "No problems. Did a quick scout of the property, nothing to report. Haven't spent time with DM yet."

She picked up breakfast and brought it home to find Dale was already up, but still in her pajamas. "I tried to sleep in, but I'm not used to that. So I cleaned a bit more."

Ari looked around. "If you say so... The place looks plenty clean."

Dale sighed. "I just have to stop thinking. What did you get? It smells greasy, and I'm starved."

"You know, you could focus on the fact this is the closest thing we've had to a morning off in a long time. Having Segura pick up some of the slack might be a really great thing in terms of quality time."

"That's true." She unwrapped her breakfast burrito. "And I do appreciate the chance to hang out for a few hours before going into the office."

"How long do we have to wait before the secret is revealed?"

Dale looked at the clock. "Well, his plane gets in at ten... figure twenty minutes for baggage check, half an hour to get here with traffic..."

"His," Ari repeated, narrowing her eyes. "Plane."

"I thought you said you weren't in detective mode."

Ari held up in her hands in surrender. "Sorry. Sorry. I'll find out everything in forty-five minutes."

Dale coughed on her food and looked at the clock. "What? Oh. Oh, damn. Oh... I'm not ready." She got to her feet, but Ari stood and got in her way before she could run into the bedroom.

"Hey. Stop. Breathe." She rubbed Dale's shoulders. "You have time to eat. You have time to get dressed and do your hair. The traffic out there is kind of bad, so half an hour to get here from SeaTac is generous and unlikely. Don't run the marathon before the starting gun has even gone off, okay?"

Dale sighed and closed her eyes. "Okay. Yes. Okay." She kissed Ari. "Thank you."

"My pleasure."

They sat down to finish their food, and then Dale went to finish getting ready. Ari checked to make sure everything in the living room was tidy, kicked her shoes into line next to the door and removed the debris from breakfast. She kept an eye on the clock and wished she was as confident as she'd sounded when she told Dale they had plenty of time. What if the plane got in early, what if this mystery man hadn't checked a bag? Traffic might magically clear up and give him a straight shot to them.

A tiny, skeptical, suspicious part of her brain wondered if the man was Isaac Hayden, but she shot down that theory as soon as it formed. Dale would never, and that was the only evidence she needed to dismiss it. But she couldn't shake the feeling that she should know who they were expecting. If she applied a little deductive reasoning, the answer was probably staring her in the face. But she'd promised she wouldn't play detective, so she didn't try to follow the threads.

It was just past ten-thirty when Ari heard a car door slam in the driveway. She called Dale, who hurried out of the bedroom smoothing down her blouse.

"Are you okay?" Ari asked.

"Mm-hmm." Dale looked at the front door with worry and apprehension.

Ari followed her gaze and saw a man coming down the stairs. As soon as she saw his shoes, she knew exactly who she was about to see.

"Oh, shit."

"Be good, puppy."

Dale brushed her hand over Ari's shoulder as she passed to open the door. Ari remained frozen where she was as the man entered. He gave Dale a hug, his body language stiff and awkward, then faced Ari with an unreadable expression. The man was a little shorter than Dale, with big ears and a ring of salt-and-pepper hair. He put down the suitcase he'd carried in, squared his shoulders, and lifted his chin in an attempt to match Ari's height.

"Samuel Frye, you remember Ariadne Willow," Dale said. "Ari... you remember my dad."

She certainly remembered him. She couldn't forget Dale's staunchly Republican father. The conservative-in-every-way, stopped talking to his daughter after she came out, and when he did contact her it was to try forcing her to her quit the agency for something safer father.

"Yep," Ari finally said. "I remember him. How have you been, Mr. Frye?"

"It's Dr. Frye," he said. "I'm doing very well, Miss Willow. I'm here to take my daughter home."

CHAPTER ELEVEN

ARI SAID, "The hell you are," at the same time Dale looked at her father and said, "What are you talking about?"

Samuel Frye looked between them and finally settled on his daughter. "You emailed me and said we needed to have an important discussion. Face-to-face. You practically begged me to come. You offered to pay for my ticket, you said it had to be as soon as possible."

"Right," Dale said.

"You paid for his ticket...?" Ari asked, trying not to calculate how much a last-minute ticket from Philadelphia would cost.

"No," Dale and her father said at the same time. "Well, yes, technically, I offered knowing he wouldn't allow it. It's a dad thing." She looked sternly at her father. "But that is *not* what we need to talk about."

Samuel said, "Then what, Dale? Did you want to show me that you'd downgraded to living in a *basement*? My god, when you told me to use the back entrance I expected a guest house, but this is beyond the pale. A basement!"

Dale bristled. "Dad..."

"This woman has you living underground in-in a rumpus

room. Teenagers should be playing Dungeons and Dragons over in that corner. This is not a person's home, Dale. I bought you a return ticket. Come home with me. You can stay with me until you get back on your feet, go back to school, get an actual~"

Dale shouted, "Stop talking!"

Ari blinked. Samuel was stunned enough to do as she said. Dale steadied her breath and moved away from her father to stand between him and Ari.

"This woman is the love of my life. This is a home. It's *our* home. It's the home we chose together, the home we're making together. I brought you here because I thought if you saw it, you might understand, but it's clear you don't. I wanted to say this to you in person.

"I'm not going to defend Ariadne to you anymore. She doesn't deserve to be explained or justified. If you don't understand what we have, that's on you, and I'm not going to waste any more time trying to make you see how lucky I am. A few months ago, I was more lost than I'd ever been. I lost myself. And Ariadne stood by me. She never lost her faith. She never wavered. I found my way back because she was holding the lifeline and pulled me in. She likes to tell people she'd be lost without me, and maybe it's true, but I don't have anything solid under my feet when she's not around. I love her. I'll always love her. She's the person I'm meant to be with. She is my family."

Samuel said, "Dale, this isn't~"

"I told you to stop talking," Dale said.

He clenched his jaw. Ari pressed her lips together, knowing a smile would be inappropriate.

"If you don't accept that Ari is my family, then... then you aren't."

"Dale," Ari whispered, lightly touching her elbow. "Maybe you should think~"

"I've thought about this. And I kept it from you so you wouldn't think about it or try to talk me out of doing it like this. I know him. I know what I have to do to get through to him." She hadn't looked away from Samuel. "I spent way too long waiting for you to see that Ari was good enough to be with me. I regret that. You should have been the one fighting. This is my family, this is the life I chose. You're welcome to be part of it, but the choice has to be yours."

'Samuel wiped a hand over his face. "Dale. Your mother would~"

"Get out."

He stared at her. Ari stared, too.

"Excuse me?"

"If you're about to use Mom in a shameful way, I don't want you in my house. In fact, you should leave no matter what. This is Ari's territory and you've never once shown her the respect a guest should have for their host. So I don't want you here anymore. You can text the name of your hotel if you want to meet up with me before you fly back to Pennsylvania, but you're not welcome here."

Samuel blinked, fuming. He looked at Ari, who didn't give him the satisfaction of looking scared.

"You asked me to shut down my business and fly across the country just so you could throw me out of some dank basement hovel?"

"I invited you here to see the life I'd built for myself. My home, my partner. This apartment fits us and our needs. I would take it over whatever two-bedroom you have in mind for me back home. And I would take the slowest days at our agency over a mind-numbing and soul-sucking lifetime as a receptionist at your dental office. I don't want to cut you out, Dad. You're cutting yourself out. This is your choice. And it's your last chance. Apologize to Ariadne for everything you've said about her, our work, and our home, and we can sit down and have a nice conversation."

Samuel picked up his suitcase. "I'm ashamed of you, Dale."

Dale said, "And I'm very sad to say I couldn't care less about what you think. Goodbye."

After a long moment in which he seemed to think she would have a change of heart, he turned and let himself out of the apartment.

Ari waited until he was out of the yard before she stepped forward and hugged Dale from behind. She kissed Dale's hair and said, "It's okay. You can relax now. I've got you."

Dale sagged against Ari, who squeezed her tighter to keep her from falling. "What did I just do?" Dale whispered.

"The bravest thing I've ever seen." She kissed Dale's cheek. "Those things you said about me..."

"You know how I feel."

"Still. Hearing it out loud doesn't get old. I love you. And I hope you know that you still have a family. Me, Mom, Milo. Other people whose names don't start with M..."

Dale chuckled and turned around to wrap her arms around Ari's waist. "I love you, too. All of you. Thank you for being here."

"I wouldn't have missed that for the world."

"But now you have to go."

Ari said, "After that? No. I need to be here for you."

Dale stepped back. "You need to go up to Bellingham, which means you have at least two hours on the road ahead of you. And honestly, I'm completely drained. That took all of my energy. I just want to collapse and sleep until sunset. You can take care of me tonight."

"Are you sure?"

"I'm sure." She kissed Ari's lips, tightening the embrace before stepping out of it. "Go. I'll sleep, and if I wake up before you get home, I'll call Segura to see how she's doing. And I really want to dig into those emails, see if I can figure out where they came from. See? I have a very full day and I don't need you underfoot, doting on me."

"If you say so." She kissed Dale's cheek and whispered, "I'm so proud of you, darlin'."

"Go," Dale said, blushing and waving Ari toward the door. "Your mystery is waiting."

Leaving was one of the hardest things Ari had done in a long time, but she had to admit Dale made a convincing argument. She also admitted to being slightly concerned Dr. Frye would be waiting in the driveway, but there was no sign of him when she finally went out to her car. Earlier she'd been dreading the drive to Bellingham, but now she was grateful for the chance to be alone in the car and think about what had just happened.

Dale was right. If she'd known in advance, she would have tried to protect Dale or at least taken the brunt of her father's anger. She'd only been able to stand there in shock, awed at how Dale handled the man whose acceptance had once been so important to her. Cutting ties with him was a huge step. Maybe even bigger than the engagement they'd finally entered into. That was something they'd have to sit down and talk about soon. Neither wanted the traditional church marriage, but there had to be something that worked for their relationship.

She didn't want to get Dale a ring just because it was tradition. And they'd already exchanged non-traditional totems of their commitment. She had her collar, and Dale had the bracelet with strands of Ari's hair threaded together with fur from the wolf. She couldn't think of anything more symbolic to use as for a wedding.

Ari was touching her collar as she crossed the city limits of Bellingham. She liked the town the few times she'd passed through. Beautiful views of Mount Baker to the east and a sparkling bay sprawling to the west, it was quintessential small-town Washington. It was the kind of place that would have a neighborhood named Lettered Streets with white picket fences and perfectly parallel blocks. The high school was a massive white colosseum with pillars on either side of the entrance. A woman pushed a stroller on the sidewalk, and there was actually an old man sweeping the sidewalk outside of a small grocery store. He waved when Ari drove by.

In other words, it was the perfect place for someone to disappear off the grid.

Ari found the address Nellie had given her on A Street, quite possibly the most generic street name she'd ever heard. It was also straight out of a storybook: a two-story Craftsman house painted baby blue, white picket fence, flagpole in the front yard. An archway spanned the front gate, which had flowers woven into the trellis. She parked at the curb and got out, making it halfway to the gate before she heard barking from the backyard.

The barking intensified when the Akita rounded the corner and saw an actual threat. It raced to the fence and jumped onto its hind legs, letting her know that she was absolutely, definitely not crossing over into its territory this afternoon. Ari took off her sunglasses and walked to stand in front of the dog, which only increased its fury. The dog had a thick white coat with patches of orange gold on its head and shoulders. There was no real violence in its bark, just a very loud and insistent warning. *Back, get back, you no go here, leave!*

"Hey," Ari said. "I'm not a threat to you or your human. I'm a friend."

The dog snarled and barked.

"Stop that." She held out her hand, fingers stiff and palm out. The dog growled as she reached for it, but then caught a whiff of something on the air that gave it pause. The growling quieted and then stopped completely as Ari took another step closer. The dog sniffed her palm and confirmed she was the source of the unusual odor. Security took a backseat to curiosity and it began to sniff more intently. Ari smiled and relaxed her fingers, turning her wrist to scratch the side of the dog's face.

"That's more like it. What's your name, buddy? My name is Ariadne."

Dale sometimes claimed she was telepathic with dogs. Other *canidae* said the same, but only when they were trying to impress someone. Ari didn't think there was anything telepathic happening, not really. She believed some species just picked up on cues humans couldn't see. Smell, body language, tone of voice no matter what was being said. The dog smelled Ari's wolf, it saw how she was standing, it heard her speaking and saying words like 'friend,' and the aggression faded.

Her theory didn't explain how she knew the dog's name was Mingus, but she was willing to ignore that until it became an issue.

She was still petting Mingus when someone at the end of the street said, "Well, now, you're going to have to explain how you managed that."

The woman was standing with her hip cocked and a bag of groceries cradled in her arms. She was about Dierdre's age which put her in her early thirties, with straight blonde hair and shockingly blue eyes. It was clear she'd been standing there for a while watching Ari pet the dog, and her expression was bemused curiosity more than anger or suspicion.

"Is this your guy?" Ari asked. "He's super-friendly."

"No, he isn't," the woman said as she came closer. "The mailman has threatened to stop coming by the house unless I lock him in the garage."

Ari said, "I guess I'm just a dog whisperer."

"Uh-huh." She unlocked the gate and let herself in.

"Are you Rudy Paviour?"

The woman stopped and closed the gate between them. Now the suspicion arrived in her eyes. "And who might you be?"

"My name is Ariadne Willow. I'm a private investigator from Seattle." She handed over her card. "I was hoping I could ask you a few questions about a case I'm working on."

Rudy looked at the card. "Seattle? You came a long way to risk I might just say no and send you away."

Ari said, "I hoped making the trip would convince you to at least hear me out."

"What do I possibly have to do with a case in Seattle?"

"It's about Dierdre Macrae."

Rudy flinched and lowered the card, then held it out to give it back. "I'm sorry you wasted your time, Miss Willow. That is not a topic open to discussion."

"Dierdre is my client." Rudy was already walking back to the house and didn't look back. Mingus followed, although he looked torn about leaving his newfound friend. "I'm afraid someone wants to hurt her. They've sent messages. One was hand-delivered to the house where she's staying."

Rudy stopped on the porch and looked at her. "What makes you think I would know anything about... oh." She looked past Ari. "Oh, I see. You didn't come out here for information. You came out here because she gave you my name as a suspect. Hah. Okay. That's really what she... She really thinks I would be capable of that?"

"Dierdre didn't give me your name. She doesn't even know I'm here. I got your address from Nellie Bain."

Rudy laughed. "She's still working with Nellie Bain? Oh, god." She rubbed her forehead and looked down at Mingus, who tilted his head back to return her gaze. "Please, Miss Willow..."

Ari said, "I need to know as much as I can about Dierdre if I'm going to figure out who is sending the threats. I can go back to Seattle right now, but then I would be left with only Nellie's version of the story. I would much rather hear your side of things."

Mingus made a chuffing sound, as if he was saying "I vouch for her, boss." Rudy looked at him and then nodded toward the house.

"If I let you in, will you tell me how you charmed my damn dog?"

"No," Ari said, "but I'll help you put away the groceries."

Rudy sighed and turned to go inside. "Fair enough."

Ari smiled and let herself in through the gate, hurrying to catch up. Mingus looked back at her, and Ari winked her thanks to him. Though Ari knew he was just blinking, Dale would have claimed the dog definitely winked back.

CHAPTER TWELVE

GOING INSIDE Rudy's house felt like a museum display of a time before technology. No television dictated how the living room furniture was arranged, and she didn't see any computers, smartphones, or voice-activated household appliances. Ari hadn't realized how much she'd gotten use to them, living in Seattle and being surrounded by billionaire geeks who loved their toys. The sole concession to technology she saw was a CD player tucked away high on a bookshelf, surrounded by stacks of jewel cases. It was the house of someone's grandmother, Ari thought, not the young woman in front of her.

She followed Rudy into the kitchen. Mingus walked between them, nails clicking on the hardwood floors. Rudy put the bags on the counter and took out a carrot. She held it out like a stick and tossed it. Mingus caught it in his jaws before it hit the floor, dropped down, and began gnawing on it like a bone. Rudy kept her back to Ari as she began unloading everything else.

"I don't want your help with this. You don't know where anything goes."

"Fair enough," Ari said.

Rudy looked back at her. "Dierdre really doesn't know I'm

here?"

"She doesn't even know I know your name."

"Good. That's good, I guess. So what version of the story did you get from Nellie?"

Ari watched her. She even moved and talked like an older woman. "You and Dierdre were best friends. You came up with the idea for Saint Artemis. You had a crush on Dierdre but she didn't reciprocate. She came to you one night in character, the two of you spent the night together, then she claimed it was Saint Artemis and not her. So you left and Nellie paid for your silence about her real identity."

Rudy nodded slowly. "That's a nice story. I might start using it myself. Much cleaner than the one in my head."

"I'd love it if you ran that one by me."

"I'm sure you would."

She finished with the groceries and poured herself a glass of lemonade. She gestured with the pitcher and Ari nodded, so she poured a second glass and motioned for Ari to follow her into the living room. Mingus hesitated at the edge of the kitchen and fell into step beside Ari. Rudy frowned down at him. "Seriously, what did you do to my dog?"

Ari reached down and scratched between his ears. "We just kind of speak the same language."

"Apparently. But I've always said dogs are the best judges of character and if you got *that* one on your side... well." Rudy sat in one of the armchairs and crossed one leg over the other, settling against the cushions as Ari took a seat on the couch. "What is the nature of the threats being leveled against Dierdre?"

"They threaten to reveal her identity. They talk about her being a coward. Hiding. The notes imply she's not just protecting her privacy, she's hiding from something. Or someone." She looked around the house. "I can't help but feel as if you're hiding, too."

Rudy said, "My name is on the mailbox."

"But you have no online presence whatsoever. Do you have any idea how unusual that is? Especially for a young woman like yourself. You must have grown up in the era of email, if not social media."

"My parents couldn't afford a computer, let alone the internet. I never considered it a hardship. Dierdre was my only real friend, so I didn't need Facebooks or Twitters to keep up with anyone. And now I read in the paper about people deleting their accounts, and it sounds like addicts coming clean. They all seem much happier for walking away."

Ari said, "Sure. But it definitely makes a private investigator's job harder."

Rudy smiled. "To answer your implication, no. I'm not hiding from anyone. I live a very quiet life in a quiet town because I like the solitude. Nellie wasn't exaggerating when she said I was paid handsomely for my silence. Every day I resist saying Saint Artemis' real name is another dollar in my pocket."

"You said there was more to the story about your falling out with Dierdre."

"Yeah." Rudy took a long drink of her lemonade, so Ari drank as well. It was extremely good, and surprisingly minty. "The first thing you should know is that Nellie's in love with Dierdre, too."

"Oh."

"She was forty when they met, and Dierdre was nineteen. Even if the feelings had been mutual, which they weren't, Nellie wouldn't have let anything happen. But everything she does comes from a place of... yearning, I suppose? Dierdre is the love of her life, and she works her ass off to make sure she gets everything she wants."

Ari said, "That must be incredibly, um... frustrating for her."

Rudy shrugged. "She seemed fulfilled when I knew her. She never tried to take advantage of Dierdre. Of course it's been over ten years since we last spoke face to face, so I suppose things might have changed. But as sweetly ironic as it might be to turn the tables and name her as a suspect, I really don't see her ever sending threats to Dierdre even if they were hollow."

The front door opened and a woman entered, already speaking. "Some asshole parked right in front of the house. Damned tourists..."

Rudy stood and so did Ari. The new arrival was older, at least fifty, with silver hair and wearing the uniform of a postal carrier. She stopped when she saw Ari and looked a question at Rudy.

"Effie, this is Ariadne Willow. She's--"

"The asshole who parked in front of the house," Ari said. "Sorry about that."

Effie shook her head. "No trouble. Right...?" To Rudy, "Everything's okay?"

Rudy said, "Yeah, everything's fine. But we have to talk about the silent thing."

"Say no more," Effie said, holding up her hands as she

retreated. "I just had to swing by to pick up my knee brace."

Rudy said, "You told me you keep that in your truck."

"I don't need it every day."

"But if it's available when you *do* need it~"

"Honey..."

Rudy sighed. "We'll talk when you get home. I love you."

"I love you, too. I'll go out through the garage so I won't interrupt again." She nodded to Ari. "Nice to meet you. I apologize for the asshole comment."

Ari shrugged. "You would have been right if I wasn't a guest. And as it is, I was uninvited."

Effie disappeared down the hall, and Ari heard a door open and close. They both resumed their seats and Rudy smiled.

"My wife."

"She seems great."

Rudy smiled proudly, but hid it behind her glass.

"Does she know about Dierdre?"

"No. She knows my money comes from a non-disclosure agreement, which means I can't discuss the terms of it even with her. She asked a few questions when I first told her about it. Is it illegal, immoral, harmful. When I said no, she assured me she didn't need the details."

"That's a lot of trust."

"That's a relationship," Rudy said. "That's faith in your partner."

Ari nodded. "So you were saying you don't think Nellie is a viable suspect."

"It's more likely that Dierdre is sending them to herself in a fugue state as Saint Artemis." She started to take a drink but stopped herself. "I mean to say, extremely unlikely. Dierdre does not become a different person when she's in costume. I've never believed that."

"She tried it on me yesterday," Ari said. "She put on a mask and introduced herself like she'd never seen me before."

Rudy nodded. "She does that. But you didn't drive all the way up here for my theories about who is sending the notes. You want to know what really happened back then, when Saint Artemis was still a newborn."

Ari said, "I think it could help me," but she couldn't say how. She felt very strongly that she needed to figure out who Dierdre was to understand why she chose to wear a mask, and knowing that could lead her to the note-sender.

"Dierdre and I were inseparable, but I admit that I contributed very little to her career. I wrote a few songs, but they were pablum compared to what Dierdre wrote. She would put on her costume and go perform at burlesque clubs and drag shows. I think she would have been happy doing that for the rest of her life. Collecting tips and working for peanuts. Everything changed when she was discovered."

A door closed elsewhere in the house. Rudy twisted to look out the front window and waved goodbye, blowing a kiss as Effie crossed the lawn.

"So she didn't go looking for representation?"

"God no. It just sort of happened. The right people sat down in the audience, they left business cards for her, eventually rent and the price of gas meant she needed more money than the clubs were paying, so she decided to call one of them back. She figured millions of people out there make albums hoping to hit it big. It was like playing the lottery for her. Maybe she'd get a few bucks, maybe it would be a bust, but why not play and see what happened."

Ari said, "But Nellie saw stars."

"Nellie Bain. The bane of her existence. Nellie believed Dierdre belonged on stage. She also wanted to fuck Dierdre, but she was nineteen, a virgin, and mostly straight. So Nellie put all her efforts into making Saint Artemis a star. Dierdre went along for the ride. She still got to play her music, she didn't have to worry about money anymore, and she had someone in her corner willing to fight for the mask."

Ari said, "The mask must have been a hard sell."

Rudy shook her head and waved her hand dismissively. "It's glam rock, performance art. It's Daft Punk wearing robot masks, or Sia hiding her face behind a wig."

"For someone without TV or a computer, you sure know a lot about pop culture."

Rudy smiled and nodded at the window she'd just blown a kiss through. "Osmosis from what she hears at work. She has a laptop and a television in her office upstairs. Just because I cut myself off from the rest of the world doesn't mean it can't find me."

Ari said, "I suppose that's true. So what happened between you and Dierdre? Why did you leave?"

"I was willing to stay. Put the night we had together behind us. But Nellie was furious. Jealous, you know? That I got to be with

Dierdre when she never would. It's not like she saw me as competition..." Rudy rubbed her jaw as she put her thoughts in order. "She acted like I'd won some contest I didn't know we were having. She started treating me like garbage. Refused to speak directly to me. Stopped sending me concert information so I wouldn't show up."

"Dierdre let her treat you like that?"

"I never told her. She needed Nellie, as much as I hated to acknowledge that. Nellie could help her a lot more than I could. So in the end I decided to take her offer to vanish. I figured it would be better for Dierdre in the long run."

Ari said, "That must have been hard."

Rudy exhaled sharply and looked toward the window, but she wasn't looking at anything outside. Ari let the silence linger. Finally Rudy snapped out of the memory and shifted in her seat.

"Whoever is sending the notes," Rudy said, "they definitely knew how to hurt Dierdre. They could have threatened violence, but they attacked her secret. That's bound to scare her more than any physical attack. She was reluctant to become famous as Saint Artemis, but it *never* would have happened as Dierdre. If she's exposed, she would be finished."

Ari said, "So it has to be someone close enough to know that was the right way to twist the knife. There can't be many names on that list."

"As far as I know, it's only me and Nellie."

"The two suspects I've ruled out," Ari said.

Rudy shrugged apologetically.

There were other names on their suspect list - the guitarist, the producer, and the other singer - but they all seemed thin. And the artist had no reason to risk losing a customer by eliminating Saint Artemis' need for masks. The three people with the means to send the notes had no motive she could figure out, and the rest of the list seemed unlikely because they didn't truly know Dierdre.

Essentially she'd just driven most of the way to Canada to end up farther back than when she'd started.

Rudy watched her. "I feel like I just threw your whole case out the window."

Ari sighed and showed her palms. "Maybe it seems that way. But you really just cleared the deck a little, and gave me some insight into who Dierdre is and how she thinks. That's valuable. And maybe one of the other suspects just got lucky when they chose an angle of attack. They might not know how big of a threat they were making. It's obvious Saint Artemis protects her identity, so it's an obvious thing to target. So we'll keep them on the board for now."

"I'm happy I could be of some help."

"You have my card in case you think of something else that might be useful." She stood and held out her hand. "Thank you for your time, and apologize to your wife for my parking."

Rudy smiled and shook Ari's hand. "She was only mad when she thought you were a tourist. It's been an issue."

"Ah. I see. I should leave you alone. I have a long drive back to Seattle."

"Good luck, Miss Willow."

Ari headed for the door. Mingus, who had been settled next to Rudy's chair for the conversation, got up and trotted after her. Ari stopped and crouched down to scratch his neck and the top of his head.

"Goodbye to you, Mingus. It was good to meet you, too."

Rudy stared in disbelief. "Okay. Honestly. What's your secret?"

Ari smiled and shrugged. "What can I say? I've just always been a dog person."

CHAPTER THIRTEEN

ARI SPENT the drive back to Seattle thinking about their suspect list and everything Rudy had told her about the origins of Saint Artemis. The person sending the notes didn't necessarily have to be on the list. Brcich, Conrad, and Morning were just Patient Zero. Any one of them could have let the secret slip to someone over the past few years. Maybe Brcich was in a new band who saw the potential in ruining Dierdre's gimmick. Or Theresa Conrad, the producer, accidentally sent a memo with the wrong line redacted. She hoped Dale would have better luck tracking the emails, but she wasn't hopeful.

She tried to look less defeated than she felt as she parked outside Dierdre's place. It was late enough that the house was once again shrouded in darkness, but she managed to get up the stairs without tripping. She was poised to knock on the door when a voice came out of the darkness to her right.

"Halt, who goes there?"

She turned toward the woman she couldn't see, but her *canidae* senses picked up a familiar scent on the wind. "Housekeeping."

"A likely story," Segura said. "You look like trouble to me. Have you ever done time...? Why don't you move along before I have to get rough?"

"I'd like to see you try."

Segura chuckled and turned on her phone's flashlight, aiming it at their feet so they were caught in the backwash.

"How'd everything go today?"

"Case-wise, not good. Dale... up in the air. I think it went well, but we'll see." She nodded at the door. "How'd things go here?"

Segura wrinkled her nose and shrugged. "Fine. She didn't seem to like me much. She came out of the bedroom and said hello when I got here, then didn't come back downstairs until close to noon. We had lunch together, but she never even looked at me. After that she was just in the studio all day. We might have said ten words to each other since this morning."

"That's strange. She seemed to open right up with me."

"I didn't take it personally. I spent most of the day with the ice queen, Nellie. She ignored me, too. Spent the whole time on her laptop and cell phone. When she finally left, I came out here to, um... recon? Is that the word? Just checking out the perimeter."

"Well, I'm relieving you of duty. Thanks for filling in today."

Segura saluted. "Happy to be of service, boss. You all set to be here tomorrow?"

"Yeah. You should stick to the office in case your parole officer comes back."

"Right. I'll leave you to it." She shifted her weight but stopped herself before she actually moved. "Oh. Melissa wants to have you and Dale over for dinner some night."

Ari said, "Dale has brought that up, too. We'll definitely make it happen." She shook Segura's hand. "Glad to have you on the team, Shae."

"Glad to be useful."

Segura left and Ari unlocked the door to let herself into the house. All the lights were on downstairs, but she didn't see signs of anyone actually being present. She listened for movement upstairs before she went through the back door into the yard to the studio. Muffled music played inside and she waited for a lull to try knocking.

"Dierdre? It's Ari. I just wanted to let you know I was here."

The music stopped and the door opened just enough for Dierdre to poke her head out. "Ariadne. Hey. Hi." She twisted to look toward the house. "Where's the other one? Shane?"

"Shae," Ari corrected. "She went home."

Dierdre relaxed and opened the door wider. She was in a T-shirt and shorts, barefoot. "Good. I didn't like her." She flinched and pushed a hand through her hair. "No, not like... she's fine. I'm sure she's fine. But she was new. I didn't really know her and she was just suddenly here. I don't like that. I like how we met. Neutral ground. That's better."

"I'll keep that in mind. Hopefully it can be me from now on. For tonight, I'll be inside if you need anything."

"Oh, actually, you can go ahead and leave. I'm about to finish up here, and then I'll crash for the night. Shae was really vigilant all day. I think I'm snug as a bug."

"Are you sure?"

Dierdre nodded. "Positive. I'll see you tomorrow."

She went back into the studio. Ari made sure everything in the house was locked and secure before she left. It was another overcast night heavy with the scent of rain, and the wolf was scratching to be let out for a run, but she quieted it. She needed to be human as much as possible during this case. Dierdre was counting on her to be available. Not to mention Dale also needed her more than ever at the moment. The wolf was a lot of things, but it couldn't support someone in emotional turmoil.

The office was dark when Ari drove past, so she continued home. She found Dale at the dinner table working on her laptop, a takeout container sitting forgotten to one side. She glanced up when Ari came in, blew her a kiss, and went back to what she was typing.

"How'd Bellingham go?"

"Not bad in general," Ari said, picking up the Styrofoam box and examining Dale's leftovers. "frustrating for the case. What is this?"

"Thai. Pad See Ew."

"Ew," Ari said.

"Never gets old, puppy. You can finish it off if you're hungry."

Ari sat down across from Dale and started to eat. "Thanks."

"Ugh, warm it up at least. It's cold."

"It's fine."

"Forget the wolf. *You're* the animal."

Ari smirked at her and kept eating. "I only stopped for lunch on the way up to Bellingham. I'm starving. Tell me about your day while I finish this off."

Dale pushed the computer to one side so it wasn't between

them. "All the emails were sent from different IP addresses, but all originated in Seattle or nearby. Someone was trying to cover their tracks."

"But they didn't count on you."

"They never do." Dale got up and went to the kitchen. She came back with a bottle of beer, which she sat in front of Ari. "It's not helpful to find out who they are, since they used public wifi, but it confirms that they're all from the person who hand-delivered the latest note." She waited until Ari had swallowed the drink she'd taken before she said, "There was something else, too."

Ari said, "Yeah?"

"Dad's flight out was this afternoon. He emailed to say he had moved it to another day."

"Really?" Ari said. "Dale, that's big."

"I don't know. It might mean he's thinking over what I said, or it might mean he's plotting ways to change my mind. Whatever his motives are, he's in Seattle for at least the next few days."

Ari said, "I'll keep that in mind."

"Your turn," Dale said. "Tell me what you found out."

Ari sighed and put down her fork. She relayed everything she'd learned from Rudy, and how it changed their suspect list to more of a general idea of who might be involved.

"So not exactly square one," Dale said when she finished. "More like a couple of steps behind square one."

"Yeah. The list isn't necessarily useless, but I'd be very surprised if anyone on it is actually responsible. And now Dierdre doesn't want anyone else keeping guard at her place, so it looks like I'll be pulling that duty for the foreseeable future. Not that I really have any leads to chase down."

Dale said, "And if anything comes up, you have me and Shae to pick up the slack. It'll be fine." She closed her laptop and stood up. "Now, if you're finished eating, go shower and brush your teeth. I'll clean up in here and meet you in bed."

"What now?" She looked at her watch. "I know we have to get up early, but I'll never get to sleep now."

"Didn't say sleep." She bent down to kiss Ari's cheek, then her lips. "This morning, I stood up to a man I've been low-key terrified of my entire life. I defended you and our relationship. And I've spent all day thinking about how I would celebrate that achievement, and I have some ideas I think you will be very interested in."

"And yet, you still chose Thai food for dinner."

Dale grinned. "That's why I told you to brush your teeth." She kissed Ari again. "Don't dally, my dear."

Ari lay back with a pillow under her shoulders, hands on Dale's waist and lips nuzzling her neck, passively enjoying the way their bodies were moving together. Dale had one hand on Ari's hip and the other on her breast. Ari's hands had done a bit of exploring before but now she was content to leave them where they were. They'd also whispered to each other quite a bit earlier, but now the only sound was Dale's heavy breathing and an occasional moan from Ari as Dale's thigh brushed against her.

Until an extremely unwelcome sound invaded the serenity of the moment. The dark was turned pale blue by the screen of Ari's phone as it chimed with an incoming call. They both groaned, and Ari closed her teeth on Dale's shoulder. She lifted her hips and pulled Dale against her.

"You know you have to answer it," Dale said.

"Answer what?" Ari said. "Don't stop."

"It's work, puppy." She reached for the phone and looked at name. "Shit. It's Dierdre."

Ari reluctantly took the phone and swept her thumb across the screen. Dale sat up and pushed her hair out of her face, perched on Ari's thigh in an extremely distracting display of curves.

"Dierdre?" Ari tried to sound normal, not breathless or frustrated. "Is everything okay?"

Dierdre whispered, "They were here again."

"Who?" Ari tapped Dale's hip and she rolled to one side. Ari sat up and put her feet on the floor, trying to switch gears. "Are they in the house?"

"I heard a b-bang on the door. On the front door. Not knocking. Like one really loud *bang*! And then nothing. I thought I imagined it. I stayed upstairs for... f-for twenty minutes but I finally had to go look to tell myself it was nothing. A skunk or something knocked over a planter or something." She sounded breathless, panicky. "But I opened the door and there was a note nailed there. It was *nailed there*." Her voice broke and became a sob.

"Go back upstairs and stay there. I'll be there in five minutes."

"Hurry."

Ari had gotten her underwear on while she was talking. She hung up and turned to see Dale had already untangled her bra and a T-shirt, and she took both with a quiet huff of gratitude. "I'm sorry, Dale."

"That's what we get for taking our time." She waited for Ari to get the shirt on, then kissed her lips. "Go, puppy. She'll probably want you to stay the night. Just text me when you have the all clear."

"I will." She nodded at the wrinkled sheets. "I owe you."

"I'll collect with interest."

Ari growled, kissed Dale again, and hurried out to find her shoes.

She didn't quite make her five minute estimate, but she was close enough thanks to late-night traffic and a heavy foot. She took out her flashlight as she approached the house, sweeping the beam over the driveway and the narrow strip of grass between properties for any evidence of an intruder. Everything looked normal, and the stairs likewise lacked any telltale muddy footprints.

She glanced up at the house to make sure she wasn't being watched, then closed her eyes and concentrated. Changing only a part of her body hurt like hell and she hated doing it, but she didn't have time to fully transform into the wolf. She needed its heightened senses now, so she let her skull shift and reshape, felt a film slip across her eyes as her features repositioned themselves into a snout. Her hands twitched, and she felt an itchiness at her back that told her the pelt wanted to sprout free, but she resisted and opened lupine eyes for a fresh look at the scene.

Animal tracks crossed the property. Rabbits and cats and dogs. She ignored those, and the headache squeezing at her temples from holding the change, and focused on people. Herself, Shae, Nellie. Two more tracks, one very fresh, fresher than Ari's own, which meant whoever left it came by after Ari went home for the night. She followed it to the street where it disappeared.

Someone had gotten out of a vehicle, gone up the stairs, and then came back down. There could be an innocent explanation for the extra scent. Maybe a dog got loose and the owner happened to catch up with it on Dierdre's property. It was much more likely that they were the ones who left the note. The trail ended with the car, unfortunately, but at least she could prove someone had been there. And if push came to shove, she could compare the scent to any of their suspects.

Ari relaxed and felt her face change back, the bone cracking noisily. She grunted and rubbed her jaw, knowing the soreness would linger well into the next day.

She went upstairs and checked the door before letting herself into the house. One nail had been hammered into the wood at eye-level. She tugged on it experimentally, holding it by the edges of the head to avoid ruining any fingerprints. It was stuck in hard enough that she couldn't budge it, so she left it in place until she could do something about it.

The only light on was over the stove, which threw strange shadows across the entire space. She stood between the living room and kitchen and listened before she spoke. "Dierdre? It's Ariadne."

"Ari?" The voice came from upstairs, muffled by a closed door.

"Stay where you are," she called back. "I'm going to make sure the rest of the house is clear."

Dierdre said, "Hurry, please..."

The open plan of the house made it easy to check for intruders. She opened the handful of closed doors and scanned them before moving on. Her sense of smell was greater than most people's even when she wasn't in wolf form and she didn't pick up any unusual or unexpected odors. No cologne, no perfume, nothing but a faint whiff of mold coming from under the sink. The note was lying on the kitchen island, and she took a moment to turn it around and read the message.

"I see you," she muttered, translating the all-caps text speech. "Who you really are. The mask will eventually fall and everyone will see what I see." She checked the back of the note and then said, "Well, okay then."

The outside flood lights washed the backyard in a glow like an alien ship had just appeared overhead, and Ari went out to check the studio. The door was locked but the front door key also worked there. Her phone flashlight pushed away the remaining shadows under the bushes to confirm no one was hiding there. When she confirmed the property was clear, she went back inside and climbed the stairs to the second floor.

"Dierdre?"

One of the closed doors opened and Dierdre stuck her head out. Her hair was tangled and pulled back in a ponytail, her face scrubbed and shining with some kind of moisturizer. Her eyes were wide, lips pressed tight together. She was in a tank top and a pair of black briefs.

"Did you see, find anything?"

"There was definitely someone out there who shouldn't have been, but they're gone now. Are you okay?"

Dierdre leaned against the door frame and hung her head. "I shouldn't have bothered you. I panicked. Freaked out. I'm sorry. This wasn't in the job description."

"It was, actually," Ari said. "Whoever we're looking for was not only on your property, they're getting bolder. Nailing a note to the door is a whole level above putting something in the mailbox. We're going to call the police~"

"No!" Dierdre said. "God! No. Police showing up here in the middle of the night, every single person in the neighborhood will be looking at me. No. Call them in the morning if you have to call them at all."

Ari reluctantly agreed. "Tomorrow. As for tonight, I can stay if you like. I don't think they'll come back, but it might help you get some sleep. I can camp out downstairs."

Dierdre visibly relaxed and nodded. "I think I would like that. I didn't want to ask. It's such an imposition."

"It's what you hired me for," Ari reminded her again. "We should call Nellie~"

"No!" Dierdre shook her head. "She'll find out in the morning. If we tell her now she'll just come running. It's bad enough I ruined your night. Thank you."

Ari said, "I just want to make sure you're safe. If that means I have to sleep on your couch every night in case they come back, then that's what I'll do."

Dierdre didn't look happy about that, but she nodded. "I'll bump up your pay if it comes to that."

"We'll worry about that later. For now, just get some sleep."

"I'll try."

Ari started back downstairs but Dierdre reappeared before she'd gotten very far. She presented Ari with a pair of pillows and a folded blanket.

"The least I can do."

"Thanks," Ari said with a chuckle. "Good night, Dierdre."

"Good night."

Ari made up the couch and lay down, taking out her phone to text Dale that everything was okay and she was staying the night.

"I get you all hot and bothered and you go sleep in another woman's house? That's gratitude."

Ari sent a sad face emoji.

Dale replied with a heart, and then: "I'll bring you a change of clothes in the morning."

"I love you."

"Love you, puppy."

Ari turned off her phone and put it on the coffee table. She listened to the silence of the house. This neighborhood was more insulated from major thoroughfares than she was used to, and she missed the intermittent hum of cars passing. Surely someone had to notice unexpected visitors in such a quiet place, like Rudy's wife and their problem with tourist parking. Security cameras had helped with the Burroughs case. Maybe the neighbors around here caught something useful. She'd have Segura go around and ask for tapes.

For now, all she could do was try to sleep and hope the excitement was done for the night.

CHAPTER FOURTEEN

THE EXCITEMENT was definitely over for the night, and continued to stay away for the next week. Nellie insisted on promoting Ari to a live-in bodyguard once she learned about the late-night delivery. Ari packed a bag and arranged for time off where Segura took over for her while she spent time with Dale. Dierdre wasn't thrilled about it, but they timed Segura's shifts to coincide with studio time, so they never had to interact. Dierdre insisted it wasn't that she disliked the other woman, she just felt she'd built up a better rapport with Ari. They had built up a trust, and anyone else was just a hired hand.

"You better be careful, puppy," Dale warned her on one of their dates. "She's trying to steal you away from me."

"I only have eyes for one redhead," Ari promised.

While Dale made it clear she wasn't a fan of Ari spending every night somewhere else, she did enjoy how much it felt like they were dating every time Ari came to pick her up. They'd go out to eat, take walks, fool around, and then Ari would have to leave before it got too late.

"Plus my dad is still in town. It's like sneaking around behind his back. It's fun. Like being a teenager again."

Ari responded by stroking Dale's hip. "Boy, it would have saved a lot of time if I'd known you as a teenager."

"But think of all the fun you wouldn't have had." She nuzzled Ari's cheek. "Tell me about one of your wild conquests from back in the day, puppy…"

"Oh, where to begin," Ari said, and proceeded to titillate Dale with a particularly juicy story.

Meanwhile, Segura did a canvas of the neighbors. All they discovered was that anyone who had security cameras was aiming them in the wrong direction to see the narrow, secluded street in front of Dierdre's house. Ari kept an eye on the street in front of the house, especially after dark, and Dierdre spent most of her time in the studio. Dale continued vetting the people on the suspect list, but still hadn't turned up anything incriminating or even intriguing enough to consider any of them viable as the sender.

After the note stuck to the door, Dierdre was reluctant to leave the house even to get food. Nellie shopped for groceries, and Ari arranged for Dale to bring them the occasional takeout order. Ari gave the nail from the door to Diana, who promised to abuse a few police resources to see if she could find any fingerprints on it. "Don't count on a miracle, though," she warned. "Even if we get a good print, which is in no way guaranteed, it's useless without something to match it against."

Ari said she understood, but she was still hoping for something tangible. None of the suspects looked likely. Lila Brcich was completely eliminated because Dale discovered she was on tour in Canada when the two notes were hand-delivered, and Theresa Conrad was moved to the 'very unlikely' column when Segura confirmed she lived and worked in Port Townsend. The shortest route to Seattle included a ferry, and the long route was over a hundred miles. The woman Dale spoke to at Cartography confirmed Conrad was at a recording session at eight the morning after the note had been left. It wouldn't have been impossible for her to make the trip and get back in time, but it was enough for Ari to consider her cleared.

That left Renata Morning. The woman wanted to collaborate with Saint Artemis, not ruin her career. If anything, she had more incentive to keep Dierdre's secret than revealing it.

Eliminating all the people who knew about her identity was both good and bad for the case. They didn't have to waste time looking deeper into the list, but it also meant the note-leaver was much more likely to be a stranger, a fan, a random threat. No amount of detective work could have gotten between John Lennon and Mark David Chapman.

She'd been staying with Dierdre for a week when their routine finally changed. Nellie arrived early in the morning and dropped a stack of papers on the breakfast table in front of Ari.

"The layout of the Callahan Concert Hall, with the areas Dierdre is likely to frequent."

Dierdre looked up from her Froot Loops. "You don't have to talk about me in the third person. I'm right here."

Nellie continued speaking to Ari. "Learn it well enough that you can navigate the place blindfolded. We're going to have rehearsals there starting tomorrow and I want you to be prepared."

Ari eagerly turned the file around so she could orient herself. "Perfect. I was starting to go a little stir crazy. This is just what I needed."

Nellie finally addressed Dierdre. "The dancers need their choreography."

"I'm almost finished with it."

"Rehearsals start *tomorrow*. They're already going in completely raw. If you're not finished, we can recycle~"

"I'll have it ready by tomorrow."

Nellie pressed her lips together and crossed her arms. Dierdre stared back at her.

"Can I finish my fucking breakfast first?"

"Fine," Nellie said. "But Tracy is expecting to see a full routine tomorrow morning, and if it isn't ready~"

"It'll be ready, Nellie. Go away. I've already had enough of you for today." Nellie remained where she was. "Don't make me ask Ari to throw you out."

Ari shrugged apologetically. "I'd do it, too. If she asked me."

Nellie huffed and retreated. "I'll leave you alone to do your work. But if you don't come through, not even Ariadne will protect you from my wrath."

Dierdre flipped off Nellie's retreating back, rolled her eyes, and went back to eating. The door slammed behind Nellie, rattling the windows. Dierdre glared across the room.

"Have you considered her as a suspect?"

Ari was surprised. "Not seriously. Should we?"

Dierdre sighed and aggressively stirred her spoon through the remaining milk. "No. Even if she really hated me, which she absolutely doesn't, she would never shoot herself in the foot."

"Not to mention the fact she's been with you for the entire tour. She could have been leaving the notes physically the whole time."

"Maybe she waited until Seattle to throw us off."

"Why?"

Dierdre twisted her lips. "I don't know." She put her elbow on the table and pressed her fingers against her eyes, furrowing her brow like she had a headache. "I hate thinking about all this shit when all I want to do is work on the show." Her voice was raspier than usual, as it often was in the morning, and Ari liked the sandpaper sound of it.

"Is there anything I can do to help?"

"Stand guard," Dierdre said. "Make me feel safe enough to concentrate. That's enough."

Ari nodded. "I think I can handle that."

Dierdre rested her chin on her hand, regarding Ari for a long moment. "How are you? How's the girlfriend? She must not like these long hours very much."

"She understands. I make time for her when I can."

"Well, if it ever gets to be too much, invite her to stay the night here. I can wear headphones or sleep in the studio if you two need privacy."

Ari laughed. "I'll keep that in mind."

Dierdre finished her cereal and stood, waiting for Ari to finish eating as well so she could take both bowls to the sink. She ran the water, but Ari stopped her.

"Let me do that. I need something nice and soothing to let my brain work on the case, and you need to go into the studio and work on the choreography."

"You're just scared of Nellie."

"Everyone's scared of Nellie," Ari said. "Go on."

Dierdre sighed and slumped her shoulders, turning away from the sink to go outside. Ari rinsed out the leftover milk and hoped Dale was having a better morning than she was. Given what she knew about Dale's plans, though, she somehow doubted it.

It was so very typical of her father, Dale didn't know why she was surprised when he texted her the address. Of course he was staying at the Edgewater. Of course he wanted to meet her there for breakfast, at the hotel restaurant, where she had to pay twelve bucks to valet her car. And then, after all of that to meet him at a restaurant which was literally in the same building where he slept, he made her wait.

She checked her watch to see it was fifteen minutes past the time they'd agreed to meet. She was too angry to decide if it would be more childish to stay and yell at him or to walk out in a huff. Either way felt like giving him a victory. So she stayed, but she didn't wait for him to order food. When he finally arrived, she was on her second mimosa and almost through her meal.

"This all looks lovely." Samuel Frye sat across from her, dressed in khakis and a golf shirt. "I hope you charged that to my room."

"Nope," Dale said. "I don't need you to buy my food for me."

Although she did regret the crab cake eggs benedict, and it was going to be very hard to see the receipt when she finally got the courage to look at it. She had a feeling this breakfast could have bought a week's worth of groceries once the tip was calculated in. She finished off her mimosa and casually waved off the waiter who would have eagerly brought her another one for the same price as a tank of gas.

Samuel ordered his own breakfast, then faced her. He looked rested, calm, but she could still sense the disappointment behind his eyes.

"No Ariadne today?"

"She's working."

Samuel said, "Lots of people cheating on their wives this early in the morning?"

Dale tightened her jaw and looked out over the water. "Are you still planning to take me when you go back to Pennsylvania?"

"I still think it would be for the best. But you are an adult. You are capable of making your own choices." He sounded like he was reading off a script. "But I can't help but be confused. You came out here for business school."

"And I help run a business. I got the agency off the ground."

"You didn't even graduate," Samuel said. "You work for a private investigator, you claim to~"

"Careful."

He sighed. "If you were gay, I believe there would have been signs..."

"No. You just believe if there were signs, you would have seen them," she corrected. "It's not about my sexuality. It's about being needed here."

"Dale, you said the same thing when your mother died. You wanted to forget about college and stay home because I needed you. And now you have to stay here because Ariadne Willow needs you. Have you taken one second to think about what *you* want and not what someone else is asking you to do."

"I'm~" She was interrupted by her phone ringing. She looked at the screen, saw an unknown number, and ignored it. She was grateful for the chance to think, to change what she'd been about to blurt out into something more mature and thoughtful. "What I want," she said, keeping her voice measured, "is to be vital to someone. I want to be loved by someone who loves me just as much, who treasures me. Ari prides herself on being self-sufficient, but when she needs help, I'm the first person she calls. She lets herself be vulnerable with me. And I know that when I need a little strength, I can go to her, and she gives me every bit she can spare. That's what you're asking me to give up."

Samuel pressed his lips together. "I did a little research on Miss Willow..."

Dale held up her hand. "What do you want to use as an attack? Her time in jail? She was falsely accused and cleared of all charges. She befriended her cellmate, a woman she's now helping get back on her feet. Or maybe the fact she was homeless for a few years as a teenager. She survived that time stronger, smarter, and dedicated to helping people who can't help themselves. That she built a business from scratch and kept it going even though she had no idea what she was doing until I showed up? What did you dig up that you think could possibly sway me about the woman I love?"

He stared hard at the table. When he spoke, much of the fire had left his voice. "Indecent exposure arrest. The year before you met her."

Dale actually laughed, falling against the back of her chair. "Oh! Okay. Yeah. Where was it, Alki Point?"

He looked annoyed. "She told you about that."

"Yeah, and I'm sure she regrets doing so given how often I've made fun of her for it. 'Let's go for a swim, Ari, but remember you need a bathing suit at this pool.' Ari was raised in a very, um, liberal household. Nudity isn't taboo to her. Hell, I probably saw her naked a half dozen times before we became a couple."

"That's sexual harassment~"

"Oh, please." She stood up. "I think we're done here."

Samuel said, "What's with the dog collar?"

Dale looked at him to see if it was a legitimate question, then sat back down. "That's none of your business."

"If you're involved in some sort of freakish sexual~"

"Hold on," Dale said. "One, BDSM isn't freakish. Two, Ari and I don't do that, not that it's any of your business if we did. Ari wears a collar because..." She tapped her fingernail on the table. There was nothing she could say that sounded like the truth, and the truth would be dismissed as ludicrous. "Ari wears a collar because she's my puppy. The agency's name started as a joke. Puppy came from that, and led to the collar."

He shook his head. "I just can't believe you would choose this life."

Dale's phone rang again. This time she silenced it without looking at the screen. "And I can't believe you'd prefer having me back home, working reception nine-to-five, going home to a little apartment... alone, because after being with Ari, I have no interest in dating anyone else."

"You're turning your back on family."

"No," Dale said softly. "No, I found my family. It's here. It's Ariadne Willow. You can be a part of it. But I'm not going to choose, and I am definitely not opting for a life without Ari in it."

After that, it seemed pointless to continue with the meal. She was almost finished eating anyway. She reached for her wallet and her father sighed and held out his hand.

"Put it on my room. Please."

She thought about arguing, but it was ridiculous to pay twenty bucks for a mediocre breakfast just for spite.

"Fine," she said.

"I'm in town for another week. If you want to have another breakfast."

Dale said, "If I have the time. Maybe. And Ariadne should join us."

His lips twisted and he looked away, out at the water.

"See you, Dad. If we don't meet up again, have a safe trip home."

She walked out and felt like she didn't breathe again until she was at the valet stand. The man went to get her car, and she leaned against the wall. She closed her eyes. Her phone rang again.

"Oh, for crying out loud." She hit the answer button and tried to keep her voice professional despite mounting irritation. "This is Dale Frye."

"*Na, Gott sei Dank!*"

Dale blinked. "I'm sorry, I think~"

"No, no, my apologies. I'm sorry, *Fräulein*. We were uncertain if this was your telephone number. We have been trying to reach you or Ariadne Willow for several days now."

"Who is this...?"

"Apologies, my name is Henrik Bayer. I am a member of a pack located near Potsdam. We've been working with Gwyneth and Millicent Willow to determine who was responsible for leaking information about the Magnusson essays. It was our hope to better protect the book in the future."

Dale accepted her keys from the valet, trying not to let the question *did he just refer to Milo as Gwen's wife...?* overtake her thinking. "Okay. Yes. We've been hoping to hear from them. Is there an update about when they might be coming home?"

Henrik hesitated. "I'm... not to be the bearer of bad news, Miss Frye, but I am sorry, I don't know that. The work was far more complicated than we'd feared. It would seem the man, um, Hayden? We've discovered he may have had several informants. We have been trying to find them all so the book can have a secure hiding place, but it's difficult. The Willows left our pack in search of someone they believe provided Mr. Hayden with vital intelligence about where the book was being kept. Before they left, Gwen made me promise to contact you if they had been gone for one week."

Dale's heart sped up. "You haven't heard from them for a week...?"

Another hesitation. "I'm sorry, Miss Frye. But I-I hoped for the best case scenario. When the week ended, I thought perhaps... perhaps they were delayed. I did not want to worry you or their daughter for a missed bus. And then I feared being a messenger of bad tidings so I~"

"How long, Mr. Bayer?"

"I am very sorry, Miss Frye." He sighed. "No one has seen or heard from the Willows in over a month."

CHAPTER FIFTEEN

THE CALLAHAN Concert Hall was, from a security standpoint, an absolute goddamn nightmare. Ari learned how big the job would be from the blueprints and her worries were only magnified when they took a field trip to the hall so Dierdre could see the stage in person without the dance team in place. The venue filled an entire city block, with public entrances on all sides of the building except for the north. The south side of the building had access to an underground parking garage, which had four elevators and stairwell access to the main floor.

The auditorium reserved for Saint Artemis sat three thousand, and Nellie informed her that all three shows sold out months ago. Nine thousand people would fill this space over the course of a long weekend, and any one of them could have been the person who was sending the notes threatening to reveal Dierdre's real name.

That was just the public area. If the stalker somehow got backstage, any number of secret passageways opened up. The talent entrance at the north of the building, the sound booth, the green rooms, anyone with the right badge could get into those areas where everything was dark, cramped, and claustrophobically isolated.

It was a huge job. Ari doubted she would be able to do it

properly with a team of twenty, let alone by herself.

She explained her concerns to Dierdre as Nellie drove them back to the house. They were both in the backseat, and Dierdre was wearing a black baseball cap and oversized sunglasses. Ari questioned the need for a disguise, but Dierdre pointed out that if the media got pictures of the same unidentified person at multiple Saint Artemis shows, the secret would be out. Ari was impressed at how far ahead they planned, but this had been their life for the past decade. They were pros at it by now.

Dierdre shook her head after hearing Ari out. "You don't have to find a needle in a haystack. Just stick close to me."

"It's not that simple," Ari said. "What if their plan to expose you involves handing out flyers on the sidewalk outside? What if they get hired for the multimedia crew and puts something into the video screens? If this person wants to expose you, they don't have to get physically close to you in order to make it happen."

Dierdre said, "Then I guess you just have to find her before the first show. No pressure."

Ari met Nellie's eyes in the rearview mirror. Nellie arched an eyebrow, implying *See what I have to deal with?*

At the house, Dierdre dismissed Ari with gratitude for everything she'd done so far. "You deserve a night in your own bed every now and again. And I do appreciate you being here, even if I sort of ignored your worries about the concert hall," Dierdre said, "I still appreciate that you're there pointing them out."

"I'll do my best to make sure you don't need added security at the shows, but I can't promise anything."

"I understand."

Ari bid her a goodnight and went home, thinking she could finally let her guard down and relax. Those hopes were shattered when she walked into the apartment and saw Dale's face.

"What's wrong?"

Dale stood up and went to her. "Come here. Sit down."

"I assumed breakfast with your dad went well enough," Ari said, her voice trembling. "I thought you'd call if you needed to vent or..."

"Breakfast went as well as I could have expected. That's not what this is about." She led Ari to the couch and sat next to her. "I got a call after breakfast. It was about your mother and Milo."

Ari tensed. "What... what happened?"

"We don't know." Dale told her about Henrick, and everything he'd told her. "Gwen had been checking in regularly up until she suddenly went silent. But she and Milo were headed out into the wilds. Not much civilization, no phone signal, maybe not even landlines. They may just be somewhere that they can't get in touch."

"For a month?" Ari snapped.

Dale pressed her lips together and closed her hand around Ari's. "We don't know what's happening there."

"You're right, we don't."

Ari got up and went to the laptop.

Dale stood as well. "What are you doing?"

"Finding a flight to Germany..."

"Okay."

"Dale, don't." Ari looked up. "What?"

Dale came closer. "I said okay. You want to go to Germany and help them, okay. You can abandon the case, abandon Dierdre, and fly halfway across the world to a place you've never been and walk into a situation you have no idea about. I don't know what you expect to do under those conditions, but if that's what you have to do, then I'm in. I'm right there next to you, puppy."

Ari stood up straighter, struggling to keep her expression steady. "It's my mom."

"I know," Dale said softly. She stepped forward and wrapped her arms around Ari and squeezed. Ari sagged against her, eyes closed. "Sometimes there's nothing you can do. Not even you."

Ari cried. Dale held her, eventually leading her back to the couch. Eventually Ari's tears went dry and she repositioned herself to lay her head on Dale's lap. Dale stroked her hair while Ari wiped the remaining tears away from her eyes.

"What time do you have to get back to Dierdre's?"

"I don't. She gave me the night off."

Dale said, "Oh. That's nice of her. Do you want to go for a run?"

Ari shook her head. "I can't. If Dierdre calls, I can't~"

"I'll go with you again. I'll have the phone. If Dierdre calls, I'll find the wolf and you can change in the car." She brushed the hair away from Ari's face. "You need to process what's going on. The wolf does, too. The easiest way to do that is on all fours, in the fresh air."

Ari rolled onto her back and looked up at Dale. "I love you."

"I love you, too."

"This time I won't let the wolf turn it into hide-and-seek. We can find a more secluded place, and I'll be sure to communicate that running wild isn't an option tonight."

Dale said, "Good."

"And you still need to tell me what happened at breakfast."

"Annoyed grunt."

Ari sat up and stroked Dale's hair. "That bad?"

"No. Yeah." She shrugged and turned her head to kiss Ari's wrist. "I don't really know, puppy. But I meant what I told him. I'm not defending you anymore. He has to get right on his own. I won't waste my time or energy trying to force him to see what's right in front of him. We have more important things to worry about right now. But he's in town for another week, so I'll probably have to see him at some point."

"I'll be there for you."

"Dierdre~"

"She can take care of herself for one dinner," Ari said. "I'll be there next time."

"Okay. Speaking of dinner, have you eaten?" Ari shook her head. Dale kissed her and got up. "I'll cook something."

Ari stood and followed Dale into the kitchen. "Do you really believe Mom and Milo are okay?"

"We can't know one way or the other, worrying isn't going to help any more than running over there would. We can hope for the best, though, and now we can keep in touch with the Bayer pack for more information."

"Right."

Dale opened the fridge, thought of something, and then closed it. "There was one other thing from the call you might find interesting. Henrick. He... he referred to Gwen and Milo as 'the Willows.' And he referred to you as their daughter."

Ari was thrown by that. She wasn't entirely sure if she was happy or distressed by the idea of her mother somehow being married to a woman young enough to be her daughter. But she knew how much Milo loved her, and she knew how much her mother had changed since they became a couple. Both of those were very good things. She finally nodded.

"I hope that's true. Maybe Mom just introduced Milo that way to make things easier in the long run, or maybe they had some kind of commitment conversation on their trip to Europe. Either way, Mom's been alone way too long. And Milo is good for her. So whatever the truth is, I'm happy for her. Happy for them both. They deserve it."

Dale cupped Ari's face and kissed her cheek. "Very mature, puppy."

"Yeah, yeah, yeah," Ari grumbled. "I just hope Milo doesn't expect me to call her 'mom,' because that is *not* happening."

Dale laughed and started putting together a patchwork plate of leftovers.

After dinner, Dale took Ari to Cal Anderson Park where the wolf could run around for an hour or so. It was green enough that there were plenty of smells to investigate, but it was clear that the wolf wouldn't be allowed to explore any wilderness. Luckily it seemed to understand, behaving by staying close to the car for the entire excursion. Dale knew that Ari must have kept more control than usual, holding a leash on the wilder nature of her other half.

Dale stayed in the car with a book, Ari's phone on the windshield mount in case Dierdre called. When they got home, they finished what had been so rudely interrupted a week earlier. Dale half expected the phone to ring in the middle of their fun, but it remained silent. They took full advantage, not stopping until they were both ready to throw in the towel.

"You're under me again," Dale said as she curled against Ari's side.

"It happens sometimes," Ari said.

Dale kissed Ari's chest. "More lately, it seems like. I'm not complaining. I just wanted to make sure you were aware of it."

Ari shrugged. "I guess... maybe a part of me doesn't want to feel like I'm holding you down. After everything that happened with Hayden it would feel a little like I'm trapping you. I don't want to trigger you."

"Oh. In that case..." She stretched up and nibbled on Ari's earlobe. "Pin me down next time, puppy. I miss feeling you on top of me."

Ari shivered and raked her fingers over Dale's ribs. "Your, ahem, feedback has been noted."

Dale grinned and settled on Ari again. "How is Dierdre's case going? Any closer to finding who sent the notes?"

"Farther away than when we started," Ari groaned. "I didn't think that was possible, but here we are. We've got a venue that seats three thousand people, and any one of them could be the one who wants to unmask Saint Artemis. I'm worried it's going to be someone I can't possibly find on any list of suspects because they're a fan who figured out her identity through luck and research."

"Want to hear my dumb theory?"

"Always."

"It's Dierdre."

Ari smiled. "It's a good theory, baby. But I don't think it holds water. If she wants to unmask herself, she could just do it."

Dale said, "Drama makes it more exciting. A mysterious blackmailer, a hot private investigator, an ultimatum..."

"What ultimatum?"

"Hm? Oh, I don't know. Like, I know your secret and you can't hide."

Ari was frowning up at the ceiling. "Yeah. But there hasn't been an ultimatum."

"There doesn't have to be if the intention is terrorizing her. Whoever is sending the notes just wants her scared. But you're right, to what end...? What's the point of sending the notes if Dierdre can't do anything about it? It's like a kidnapper calling to say they have your kid without giving ransom demands. And if the threat really is just to warn her that an unmasking is coming, then Dierdre can remove the fear by just unmasking herself on her own terms. The notes are just giving her an opportunity to protect herself by taking her power back. It seems like an exercise in futility. Right? Puppy...?"

She lifted her head and saw Ari was asleep. She smiled, kissed Ari's chin, and put her head down. She would organize her thoughts and recap the theorizing in the morning.

CHAPTER SIXTEEN

THE MASK covered the wearer's face entirely. There were no holes for her eyes or mouth, just a shapeless egg that reflected enough light to make it look like the glow was coming from within. Ari turned it over in her hands a few times before she finally shook her head to admit defeat.

"I give up. How can you possibly use this in concert?"

Dierdre grinned. "Put it on."

Ari raised an eyebrow but lifted the mask - more of a helmet, really - and slipped it over her head. It was completely black inside, but she felt something like the padding around binocular lenses at eye level. Dierdre steadied the mask.

"Okay, close your eyes."

Ari did as she was told, even though it seemed pointless, but then she saw light through her eyelids. She opened them carefully to see a blurry and fishbowled version of the living room. Dierdre was standing close enough that her features were distorted when she smiled. She had her hands on either side of the mask.

"Can you see me?"

"I can," Ari said. "What is this?"

Dierdre pointed. "There are miniature cameras right here and here, embedded in the mask and covered with one-way glass. You can see them in a dark room, but natural lighting is enough to make them opaque. I wear a mic on my collar that picks up my voice from the neck-hole. The downside is that it gives my voice a horrible echo. This was the last time I let Edith cover my mouth. But I love the mask. It's my absolute favorite. I wear it sometimes for public appearances or when it doesn't matter if my voice is a little muffled."

The cameras turned off and Ari eased her head out of the helmet. "I have to admit, it's pretty cool. I can't imagine it's very comfortable after a three-hour show."

"God no." Dierdre took the mask back and returned it to the protective case on the coffee table. "Edith makes them as comfortable as possible, but there's only so much she can do. At the end of the day, most of my face is still enclosed in a shell."

"Is it worth it? Protecting your privacy is a big deal, I know, but you have to assume the truth will come out eventually."

Dierdre considered the question. "I want to do this for a long time. The rest of my life, hopefully. And yes, eventually people will know my real name. But I figure I'm going to enjoy the anonymity for as long as I can before I'm forced to be a celebrity every minute of every day." She gestured at the computer. "Whenever I feel overwhelmed by the routine, I go on Twitter and I find photos of Anna Kendrick out at lunch or Keanu Reeves on the subway, and I'd know I was making the right choice. Which is ironic, because I'm hiding to prevent pictures like that being taken of me. But I can go down to the Whole Foods and no one would look twice at me. I'm terrified of not being a person and just becoming a commodity."

Ari hesitated before she asked the next question, which would reveal an invasion of privacy, but she'd exhausted every other avenue and she needed to know.

"What about the, ah... the chat rooms?"

"What chat rooms?"

Ari cleared her throat. "Back when I first started standing guard, you let me use your laptop. I snooped around. I found the chat logs."

Dierdre looked at the laptop. Her expression was unreadable. "Oh," she said. "That was private."

"I understand. But I also need to know as much as possible. If someone you chatted with might have realized they were talking to the real Saint Artemis. Maybe you slipped and gave something away, or they were trying to scam you and only found the truth by accident. But there's a chance that whoever is on the other end of those conversations is the same person sending you the notes."

"They're not."

"You can't..."

"I know because Nellie digs up dirt on *them*." She sat down on the couch and put her elbows on her knees. She covered her face with both hands, then sat up with a heavy sigh. Her cheeks were flushed, making the freckles stand out more sharply than usual. "Nellie found the chats last year. She scolded me, but she said everyone needs to let off a little steam, so she wouldn't tell me to stop. But she wanted the names and profiles of everyone I talked to. She didn't actually read the chats, but it was humiliating. It was like telling your mother everyone you'd banged and letting her do research on them. If anybody I chatted with even hinted at knowing my true identity, Nellie would know about it."

Ari sat down on the table facing Dierdre. "I guess dating can be a pain, even with your identity concealed."

Dierdre scoffed and shook her head. "You can't imagine. I'm always touring. And when I stop somewhere long enough to actually settle a little, I have to work on an album or design a mask or work on choreography for my damn shows. If it wasn't for the internet, I'd never get any action."

"That's a shame," Ari said. "You're a gorgeous woman."

"Hah. Thanks." She wrinkled her nose and scratched behind her ear. "I feel all awkward now..."

Ari considered what she was about to say before she actually said it aloud. "Okay. Look, I'm dealing with some family stuff right now, and I could really use a night out. You've been locked up in this house the whole time you've been in Seattle except for one trip to an elementary school. We both need a night out."

Dierdre sat up straighter. "A night out...? I don't know. I don't really do nights out."

"All the more reason to do one now. I may not be the world's best tour guide, but I know my way around some of the best lesbian clubs in town. What's the point of wearing a mask to protect your anonymity if you never take advantage of it?"

"Nellie would hate it," Dierdre said, then held up a finger. "I'm putting that in the pro column, by the way. What the hell? Some drinking, some dancing, it'll be fun."

Ari smiled. "I'll call Dale and have her bring me a change of clothes~"

"Mm-mm," Dierdre said, standing up. "How long did you say you and Dale have been together? Ten years?"

"Around that, yeah."

Dierdre moved toward the stairs. "She's seen all the nice clothes you own. Hell, she probably helped you pick most of them out. I have some outfits, and we're a similar build. So you can borrow something of mine and really blow her away."

Ari stood up as well. "Shouldn't Dale get a chance to wow me, too?"

"Sure," Dierdre said, "but... I mean, I've only seen her in passing when she dropped stuff off for you, but I don't think I have anything that will fit her."

"Right. We'll figure something out."

She followed Dierdre up the stairs and pushed down her guilt at having fun when her mother and Milo could be in extreme danger. Dale was right. There was nothing they could do to help, and right now Ari had a responsibility to Dierdre. Right now, that responsibility included showing her a great night out on the town.

Ari liked the logo of Sea/TT/Les so much that she once bought a T-shirt with it: the words SEA and LES, separated by two rainbow-hued Space Needles. It was the perfect place for Dierdre to experience the gay nightlife of Seattle. She borrowed a blouse Dierdre said was "deep crimson" with a pair of grey slacks, and she even allowed her to apply just a touch of makeup. The tie was the exact shade of the blouse, rendering it almost unnoticeable from a distance.

She felt self-conscious in the outfit but, when she answered the door, Dale said, "Hey, puppy, I-yow-wow..." She took a step back and examined her from head to toe.

"You like it?"

"Will Dierdre let you buy it from her?"

Dierdre was on her way downstairs and overheard the question. "Please, it looks better on her than it ever did on me. She can have it." She was in a white dress that left her right shoulder exposed and exposed just enough of her thigh to entice without being too blatant about it. Her hair was artfully tousled in a way that told Dale she'd spent a lot of time making sure it looked like she hadn't spent any time on it. "I tried to convince her it would look better without the collar, but apparently that's no-go. Symbolism. I respect that."

Dale smiled and touched Ari's collar. Her outfit was the least flashy among them - a low-cut white top and a black skirt - but she caught Ari stealing glances as they walked to the car. Ari had never stopped looking at her that way, it was still nice to get proof that her long-term girlfriend had a crush on her. They were taking her car instead of Dierdre's, just in case someone had been watching the house and knew what she was driving. Ari got in the front seat, and Dierdre climbed into the back.

"Just because we're having fun doesn't mean it's a night off," Ari said once they were on the road, twisting in her seat so she could look at Dierdre. "We're going to take a long, winding route and see if anyone seems to be following us. We're only going on to the club if it's all clear."

"Deal," Dierdre said.

"And once we're there, I want you to check in with me as much as possible. I'm going to stay by the bar and watch the people around you."

Dale clucked her tongue. "My lady finally takes me out on the town, and she spends the whole time checking out other women. Typical."

Ari grinned and put her hand on Dale's knee. "Don't worry about the fact we're there. Enjoy yourself. I don't know the meaning of the word awkward."

"It's true," Dale said. "This is a woman who used to regularly strip down in front of me when I was just her secretary."

"I'm sorry?" Dierdre said.

Dale kicked herself for the slip. "It's not as harass-y as it sounds."

Dierdre said, "That's comforting. So how did you two meet?"

"Um..." Ari looked at Dale. *I was in wolf form, and a bunch of teenagers had me cornered. Dale saved me, scared them off, gave me her cheeseburger. Later, I transformed in her apartment and scared the crap out of us both.* "It's a long story," she said out loud.

"Not that long," Dale said. "You know how sometimes you just bump into someone and you realize she's exactly what you need, right at the moment you need her? That was it, for both of us. I had no job, no money, no prospects. Ari had no idea how to run a business on her own. We ran into each other, got to talking, and I became her first employee. And the rest is history."

Dierdre grinned. "I love it. The whole boss-employee fantasy.

How long were you working together before things changed?"

"About... four years?" Ari said, looking to Dale for confirmation. She nodded, so Ari said, "Yeah. Which means we've known each other for over a decade."

Dierdre whistled. "That's... that's something. I know I'm still pretty young, but I feel like each year it's less and less likely I'll have a love like that. Unless I know the person right now, I'm going to have to meet them soon to have decades worth of history with them. And honestly, I don't know that many people."

"There's still time," Ari said.

Dale looked at Dierdre in the rearview mirror. "Honestly, a decade or five minutes, when you find the person, it'll feel like you've known them your whole life. And even if you don't feel that way, it won't matter because... they're your person. They're the one you've always been meant to share your life with."

"I hope you're right."

Ari said, "I've come to the conclusion Dale is usually right. Now I just assume that immediately. It's saved me a lot of time over the years."

Dale drove through the neighborhood like she was a tourist trying to find a specific landmark. At one point she pulled into an alley and Ari got out, walked back to the sidewalk, and watched the street for five minutes. When she got back in the car, she programmed Dale's GPS with the meandering route she'd plotted to the bar.

"All clear?" Dale asked.

"Looks like it. But keep an eye out."

She was hyperaware, focused on every vehicle that looked slightly similar to any she'd seen before. There were so many black sedans and white sports cars in the city. She also saw a UPS truck and three gray Amazon vans out making late deliveries, but closer inspection revealed they all had different drivers. Eventually Ari declared they were safe enough to proceed to their final destination.

There was no line to get in at Sea/TT/Les, but inside it was practically standing room only. Ari held Dierdre's wrist with a loose grip as she scanned the room. At least a hundred people, maybe a little more, and a live band playing onstage at the other end of the room. There were gaps along the bar, and Dale hoped she and Ari could stake out a little piece of land for themselves.

"Have fun, but be aware. If you see anything that freaks you out, let me know."

"Yes, mom."

Ari tightened her grip. "Hey. Look, I don't want to become Nellie, but I want you to take this seriously. We're talking about your safety here."

Dierdre patted Ari's hand. "I am. I promise. I'm just excited. I never get to go out and hear music." She looked around like a kid at a theme park, scouting which ride she wanted to hit first. "I won't let you down, Ariadne."

"Okay," Ari said. "Go, have fun."

Dierdre hurried off. Dale pulled Ari close and put an arm around her waist, guiding her to the bar.

"You got all commanding on her. That was kind of sexy, puppy."

"Yeah? You like when I take control?"

Dale kissed Ari's cheek. "Just as long as you remember who is holding *your* leash."

She ordered them both drinks and, while Ari kept an eye on Dierdre's progression through the crowd, Dale took the opportunity to appreciate where they were. She saw a woman she recognized from television, an anchorwoman for Ari's preferred news channel, but etiquette demanded she ignore that familiarity and move on.

She focused on a brunette at the end of the bar, a gorgeous woman with thin arched eyebrows, a square jaw, and incredible dark eyes. Dale knew she'd seen the woman somewhere before, but she couldn't place her. While she was staring, the woman pushed the wave of dark hair away from her face and casually looked down the bar. Her eyes hesitated on Dale, switched to Ari, jumped back to Dale, and then her lips spread into a wide smile. She pushed away from the bar and started moving through the crowd toward them. The smile was friendly, but Dale was still nervous.

"Oh shit. Puppy. Nine o'clock. We know her. Friend or foe?"

"Who...?"

"Purple blouse. Brunette."

The woman closed in on them. "Well, hello there," she said when she got close enough to be heard over the music. She held out her arms. "Fancy meeting you here."

"Val Byrne," Ari said, mostly for Dale's benefit as she accepted the woman's hug.

The name was enough to tick Dale's memory. Valerie Byrne was the doctor at King County Correctional, the woman who had gotten Ari the help she needed to stop her transformations while she was in prison. They'd met briefly at Gwen's house during that whole ordeal, and Dale blamed her faulty memory on everything else that had been going on at the time.

Val ended the hug with Ari and switched to Dale, who happily accepted now that she remembered who she was. "It's great to see you again."

"Same, same," Val said, stepping back. "Everything okay? The drug wore off, your old friend is back and everything?"

"Oh yeah," Ari said, still keeping half her attention on Dierdre. "Shae Segura got out recently. She's been working with us while she gets back on her feet."

"She mentioned that. Good for her. I love hearing about ladies making good choices when they leave us." She followed Ari's gaze onto the dance floor, then realized what was happening. "Oh, shit. Are you working? Am I interrupting a case?"

Ari smiled. "Sort of and not really. It's fine. I'm just, ah... chaperoning a little bit. You're fine."

"Are you sure? I can make myself scarce."

"Honestly, it's okay," Ari said. "Dale will probably be happy to talk with someone who isn't constantly looking everywhere else in the room."

Dale grinned. "I didn't want to say anything. But since it's been said..." She offered her hand to Val. "Would you like to dance?"

"I was starting to think nobody would ask." Val took Dale's hand. "Enjoy your surveillance, detective."

"Watch out for your toes with this one," Ari warned.

Dale swatted at Ari with her free hand, winked, and let herself be led out onto the dance floor.

CHAPTER SEVENTEEN

"CAN I buy you a drink?"

Dierdre turned, her expression neutral, but she smiled when she realized the offer had come from Ari. "Hey! Sure, I always let good-looking women with great taste in clothes buy me drinks."

They headed for the bar. "How's everything going?" Ari asked, as quietly as she could without being muted by the overall noise of the club.

"It's fantastic." She grabbed Ari's elbow, leaned in, and repeated for emphasis: "Fan-*tas*-tic. I've danced with three different women. I think they were forming a line when you swooped in and stole me away. They might think you're kind of a jerk."

Ari said, "Well, I guess I won't be hooking up with any of them tonight."

Dierdre laughed. "Seriously, though, these women! They're all amazing. I think I actually had a shot with one of them."

"Dierdre... you're a gorgeous redhead who knows how to dance, dressed like a million bucks. You have a chance with *all* of them." Ari swept her hand to indicate the room. She guided Dierdre to one side of the bar, a dead zone where the music wasn't quite as loud and they wouldn't be crushed from all sides by people looking for a drink.

"Well, not all of them," Dierdre said, ducking her chin to hide her blush. "Where's the lovely Lady Frye?"

"An acquaintance of ours showed up, and they've been dancing for a while." She twisted and almost immediately spotted Dale in the crowd. She and Val were doing complicated moves that Ari supposed could be, in some context, considered a dance. She indicated them with her chin. "Right there."

"Wow, your friend is hot, too. All these women are so hot, Ariadne!" She whimpered. "Do you, um... really think I have a shot with my choice of them?"

Ari said, "Oh yeah." She realized what they were discussing was more difficult than it would be under normal circumstances. "Are you thinking about maybe..."

"I'm thinking maybe." Dierdre's cheeks were flushed, her eyes wide and scanning the crowd. "I thought, you know, before we got here, that just dancing with a bunch of women would get the itch out. But now that I'm here... now that it looks like all I have to do is ask... I don't know. Please tell me it's possible. Please don't be a Nellie killjoy..."

"It's possible," Ari said, considering the logistics. "You can't bring her back to the house, and you shouldn't go to hers. A hotel. That makes the most sense for a random hookup, right? Safer for both of you. Text me where you end up. The name of the hotel, the room number..."

"That might look a little suspicious," Dierdre said. "I don't want to freak her out by texting the room number to someone she doesn't know."

"Good point. That's a little questionable." She chewed her bottom lip. "Okay. Play it by ear. If you think the person is trustworthy enough to take her to a hotel, then I don't need to babysit you."

Dierdre raised an eyebrow. "Really? You're willing to not know where I am for an entire night?"

"Sure. There aren't a lot of alternatives other than putting the lady through a background check. And everyone deserves a night out."

"Nellie's going to kill you."

"You didn't hire me to worry about how Nellie felt. When was the last time you slept with someone?"

"Three years."

Ari said, "Okay. Yeah. I don't need to know where you are until eight o'clock tomorrow morning. Maybe later. If you do leave with someone, find me to say goodnight so I can get a look at her. Other than that, I'm not going to babysit you."

Dierdre looked at the crowd again. "Things just got interesting."

Ari laughed and patted Dierdre's shoulder. "Choose wisely."

Dierdre rejoined the crowd, and Ari saw several women change course to cross paths with her. Nellie might get mad, and there was a small chance she'd just made a horrible error, but the stalker hadn't been violent. She was fairly certain the stalker didn't even know where they were tonight. The risks were minimal enough for her not to worry. She would be vigilant until Dierdre left the club. After that, she was a grown woman, and Ari knew she could take care of herself.

When the band shifted to a slower song, Val shifted her weight away from Dale to indicate she was willing to go back to the bar. Dale put a hand on Val's hip and pulled her closer. Val smiled and put a hand in the small of Dale's back. Dale was just a little taller than Val, a difference she appreciated after years of being the short one in the relationship. She looked around to see if anyone was paying attention to the doctor.

"Hopefully I'm not ruining your chances of catching someone else's eye."

"I wasn't exactly fighting them off before you showed up," Val said. "Besides, dancing with you, I'm the, uh... the forbidden fruit. They see me dancing with you, I suddenly become desirable. Everyone wants what they can't have."

Dale said, "In that case, you're welcome."

"Even if no one approaches me, it's nice to just be out. To unwind a little. Working at a women's prison isn't as bad as it would be with men, but the prisoners tend to take out their frustrations on anyone who is available. You can only get called a bitch or less kind words so many times before it gets under your skin." She tightened her grip on Dale a little. "It's nice to just dance with someone who has a nice smile and smells good."

"You don't smell so bad yourself, doc."

Val arched an eyebrow. "Are you sure Ariadne is okay with us dancing together?"

"Absolutely. Ari doesn't get jealous. I think it's part of... you know, who she is, if you know what I mean. They have different rules when it comes to relationships. Monogamy. We've been completely monogamous, but in general... the others don't mind a little exploration."

Val nodded thoughtfully. "I've heard that from some of the others. There are partners, and then there's the pack. It must be so odd. Being with someone... someone different."

Dale shrugged. "There are adjustments, sure. But every relationship has unique hurdles. If I was in a wheelchair, it would affect where we lived. If Ari had allergies, we might have to move somewhere with better air. Her uniqueness is just a little more unique than most."

"I suppose that's true." She smiled and tilted her head to the side. "You know what's strange? I work in the prison, and all the *canidae* in there are on the drug. Obviously. So I've never actually seen any wolves."

"Really?"

Val shrugged. "When would I have a chance? I suppose I could look them up after they get out and ask them to show me, but that seems weird, don't you think?"

"Yeah. Wow. But if you've never seen it... that's a heck of a thing to take on faith."

"My father was a hunter. He was telling me about them since I was a little girl. Honestly, it's harder for me to remember that other people don't believe in werewolves." She whispered the last word. "They've never been myths to me. But you must have seen it."

"Countless times," Dale said. "It used to freak me out. But now... it's beautiful."

Val said, "If Ari ever wants to run the wolf by my apartment, let me know and I'll leave out a nice juicy steak for her."

"I'll let her know."

Dale looked past Val and saw Ari at the bar, alone, still policing the crowd. When her eyes found Dale, she stopped and the corners of her mouth curled up in a smile. She winked. Dale winked back. Ari put a hand on her own ass, then pulled it away with her other hand, waving a "no-no" finger at Dale. Dale pouted her bottom lip. Ari grinned and continued her surveillance of the crowd.

An idea formed in Dale's mind. It was something she couldn't have said she expected, but also one that wasn't completely out of the blue.

The song ended and Val stepped back. "I'm going to get something to drink. Maybe see if anyone was successfully tempted into making a move on me."

"Fingers crossed," Dale said.

She watched Val walk away, then began making her way through the crowd to Ari, formulating what she was going to say as she walked.

Ari rested her hand on Dale's hip as she rejoined her at the bar. Dale slid her hand across Ari's stomach and motioned to the bartender for a drink. She noticed that Dale had worked up a sweat, seeing the gleam on her forehead and also picking up a whiff under her perfume.

"How was the dance?"

"Good. Great." She drummed her fingers on the bar. "How's Dierdre?"

Ari said, "Reborn. Honestly, we should have done this on day one. She's having the time of her life."

"Awesome. Good. Great."

Ari looked at her. "You're repeating yourself, babe. Everything okay?"

Dale nodded. "Yeah. But I was thinking about something." She turned to face Ari, her elbow on the bar. "So. You remember during the Burroughs case, when one of the twins came on to you, and you said 'no, no, I'm with someone,' and she said, 'well, okay, bring her along,' but you thought it would make me a third wheel or left out or~"

"Elizabeth," Ari said. "And it would be weird because she made the offer without ever seeing you, so it would've felt like you weren't really a part of it. Why are you bringing this up?"

Dale twisted and looked at Val, who had ended up at the other side of the bar. Ari followed her gaze, then they looked at each other again. Ari raised an eyebrow.

"I guess that *was* a good dance."

Dale laughed. It was slightly more nervous than usual. "She's beautiful. She knows both of us. She kept you safe and took care of you when I couldn't. That's already enough to raise her up in my books." She touched Ari's hip. "We talked and she got me thinking about all the things you're giving up by not being in a pack, or having a partner who is like you."

"Where do threesomes come into that?"

"I stayed with Milo's pack when you were in jail. Those wolves jumped from bed to bed like they were playing musical chairs. I'm not saying we have to do anything. I didn't say anything to Val. But I'm thinking about it."

Ari considered the suggestion. She hadn't expected anything like this to come up, tonight or really ever, but now that it was on the table, she couldn't help be intrigued. She looked at Val, who was legitimately beautiful. She had dark features and a smile that could be warm and welcoming or devious depending on the way she tilted her head. She was the sort of woman Ari would absolutely have been drawn to before she was chosen by Dale.

"Are you sure now is the best time to introduce someone new to the bedroom? Things are back to normal after everything with the book, but do we want to push it?"

Dale took Ari's hand. "This has nothing to do with that. I wouldn't be making the suggestion if I thought there was a chance I had any lingering aftereffects. This is about you, and your wolf, and letting you explore part of who you are that you might otherwise ignore." She moved closer. "Look, I like the idea of a threesome. I know you do, too."

Ari slowly grinned. "It's usually better in theory than in practice..."

"So is going to the beach, but it's still a great way to spend the afternoon."

Ari laughed.

"And I don't think we'll ever find another candidate better suited than Dr. Byrne. She knows both of us. She knows your secret. We both trust her. We both think she's attractive. The only real stumbling block is that you have to watch Dierdre, but... what?"

"That... might not be an issue. I gave Dierdre permission to go radio silent if she found someone she liked. I've been watching her and she's really running through her options."

Dale said, "Really... well, then. It looks like all the stars are aligning in our favor."

They both looked down the bar at Val, who was waiting for the bartender to take her order.

"I guess there's just one other person we need to convince," Dale said. "So... which one of us is going to do it?"

Ari held out her fist to do rock-paper-scissors.

Dale laughed and brought her fist up as well.

CHAPTER EIGHTEEN

ARI WOKE to see the back of an unfamiliar head, a wild tangle of black hair falling across a shoulder that was more tan, more slender, than Dale's. She blinked the image into focus and became aware of the much more familiar curves pressing against her from behind, the weight of Dale's hand on her hip. They were all naked, but someone had at some point attempted to pull the blanket up over them all. Ari took a deep breath and a variety of scents washed over her, waking her memory.

"Would you like to come home with us?"

Val, starting to laugh, then looking at Ari, her smile fading as she realized this wasn't a joke or meaningless flirtation.

"Yes," she said, finally convinced the offer was sincere. "Yeah, I think I'd like that very much."

They were at home, in their bed. She remembered kissing the dark of the living room, the odd sensation of kissing someone who wasn't Dale. Her heart had sped up at the wrongness of it until she felt Dale's lips on her neck. She remembered hearing Dale breathing hard as Val bent down and kissed her through the lace of her bra. It turned out the doctor liked breasts, and Ari knew Dale's were lovely to explore. Dale's fingers tightened into a fist in Ari's hair and they kissed as Val did more things with her tongue.

"I want to see her with you," Val said, kneeling on the foot of the bed, wearing only her underwear. *"I want to watch the two of you."*

They'd obliged, both of them almost aggressive due to the arousal of being watched. And then Ari felt a hand between her legs, and then a mouth was on her, and then...

"Puppy," Dale whispered now, sliding her hand up over Ari's stomach.

"Sh," Ari said.

Val looked over her shoulder. "It's okay. I've actually been awake for a while."

"Oh."

Val rolled onto her back. "Last night was not what I went out looking for," she admitted. "But damn if it wasn't exactly what I needed. Thank you. Thank you both. You're... amazing. You're so beautiful, and watching the two of you make love was... one of the most... erotic things I've ever experienced."

Dale rested her chin on Ari's shoulder. "We should thank you, too. Watching Ari like that... usually I'm a little distracted at the key moments. It was nice to let someone else focus on the work so I could watch her."

Ari reached back and stroked Dale's naked hip. "I think we all benefited from what happened last night."

"It was a hell of a night." Val leaned closer and kissed Ari's lips, then Dale's. "I don't know what threesome etiquette is, but if you ever want to fool around again, I can leave you my number."

"Never say never," Ari said.

"I won't take it personally if this was a one-time thing. Some things need to be a one-time event." She pulled the sheet up higher and looked around the room. "There's also, um... the question of how to gracefully exit a threesome. Bathroom?"

Dale pointed. "Right through there. Extra toothbrushes are in the drawer, towels under the sink if you want to take a shower."

"Thanks." She started to get up, then looked back at them. "Thanks for the sex. You're both really great at it."

Ari and Dale both laughed, then looked away so Val could gather her clothes and duck into the bathroom without feeling awkward. Ari moved onto her back and Dale shifted her weight until she was lying on top of her. They kissed, and Ari traced circles on Dale's sides at the bottom of her ribs. Dale shivered and slipped her tongue into Ari's mouth, moving her hands up into Ari's hair.

Ari brought one leg up and hooked it around Dale's to pull her lower body closer.

"A two-some?" Dale said against Ari's mouth. "How vanilla of you..."

"You're too good for the classics now?" Ari said.

Dale shrugged. "I'll hear your arguments in its favor, but you better make a damn good case."

What happened next was quick, but it felt brand-new. She'd seen Dale in a new light thanks to Val, from enough distance to remember what it was like when they were new lovers. She'd been kissing and touching and holding Dale for almost a decade, and now she could imagine doing it for ten more, twenty more, as many more as they had left.

Val came out of the bathroom as they were finishing, and she sat on the edge of the bed to watch the grand finale. Ari lifted her head and brushed her hair back, smiling up at Val.

"Hey. We have cereal if you want breakfast."

"I think I'm just going to call a Lyft to get back to my car. But I want to thank you both for an absolutely amazing evening. It has, um..." She searched for words and then laughed with a shake of her head. It made her hair bounce against her cheeks and she tucked it behind her ears. "It definitely raised the bar for the next time I go out."

Dale pushed herself up on her elbows. "Let us save you the walk of shame. Have some breakfast while Ari and I shower, and one of us can take you back to your car."

"I don't want to be an imposition..."

Ari said, "You won't be. You'll be making us breakfast while we shower."

Val laughed. "Okay, I guess that's fair."

"One more thing," Ari said.

Ari got out of bed, letting the sheet fall away without a second thought. Val's cheeks reddened and she turned away out of instinct, then looked back with her hand against her cheek. Ari walked to the foot of the bed and crouched down. Dale, anticipating what was about to happen, pulled her knees up under the blankets and rested her arms across them.

"Dale says you've never seen a wolf."

Val's eyes widened. "Oh, shit. Really?" She looked at Dale, then quickly back at Ari. "I-I really don't want to force you into~"

"I'm happy to do it."

Ari bowed her head and hunched her shoulders. She typically despised transforming as a spectacle, but this was a special case. Everything Val had done for her and *canidae* in general made her a unique case. Her skin rippled and changed, her vision shifted, and she widened her mouth to find the jaw much longer when she closed it around a thin tongue. She arched her back and steadied herself on four paws before rising to her full height and lifting her head to look at Val.

"Oh my God."

"It's something, huh?" Dale said.

Val got down on her knees and scratched Ari behind the ears. There were tears in her eyes. "That was like seeing a miracle. Thank you, Ariadne." She pressed a kiss to Ari's muzzle, hugged her neck, and stood up, turning away to wipe her cheeks. When she had composed herself, she looked back to see Ari sitting on the foot of the bed in her human form. She blinked in surprise.

"You can do it that fast?"

"It's usually not advised," Ari said, breathless. There was a sheen of sweat all over her, and her every muscle ached like she'd just run a marathon. "But a shower is waiting, so it will be fine."

Val said, "Well, then. Okay. After that, I think breakfast is the least I can do. I'll see what I can find in your kitchen."

Dale used the massage feature in the shower until Ari's pains were gone. They came out to discover Val had used the time to make something called Cloud Eggs. "Beat the egg whites, salt and pepper, lightly brown and then add the yolks. Cook a few more minutes and voila."

"Voila, she says," Ari muttered. "Magicians usually say abracadabra."

"Medical school," Val said. "This takes about ten minutes and it's delicious. I'm just lucky you had all the ingredients."

Dale volunteered to drive Val back to the club, and said she'd find ways to keep Segura busy at the office. Ari, meanwhile, found a text on her phone from Dierdre revealing she'd taken someone to the Hotel Andra. She'd done as requested and introduced Ari to the woman before they left together. Ari couldn't remember the woman's name, but she knew Dierdre looked ecstatic and a little nervous about what was about to happen.

She kissed Dale goodbye and, unsure of the protocol, gave Val a kiss on the cheek before she left.

She drove to the hotel and went up to the room from Dierdre's text. She heard shuffling inside, the heavy stomp of a foot on the floor, and then a quiet curse before she heard the lock disengage. Dierdre swung open the door with one hand while pushing her hair out of her face with the other. The motion made her robe swing open to reveal she was wearing a pair of lacy red panties and nothing else.

Ari laughed and looked at the ceiling. "Maybe should have tightened the belt before you answered."

"Oh, shit!" She tugged the two sides together. "Sorry."

"Don't be. That's actually the third pair of nipples I've seen this morning."

Dierdre whistled. "Someone's living their best life." She retreated back into the hotel room. "Come on in. I obviously still need a little time to get ready."

Ari closed the door. "Hotel Andra," she said, eyeing the spacious room. "We didn't really talk about laying low, but the woman you brought here~"

"Shannon."

"Right," Ari said. "She must have wondered how you could afford a place like this."

Dierdre kept her back to Ari as she shed the robe, trading it for her bra and the dress she'd been wearing the night before.

"I figured it was suspicious that I was bringing her to a hotel in the first place. I could have been a murderer. So I thought rather than taking her to some Best Western, I might as well go all out. A psycho killer wouldn't pay two hundred bucks for a room at a boutique hotel just to get laid, right?"

"Probably not." Ari sat in an armchair which was positioned to look out the window at a vista of Elliott Bay. She couldn't stop herself from saying, "Wow," when she saw the view.

Dierdre laughed. "Shannon said that, too. She had her hands on either side of the window, and she looked out at the water while I~"

"Whoa, whoa," Ari said. "Nope. Don't need the details."

"Fine, fine. Has Nellie called you?"

Ari said, "No... should she have? I assumed we'd get back to the house before she got there."

"We might." Dierdre kept her back turned.

"Dierdre? Why would Nellie have called me?"

"I might have texted to let her know not to freak out if the place was locked because we weren't there." Ari sighed, and Dierdre finally looked at her. "I didn't want her to worry!"

Ari shook her head. "No, you were making sure we didn't get away with it. You wanted her to know you were misbehaving."

Dierdre started to protest, then held her hands out in surrender. "Maybe I did. Maybe part of the thrill last night was knowing how much Nellie would hate it. How much she would absolutely despise the fact I was out having fun."

"To be fair," Ari said, "you *are* being threatened. And you're the one who decided you wanted to protect your identity at all costs. Dierdre may act like a warden, but you're the one who gave her the key."

Dierdre twisted her lips into an irritated grimace. "Fine. You may have a point."

"I have to ask this question, Dierdre. Is it still worth the effort? The mask, the secrecy, the whole Saint Artemis façade? The only thing the person sending threats has against you is that they know your real name."

"Are you kidding me? It's worth even more now. Do you think last night could have happened if my face was on *Settle In, Seattle* or *Colbert*? I told Shannon that I was a journalist. I could do this in every new city if I wanted."

Ari said, "But it still wouldn't be your life. Your life would be lived behind closed doors, and in studios. You can't live like that, Dierdre."

"I've been living like that just fine."

Ari paced toward the window and looked out at the water.

"For a long time," she said, "I hid part of who I was. It's one of those secrets you have to tell a significant other if you want to have any trust at all in your relationship. But it's also not something you can just blab to someone on your second date. So I didn't get close to anyone. I had a lot of nights like last night. Fun, sure. Exciting. Great sex is great sex. But when I finally found the person I could trust, the person who knew everything about me... I wouldn't trade that for a million one night stands."

She turned to look at Dierdre, who was staring at the floor.

"I'm not saying it's the right option for you. All I'm saying is that you should consider it. I think you'll be happier in the long run, and as a bonus, it'll take away the power from the person stalking you."

"I'll consider it," Dierdre said in a small voice. "But it's scary."

Ari put a hand on Dierdre's shoulder. "I know. The big things always are. Come on, let's go before Nellie puts out a missing person alert."

Dierdre checked out of the hotel, and went over the day's schedule as Ari drove her back to the house. Nellie was out the door before Ari could turn off the car's engine, marching down the stairs so she could meet them halfway.

"What in the world were you thinking, Miss Willow? Do you have any idea the danger you put her in? If this note-sender saw her leave, they could have come into the house and done any number of things while you were out doing god-knows-what."

Dierdre said, "Getting laid, Nellie. I was getting *laid.*"

"You... oh god." Nellie looked at Ari with an expression of horror and disgust.

"Not *her,*" Dierdre said, then added a quick, "Not that you're hideous, you know what I mean," to Ari. "We went to a club. I met a woman who wanted to fuck me, and I let her do it. I let her do it a couple of times, actually."

Nellie said, "You... A *stranger?* Good lord! We hired you for protection, and you take her out to some, some nightclub, and let her go off with some woman you've never even met." She exhaled sharply and pushed her hand through her hair. "I'm sorry, Miss Willow, I've given you enough leeway. This cannot be overlooked. You're fired."

"No, Nellie, *you're* fired."

Ari and Nellie both looked at Dierdre. Nellie scoffed. "You can't be serious."

"I don't need you anymore. There are a dozen managers out there who would kill to have your job, and they wouldn't take the liberty of micromanaging my whole life at the same time. I'm your client, not your daughter."

"After everything I've done... everything I do for you every day..."

"You fought for my career, and I'll always be grateful to you for that, but Saint Artemis is established now. I can tell people I need my mask and they'll go along with it because I've proven I can make them money. There's no need to fight every single step of the way anymore. We won. Saint Artemis exists."

Nellie's eyes filled with tears. "You're going to regret this, Dierdre." She didn't say this as a warning, but instead as a plea, a warning. "We can~"

"We're not going to do anything, Nellie. Go. Leave."

Nellie looked at the ground to compose herself, then looked at Ari. She was expecting anger, or some sort of insult, but Nellie surprised her.

"Keep her safe. I don't care what you have to do. You're all she has now."

Ari nodded. "It's my job."

"Yeah." Her voice was small and weak. She smoothed her hands over her blouse, looked at Dierdre again, and finally walked away past Ari.

"That was a little harsh," Ari said once Nellie was gone.

"Yep," Dierdre said, brushing at her eyes before heading up the stairs to the house. "Come on. I want to shower and change clothes. We've got a long day ahead of us."

Ari looked back at the sound of Nellie's car starting, then followed Dierdre inside.

CHAPTER NINETEEN

DALE ONCE heard it took twenty-eight days to form a habit. That was also about how long a *canidae* could go without transforming; she wondered if there was some kind of correlation. Routine days turned into weeks, and soon their new arrangement seemed as normal as anything. Ari spent her nights and the vast majority of her days at Dierdre's house or acting as security when she went to the Callahan to rehearse. Segura was assigned new cases, jobs Ari would have otherwise turned down because she was focused on Dierdre. Surveilling spouses suspected of infidelity, following people on workman's compensation cases, and process serving. She helped Dale do background checks for job applicants at a bank. The nights Ari spent at home, Segura was parked across the street from the house watching for any suspicious activity.

Ari introduced herself to the security at the Callahan, letting them escort her to every nook and cranny of the concert hall. There were a concerning number of places where a 'bad actor' might hide or gain access to the building without being screened by security. Management offered to install metal detectors at every entrance and exit, but Dierdre vetoed the idea.

"It's just a precaution," Ari argued.

"It's a slippery slope from this to every public event being wrapped in barbed wire and electric fences. There will be security at the main entrances. That's already more than I'd like."

Ari relented, but she wasn't happy about it. She revealed all of this to Dale during one of the few nights they were able to spend together. Dale missed having Ari in her bed every night but, on the nights Ari was there, she felt guilty and couldn't stop worrying about Dierdre being all alone in her house across town.

Dierdre continued to prepare for her shows. She introduced herself as the dance instructor and said she'd been with Saint Artemis "from the very beginning." The choreography was as detailed and intricate as a Broadway musical, and Ari had no idea how Dierdre would be able to pull it all off without gasping, panting, and losing her breath. She brought up this question in the office in front of Segura, who had a theory.

"Have you ever seen *The Prestige?*"

"Dierdre does not have a twin sister."

"Are you sure about that?" Segura asked. "The twin could be the one sending all the notes."

Thirty-six hours later, Dale was able to tell Ari that she was ninety-five percent certain Dierdre was an only child. Ari privately admitted to disappointment; it would have been a nice dramatic way to solve the case. But if there was a lookalike, there would be no reason to employ masks. And Ari was a hundred percent certain that there were no other people staying at the house who could swap places with Dierdre when she wasn't looking.

"It's impossible," Ari said.

"Says the woman who can transform into a wolf," Dale said.

Ari only shrugged.

The nights they were together were mostly spent trying to get more information about what happened to Gwen and Milo. Henrik Bayer was the only person they'd been able to contact with any regularity, and even he only had access to a landline with spotty reception. He wasn't aware of everything Ari's mother had done in Europe but he'd managed to give them the broad strokes.

Gwen brought back the book of essays which could be used to brainwash people into becoming hunters. The pack which had spent generations protecting it was dead, killed by Isaac Hayden. No one seemed to know how he'd even managed to find out the book existed, let alone where to find it. Its location was a closely-guarded secret among *canidae*. Gwen refused to hand the book over to anyone until she knew the whole story. Gwen and Milo were the only two above suspicion, since they'd been on another continent at the time, so the investigation fell to them.

They'd now been missing for two months. No sign, no word, not a single indication of where they might have gone. Ari put on a brave face, but it was blindingly obvious to Dale that the questions were eating her alive. She barely slept on the nights they shared a bed, and she had a feeling more of her nights at Dierdre's were just as sleepless. She wished there was something she could do, some way she could help, but short of flying to Europe and beating every bush, she didn't know what help she could be.

The only bright spot of the past few weeks had been her father finally returned home. He'd called a few times before he left, still trying to convince her to come back with him, but Dale always hung up when he brought up the topic. And now, since his return to Pennsylvania, it had been silence. She hated it, hated the rift that had opened between them, but she would stand by her defense of Ari. She refused to accept the blame, and she wouldn't be the one to reach out.

In the meantime, she kept the business running. She collected payments, paid the bills, and waited for the inevitable shakeup that would shatter the current status quo.

One event that broke up the monotony happened on a morning not long after Dale's father left. Ari spent the night at home and left the apartment to get breakfast. A large black sedan was parked in front of the house and, as she approached her car, a man got out of it and started up the driveway toward her. He lifted his hand in greeting, smiled warmly, but Ari still repositioned her key so it jutted out between the middle fingers of her right hand.

"Ariadne Willow," he said, like a fan meeting his idol. "You're a tough woman to track down. You're hardly ever at your office and seem to be spending all your nights away from home. I finally had to pull a stakeout just to maybe catch a glimpse of you. Now here you are."

"You must be Shae's parole officer." She let the keys slip back into her palm and stepped closer. "Mr. Terrence, right? I've been expecting you for a while now."

He laughed. "Yeah, I like the element of surprise. Tell someone you're coming, they expect a visit in a day or two. Give it a week, two weeks, three, they let their guard down a little. Also, you can call me Michael."

"Okay. How can I help you, Michael?"

"I don't want to keep you from wherever you're rushing off to now. This case you're working seems to be taking up a lot of your time."

"It's pretty much twenty-four seven."

He nodded thoughtfully. "Yeah. Certainly does look that way." He sighed. "I won't play the tough guy here. The truth is, while I've been waiting for you, I've confirmed Miss Segura is checking in at your offices every single day, usually twice a day. She's more reliable than you are, in fact. And I've spoken with your partner, Miss Frye. I wish all my parolees had someone like her watching over them."

Ari smiled. "Yeah. She's a good one."

"I don't love the fact that she's working for a PI. Lots of potentially bad influences there. I wanted to meet you to confirm you'd do your best to keep her away from that element."

"Absolutely."

"If you didn't, I believe Miss Frye would. So I'm not worried about that. And you're dedicated to your work. That's commendable."

Ari watched his face. He watched her.

"But you don't seem very relaxed," she finally said.

"No. Nope. I'm not. Because, Miss Willow, I've been doing this a while and I think someone is lying to me. I get this itch. I don't know where it's coming from, but it's not going away. I thought it might be you. But I've looked into you. I know the skeletons in your closet and I'm okay with them. You're a good influence on Shae."

"The itch might just be an itch."

Michael smiled, shrugged. "Yeah. Maybe. But it's going to be hard for me to let it go. I can't leave a puzzle unfinished, even if I can see ninety percent of the picture."

"I hope you find some relief soon, then."

"Me too. Have a great day, Miss Willow."

"You too."

She watched him walk down the driveway, letting her smile fade just a little. She had no idea what he knew, what secret he thought he was sensing, or how deeply he would dig, but she added him to the growing list of things she needed to be cautious about.

"It's been a month," Ari said. "There hasn't been a note, or even an email."

Dierdre said, "Maybe they gave up. Maybe you scared them off."

"Or maybe they're past the point of warning you," Ari said. "I don't know what the lack of contact means, and that concerns me."

They had just finished dinner and were still sitting at the table with the dirty dishes in front of them. Dierdre picked up her wine glass, realized it was empty, and went to the kitchen for a refill.

"So what are we going to do? Put out a flare and tell them to cough twice if they're still watching?"

"Actually, that's sort of the plan. The last note was delivered on a night I wasn't staying here. I think they might be trying to avoid me. So I think tonight, we should pull back."

Dierdre stopped pouring in time to prevent a spill, looking up, startled. "What? You're leaving...? Sorry. I-I know you have some nights off, but I've gotten used to having you or Shae around." She looked at the windows as if she expected monsters to be looming behind the glass.

Ari went to join Dierdre in the kitchen. "We're not really going to be gone. I'll have Segura nearby, but out of sight, so she can be here in a moment's notice."

"Where will you be?"

"Watching, out of sight."

Dierdre narrowed her eyes. "You've said that before. It's strangely ominous."

Ari shrugged. "Tricks of the trade. I promise you, I'm not going to be far away. I want to see if giving the impression of leaving you alone is enough to draw the person back out."

"You know," Dierdre said, staring into the wine, "it's also been a month since I told Nellie to leave. Maybe... the note-leaver lost access."

"The thought occurred to me," Ari admitted, "but I didn't want to upset you. We looked into that possibility. Segura checked up on her, and she's keeping her distance. She's still in Seattle, though. I think she's waiting for you to call her back."

Dierdre said, "Well, she's going to be waiting a long time. I finally feel like a free woman for the first time in years. When these shows are over, I'm going to take a few weeks for myself and forget all about her. Hopefully the notes will have stopped by then as well. I can take my time finding her replacement and just actually relax."

"If you're sure," Ari said, opting not to point out Dierdre had just gotten close to panicking at the thought of being left alone for one night. "Like I said, Segura will be nearby. I'll be around, even if you don't see me. But if you can't see me, then the person we're after definitely won't be able to see me."

"Okay. I trust you."

"If anything happens, Segura will be here in a flash. I'm going to focus on pursuing anyone that trespasses."

Dierdre said, "Sounds dangerous."

Ari shrugged. "That's the job sometimes. Just go about your normal routine, keep all the doors and windows locked. If you hear anything, call Segura."

"You won't be reachable?"

"I can't exactly be inconspicuous if my phone lights up with a call."

"Right. Okay." Dierdre sighed and looked out the window. "I can be brave for one night."

Ari said, "Fingers crossed it'll be one of the last times you have to worry about it."

She left the house just after dark. Segura was parked across the street, as she was every other night Ari took off. Ari spun her finger in a circle as she approached the car, and Segura rolled down the window.

"That stopped being accurate years ago," Segura said. "The rolling motion. Cars haven't had window handles since I was a kid."

"It's still applicable," Ari said. "Rolling, roll down, it symbolizes the word rather than the action. We're not going to change it to holding down a button. That's way too obscure for charades."

Segura gave in and looked out the windshield. "I haven't seen anyone lurking."

"Doesn't mean they're not watching. They somehow knew I wasn't here the last time they left a note. When you leave, go at least a mile before you come back."

"Exactly how far away should I park?"

Ari considered the question. "There's a side street about a block back that way. Every time I pass it, there's about a dozen cars parked at the curb. Try to squeeze in there. You won't stick out quite as much. If I see anything, I'll let out a howl."

"I'll keep my podcast turned down low."

"Good luck," Ari said, laughing as she patted the car door and backed up.

Segura left, and Ari got into her own car to follow her. She drove to the office because it was closer to Dierdre's house than going all the way home. Dale was waiting for her.

"Got everything you need?" Dale asked as Ari undressed.

"All I need are my eyes and ears," Ari said. "And you, of course. Always you."

Dale kissed Ari's lips. "Good luck, puppy."

Ari winked and got down on her hands and knees. She closed her eyes and began to transform.

Becoming the wolf was nowhere near as painful as it had once been. In fact, sometimes it actually felt good, like cracking her knuckles or having her back popped. But even then, the sensation became uncomfortable when it was every single joint popping simultaneously. Ribs contracted, squeezing organs, and her shoulders repositioned themselves, forcing her back to arch as fur erupted from newly-thickened skin. Dale was on her knees in front of her, cupping her face, so she had to feel when Ari's skull snapped and reshaped itself into a longer, thinner version.

When Ari opened her eyes, she saw Dale smiling at her. "All good, puppy?"

Ari licked her face. Dale laughed and raked her fingernails through the thick fur.

"Be safe. And I'll try not to worry about you too much."

Ari harrumphed.

"Yeah, yeah, but it's a good lie and I'll never stop trying." She kissed the top of Ari's head. "Go. Be a hero."

She opened the door and Ari headed out.

The wolf knew this was a work night, that it was only out to be Useful, so it stuck to the plan. It followed the route back to Dierdre's house and only made deviations to avoid being spotted and captured, locked up in some kennel. Neighborhoods like these went to great lengths to prevent strays from roaming their streets.

Ari loved traveling the city as the wolf. The smells were turned up to eleven-hundred, and every bush, tree, and alleyway was alive with a vibrant stink of life. Even decay was beautiful to a wolf's nose, and she gave in to the wolf's instinct to stop and investigate a few of the more pungent spots.

Eventually she arrived at Dierdre's house. She eyed the front door to make sure a note hadn't been left in her absence, then wandered into the bushes alongside the property. She hunkered down, chin on her forepaws, and waited. Wolves were excellent hunters, practiced at conserving their energy for the perfect moment to pounce and take down their prey. Her eyes moved constantly, tracking an opossum as it shuffled across the street. Her ears twitched when two raccoons argued over ownership of a trash can. She could sense the birds slumbering in the trees high above her head.

After an hour she got up to stretch her legs and check for signs of any other lurkers on the property. Someone nearby was smoking pot, and the scent wafted on the breeze.

The wolf wanted to run. She could feel it in her joints, like a tremor running down from her spine. She roamed into the backyard and promised herself a few quick laps around the perimeter if there wasn't any action by four in the morning. The wolf begrudgingly agreed and moved back into the front yard to resume its vigil.

She had just started to settle down in her hiding spot when someone on a bicycle came weaving down the street. Ari went completely still and became a shadow among shadows. When the cyclist stopped and planted his foot on the pavement, she lowered her head and suppressed a low growl. Her ears flattened against her skull. Only her eyes moved as she tracked the man, who swung his leg over the bike, looked both ways, and then moved toward the house like a deliveryman in the middle of the day.

He took the steps two at a time, stepping on the balls of his feet to minimize the noise. He took a piece of paper out of one coat pocket and a hammer out of the other. He brought both hands up at once to sink a nail into the door, then spiked the paper down onto it. He turned and descended the stairs as quickly as if he'd been on a zipline, not breaking stride to cross the lawn. He threw a leg over his bike and was moving like a starter pistol had been fired.

Ari got to her feet and gave chase. She waited until she was at the intersection leading to Segura's car before throwing her head back and letting out a low, mournful howl.

The cyclist looked over his shoulder at the sound, his bike weaving until he was able to correct its course. He hunched his shoulders and put on an extra burst of speed. Ari let the wolf know the leash was off and she felt more energy surging through her legs. Her feet barely seemed to touch the pavement.

Her quarry headed north, and she never let him get more than two blocks ahead of her. She kept close to buildings, ran under trees and through bushes. They went over a moss-covered stone bridge near the arboretum, its stately lamps glowing ghostly in the night. She chased him through Montlake, and the wolf in her howled in joy. First playing prey with Dale, and now she was predator. This was the most fun she'd had in ages. She'd been caught by Dale, but she was not going to let this man get away. He would not escape.

Farther north, even farther. She let him cross the Montlake Bridge alone, confident she could make up the distance between them before he had a chance to make a turn.

They passed the university and still the cyclist showed no signs of ending his ride. Ari didn't care. She could have run all the way to the Canadian border and back. Her adrenaline was spiked and she wouldn't rest until she'd reached the finish line. She so rarely got to cross the bridge, so new scents and sights was an added bonus even if she couldn't explore as much as she would have liked.

Finally, the man turned onto a side street and slowed down, his mad race dwindling down to a leisurely midnight ride. He let go of the handlebars and sat up straighter as he casually pedaled down the quiet, fast-asleep streets. He was completely unaware of the wolf on his trail. It was harder to hide in this little suburb, but he hadn't looked over his shoulder in quite a while.

Ari guessed they had gone over four miles, and the wolf was ready to go another four, a full dozen, but she calmed it down.

The cyclist pulled into the driveway of a cozy-looking house with a like-new fence and a lawn that looked like it had been manicured for a magazine. He walked his bike into a shed at the top of the driveway, locked the door, and went up the side stairs into the house. Ari crouched on the sidewalk and waited until she saw a light in an upstairs bedroom switch on. She sat down, head held high. If she could have grinned, she would have. As it was, her eyes shone with pride.

Gotcha.

CHAPTER TWENTY

ARI SPENT the rest of the night scouting the neighborhood to guarantee she would be able to find the house again once she was in human form. She looked at the street signs, but she could feel herself forgetting the words on it even as she looked away. Sometimes the wolf's mind could retain the numbers and letters of an address, but she wasn't going to force it on something this important. Things she learned as the wolf often faded into a dream-like haze as soon as she changed back, but she could hold on to the important, case-related facts like faces, houses, and buildings. If she looked hard enough, she knew she would recognize this place if she saw it again.

She walked from one corner to the other, cataloguing smells and taking note of landmarks she passed. Every fifteen minutes she stopped and stared at the house to burn the details of it into her memory. It was a nice house, in a nice neighborhood. There was a park one block away, which would help future exploration. There were cement planters on the porch. Purple and white flowers. Two trees on the sidewalk with branches shaped like a Y and a W. She called them the 'you're welcome' trees. At one point she passed a fence and felt more than heard a dog on the other side. She crossed the lawn and smelled the grass.

Who are you? What are you doing? The dog's thoughts passed to Ari the way she'd communicated with Rudy's dog, Mingus.

Looking for someone bad. Need to find them again later. Memorizing. Need help?

She considered the request. *Can you tell time?*

Know it's Bedtimes now, until First Walks.

Ari thought, then told the dog, *Tomorrow, when the sun is way straight up above, can you howl? A single long yipping howl.*

Will help you catch baddie. I'm Laffy.

Hi, Laffy, I'm Ariadne. Remember, when the sun is way up high.

Howl for Ariadne. I'll do it!

Ari thanked him and went back to the street. When she was confident she could identify the house amid a thousand other similar residences, she left the neighborhood and headed south. She took the straightest route possible and tried to hold it in her mind so she could copy it in a car. She went slow. She paused at each corner to make a note of any businesses that might help keep her on course when she returned.

It was almost six in the morning when she finally got home. The sky was just beginning to change color from the imminent sunrise, and she could hear more cars on the street as people went to work. She was so exhausted that she was unlocking the door with human hands before she realized she had transformed. She crawled into bed and faceplanted on the pillow, staying awake just long enough to hear Dale say, "Puppy...?"

The next moment she was aware of had to be several hours later, judging by the light coming in through the window. She grunted and pushed herself up, rolled over onto her back, and watched Dale appear in the bedroom doorway.

"Long night?"

"Eight miles," Ari said, stretching and pressing her shoulders into the pillow. "But I know where we can find our note-sender. What's going on with Dierdre?"

"She's terrified. She's called a couple of times asking where you were. I told her you would have an update this afternoon, but you'd been up all night and needed to rest." Dale came into the room, taking her phone out of her pocket. "Segura stayed with her last night. The note was more of the same." She tapped the screen and read from a text message. "We show you our faces, while you hide yours and scream your lies."

Ari rubbed her eyes. "He rode a bicycle four miles to the house and then four miles back just to leave that note. Why?"

"To make a statement," Dale said, "in more ways than one."

"I wish I knew exactly what that statement was. He obviously takes issue with her having a secret identity, but he's not demanding to have her unmasked. He's not asking for anything."

Dale twisted and picked up Ari's left leg so she could massage the calf. "He obviously wants something. He's gone to all this trouble, he has to have some kind of endgame. He already escalated from emails to leaving actual notes. I don't want to know what the next step is."

Ari said, "No, me neither."

Dale tilted her head to the side, an indication she was trying to work through a knotty problem. "You said you followed him how far?"

"Eight miles round trip. He lives four miles away. Ravenna."

"That's far," Dale said. "So... if he wasn't around to spy on Dierdre's place, how did he know what nights you weren't staying there?"

Ari opened her eyes and pushed herself up on her elbows. "That's an excellent question." She looked at the time and groaned. "I have to get up and shower. We need to be in Ravenna at noon. I arranged for a dog to send out a howl in case we get lost." She got out of bed and bent down to kiss Dale's lips. "Good morning, my love."

"Good morning," Dale said. "I'll call Segura and let her know when you'll be relieving her."

"Have her check the house for any kind of surveillance. Camera, audio, anything that might tell Mr. Bicycle Man I won't be there."

Dale agreed and returned to the living room as Ari went into the bathroom to shower. Dale had raised some interesting points. How did Bicycle Man know she wasn't at Dierdre's house? Could the timing possibly be dumb luck...? She highly doubted that. Maybe once, but not twice. And what did he hope to accomplish with the notes? Did he just want to scare her or was he dangerous?

She ducked her head under the faucet and let the water wash down her back. They were so close to learning who the man was, but she had a feeling that learning his identity was only the beginning to solving the mystery.

It was reasonable to expect Bicycle Man would recognize not only Ari and Dale, but both of their vehicles from whatever surveillance he had on Dierdre's house. The best option was to borrow Gwen's car, which had been sitting unused at her house since she and Milo went to Europe. Ari felt incredibly awkward taking her mother's car when her fate was still up in the air, but she didn't have time to analyze her emotions if she wanted to get to Ravenna by noon.

She let herself into Gwen's house using the spare key. Even though she knew it was empty, she paused on the threshold and listened for signs of life. The air was cold and completely still. There was once a time she'd sworn she would never set foot in this house again. She vowed she would never speak to her mother again. Recently she'd felt that same anger when she discovered where Gwen's money came from. She was stealing from hunters, rich assholes who would only use the money to hunt wolves.

Dale had gone to the garage and returned with the spare set of keys. She watched Ari scan the living room, waiting patiently. Finally Ari looked over at her.

"You okay, puppy?"

"What if they're not missing? What if..." She looked around the living room again. "Mom knew I was angry with her for the stealing. If she thought I was going to cut ties with her again, maybe she decided to beat me to the punch. She's in Europe, she's with the woman she loves. It could be a fresh start. No judgmental daughters to worry about."

Dale came closer. "Do you really think she would do that to you?"

"I did it to her," Ari said.

"You were just a kid. You're more mature now. You know you can be angry with someone and still love them." She rubbed Ari's arm. "I know this boils down to me comforting you by saying your mother and our friend are actually in danger, but she wouldn't just walk away from you, Ari. She'd never do that."

Ari put an arm around Dale's waist and kissed her hair. "Thank you, babe."

"Come on," Dale said, shaking the keys. "We better get going."

They did their best to go incognito with sunglasses and baseball caps, but there was only so much they could do to hide their faces. Ari had a small bag of disguises she rarely used, but Dale found a blonde wig and used a bright pink lipstick to reshape her mouth.

Ari glanced over at her on the drive up and couldn't resist a smile.

"Who is this supposed to be?"

Dale affected a Southern accent. "Why, this is Miss Katie... um, Sunflower. Ah just cain't wait to see a real life big city."

Ari chuckled. "Keep that wig handy for after the case."

"Roleplay?" Dale said in her normal voice. "Kind of a step backward from having a threesome, isn't it?"

"Oh, I see. We have to keep escalating?"

"Yep."

"What's above a threesome?"

Dale looked at her over the rim of her sunglasses. "It's simple math, puppy."

"So a foursome. Then a five... fivesome? Sixsome... These are getting awkward, and to be honest, I don't think there are that many people in Seattle I want to have sex with."

"Well, you better start looking. This time next year, we're going to be well into the double digits."

Ari blew out through her lips. "Boy, sex with you is getting to be a real hassle."

Dale chuckled and leaned over to press a loud kiss to Ari's cheek, leaving a cartoonish red mark. She wiped it away with her thumb.

"Twosomes are just fine, as long as you're the other one."

"Good to know. I was about to ask a lot of acquaintances for some very strange favors."

Dale smiled and watched Ari's expression. "How are you doing?"

"I don't have to really pay attention to the small things until we get across the bridge."

"No, I meant... being in Mom's car. With everything."

"Oh." Ari was quiet for another few seconds, processing her answer. "It's... I can handle it. I can smell them both all over this car. Mom stronger than Milo, but they're both here. It's not overwhelming. I can put it aside until we get our car back. How about you? Calling her 'Mom' when your father was just here."

"It's never felt more right to call her that."

Ari squeezed Dale's thigh. "There was a time I thought I'd never call her that again. Now I hear you saying it, and... I don't know. It feels really nice, darlin'."

When they got over the bridge, Dale stayed quiet so Ari could find the right neighborhood and focus on retracing her route. She had a directory called up on her phone so she could do a reverse-search once they had an address. At one point Ari pulled to the curb and chewed on her thumbnail as she looked up the street, then twisted to look back the way they'd come.

"C'mon, girl," Ari whispered.

"Close your eyes," Dale said. Ari looked at her. "Trust me." Ari closed her eyes. Dale said, "It looked different at night, and you're turned around. We turned right after the Safeway, and its parking lot would have been all lit up with security lights. You must remember seeing that. What do you remember seeing at the same time you saw the store?"

Ari furrowed her brow. "Big trees. Lots of darkness, closed businesses. Big green house on a hill, with a retaining wall. There was..."

Her eyes snapped open. She pulled out onto the road and turned around, going back and taking a left instead of a right.

"Thank you, Dale."

"Happy to help."

They were in a neighborhood now, and Ari slowed down as much as she could without looking suspicious. She carefully examined each house they passed.

"Why do so many of these houses have the same damn fences and flowers?"

Dale reached over and put her hand under Ari's hair to massage her neck, putting two fingers on either side of the collar. Ari squirmed away from her.

"That's not helping. Thank you for the thought, though."

"Is there anything I can do?"

Ari shook her head. Dale could see the worry in her eyes. The street names were all numbers, and Dale knew the wolf had a hard time remembering numbers.

"I can't believe I lost him," Ari muttered, then smacked her palm against the steering wheel. "I had him. I *had* him!"

Dale looked around as if she could spot something familiar. Even if she'd been with Ari for the chase, she'd never spent more than a few minutes in Ravenna.

"Wait. Have you ever been to Ravenna?"

Ari shrugged. "I don't know, once or twice maybe."

"Can you smell yourself?"

"What?"

Dale said, "If you were the wolf, could you pick up your own scent? If you haven't been to Ravenna, then it stands to reason the only places you might smell yourself would be places you were last night. I'm not sure how that whole thing works..."

"I think it might work," Ari said, sounding excited. "It's worth a shot."

They parked and Dale moved behind the wheel and kept watch for any witnesses. Ari got into the backseat and quickly stripped out of her clothes. A few seconds later, Dale got out of the car and opened the back door. The wolf jumped down, tilted its head back to scent the air, then gave an excited yip before it took off running west.

"Wait! Damn it, Ari, let me get back in the car..."

All the uncertainty was gone now, and Ari didn't hesitate when she arrived at an intersection. The only time she stopped was to look back and wait for Dale to catch up. Eventually Ari stayed at the curb until Dale pulled up to the stop sign. She came up to the car, so Dale leaned over and opened the passenger side door. Ari hopped in and scrambled into the backseat. Dale had to stretch to get the door closed, then twisted to look at the naked woman who had replaced the wolf in the backseat.

"That was brilliant, Dale," Ari said, pulling her clothes back on. "I picked up my own scent immediately."

"Gross," Dale said, smiling. "Is it here?"

"A few blocks north," Ari said, "but I can navigate from here. There's a playground."

Dale faced forward. "Just tell me where to go."

Ari gave her directions as she finished dressing. There was a parking lot by the playground where she could sit without being too conspicuous. As soon as Dale stopped the car, she heard the mournful looping howl echoing from a nearby backyard.

"That's my friend Laffy. Good pup." Ari took out her camera and leaned across the seat to snap pictures of the house.

"Can you zoom in and get an address for me?" Dale asked. Ari told her, and Dale opened her phone to see what she could find. "The house belongs to a William and Janice Martell. You think your Bicycle Man could be a Bill?"

"It's possible. I... shit, look. There he is."

Dale slid down in her seat even though they were far enough away he would have to be psychic to know they were there. He had his head down, hands in his pockets, as he walked slowly around the side of the house to the shed. He unlocked the door, took out his bike, and smoothly climbed onto it before he coasted down the driveway. He came toward them, so Ari tugged down the brim of her cap and turned her head so he couldn't get a clear look at her. She glanced up as he passed, and then looked to Dale to confirm what she'd known the second they'd seen him.

"That's the person leaving the notes?" Dale asked.

"Yeah," Ari confirmed. "That's who I saw last night."

Dale slumped. "Shit."

"Yeah."

Bicycle Man couldn't have been older than eighteen, and even that was being generous.

Their bad guy was just a kid.

CHAPTER TWENTY-ONE

ARI TOOK over driving for the trip back so Dale could dig around online for information about Bicycle Man. She quickly discovered their culprit was Philip Martell, the son of William and Janice. Despite his apparent youth, he was actually twenty-one. Dale found his social media and did a little digging. When they got back across the bridge, Ari found a place where she could park looking out over Lake Union. Dale had packed a lunch for them both, and she filled Ari in on what she'd learned as they ate.

"He hasn't posted much. Check-ins at the movies, restaurants, some touristy stuff like the Space Needle and the Ferris Wheel. He dropped out of U Dub last year and since then he's been working, um... wow, a few jobs. Cashier at that Safeway, a bowl artist at Poké Fresh, delivery for Marco Polo..."

"He delivered pizza on a bike?"

Dale shook her head. "I assume he had one of those, um, bike rack things that would hold it. Or maybe he had a car but lost it, sold it, whatever." She tapped the screen and scrolled. "He has Saint Artemis listed as one of his favorite musicians."

"That's promising," Ari said. "So he dropped out of college, did a bunch of dead-end jobs, possibly lost his car. That's a hell of a year."

"It might make him turn on someone he once admired."

"Did he post anything around the time Dierdre started receiving the emails? Go back about three or four months."

Dale explored. "No inciting incident, or at least nothing he posted about. Maybe it was a private breakdown." She put down the phone and looked out at the water. "There's still a lot we don't know."

"There's a lot we don't really *need* to know." Ari sounded like she was trying to convince herself. "All we have to do is keep Dierdre safe. Now we know where the threat is coming from. We know his name, we have pictures... right?"

"Yeah, he has a few pictures online."

"We can get those to security at the Callahan. It'll be a lot easier to keep watch for one guy than scanning every single audience member. We can give his name and address to Diana, and she'll get him on a harassment charge. It's a misdemeanor, but it's something at least. I don't know if he'll actually get jail time for the notes he's sent, but he's trespassing now. Dierdre could get a restraining order and that would make any further harassment a felony."

Dale said, "Look at you, puppy, getting all lawyer on me."

"Ariadne Willow, Wolf at Law."

"I would watch that show. So what's the plan with Dierdre?"

Ari said, "I promised to keep her safe until the show. I imagine I'll tell her what I learned, she'll get the restraining order, and I'll stay on as her bodyguard to make sure Philip doesn't violate it. I'll stay on until she leaves town. The threat should be completely eliminated at that point."

"Unless he follows her."

"I think that would be a level of escalation beyond what he's capable of. He waited until she was actually in town before he started leaving physical notes. When she leaves, she'll be out of reach."

"I hope so. I know it's not really relevant, but I'd really love to know how he knew where she was staying, how he figured out who she was, how he knew what days you or Segura weren't staying at the house so it would be safe to leave notes..."

Ari nodded. "Dierdre needed a place with a studio. There can't be all that many of those, even in Seattle. Easy for him to narrow it down if he knew she was coming. I intend to keep digging. If he took advantage of a gap in Dierdre's security, she needs to know about it so this won't happen again."

They finished eating and Ari drove the rest of the way to the office. "I'll have Segura give you a ride home. Thank you for coming with me today."

"I love a good road trip, especially with a mystery. And good company." She leaned across the console and kissed Ari. "I love you, puppy."

"I love you too. Have a good day."

Segura had texted they were already at the Callahan, so Ari headed there to relieve her. She was immensely grateful for the extra help on this case. She wasn't sure how they would have pulled off round-the-clock security without a third person to handle the overlap. The original offer was that Segura could have a job until she found something more permanent, but Dale said she'd been a great help around the office, and she was knocking out some of their smaller clients while Ari was occupied with Dierdre. She might have to crunch the numbers and see if they could afford to keep her on permanently.

Dierdre was onstage with her dancers when Ari arrived. She stayed at the back of the auditorium, taking one of the seats which left her mostly out of sight in the shadows under the balcony. She watched as the six women went through their routine. The music was playing from something just off-stage with no speakers, so the sound only barely reached where she was sitting.

She had only been there a few minutes when Segura appeared and took the seat next to her. "Was this a test? To see if I would notice someone sneaking in?"

"Let's say yes, because it makes me look cleverer."

Segura snorted. "Nothing to report from last night. She was really shaken up, but she finally went to bed after I assured her you were trailing the bastard leaving the notes. I got Dale's text... did you really find the guy?"

"Yep. Philip Martell. Lives in Ravenna."

"Ravenna...? Hell, that's a long run."

Ari stretched one leg out. "Yeah. The wolf loves it, though. I haven't let her run like that in way too long. The hard part will be keeping her locked up tonight. How was Dierdre this morning?"

"Shaken up. Wondering where you were, but understanding that you had to sleep off the big chase last night. She's itching for an update. I thought I'd let you be the one to tell her all the juicy new details."

"Thanks. I'll let you head home, too. It's been a long day for you already." She held out her fist and Segura bumped it. "Give my love to Mel."

"Give hers to Dale."

Ari nodded. Segura stood, stretched, and left. Ari waited until the song ended before she started down the aisle. Dierdre saw her coming, cupped a hand over her eyes, and smiled.

"Ariadne! Come on back into the green room. Everyone, take fifteen!"

"Thanks for helping out with this."

Diana Macallan smiled. "It's kind of my job, Dale. But you know I'm always willing to help out when you and Ari need a hand."

They walked together up the driveway of the Martell house, Diana in the lead and looking very official in her blazer and mirrored sunglasses. It was sometimes hard for Dale to remember that Diana was one of Ari's ex-girlfriends. They were together when they were both very young. Diana was still a patrol officer, and Ari was a young, dumb investigator who abused their relationship to get information on someone. They'd both grown up quite a lot in the intervening years. Diana was married to a wonderful woman named Lucy, and she'd long ago forgiven Ari for violating her trust.

Now Diana had agreed to officially inform Philip Martell that Dierdre was filing a restraining order. She'd explained that a lot of times, just getting a court to issue the order was enough to make a stalker back off. When Dale asked about the other times, Diana said, "We'll worry about the other times when we have to," which was not exactly reassuring.

Diana knocked on the front door and turned to look down the street. "How'd Ari find this place?"

"Went for a run."

"Long run."

"She's gone farther," Dale said. "But yeah, this is pretty far."

The door opened and Diana immediately transformed, adopting an authoritative stance with her shoulders squared and her chin high. The man who answered the door looked at her, then Dale, and narrowed his eyes as he focused on Diana again.

"Help you ladies?" he said.

"William Martell? I'm Diana Macallan with the Seattle Police Department. I was wondering if your son was at home."

His suspicion immediately switched to irritation. "Shit, what's he gone and done now?"

"Has your son had a lot of trouble with the police?" Diana asked.

William sighed and rested his hand on the door frame. "No, but it was only a matter of time. Can't stick with school, can't stick with a job, out riding that damn bike of his until all hours of the morning. When he's actually here, you can't get two words out of him. So what's going on? Is it drugs? My wife thinks he's started using."

Diana smiled. "We just want to talk with him."

"The boy's an adult. I don't have to let him stay here, but his mom is worried he'll end up living on the streets. If it was up to me, I'd have kicked his ass to the curb as soon as he dropped out of school."

"Could you have him give me a call when he gets back?" Diana asked, holding out her card. "We really just want to have a conversation with him."

William took the card, heaving out another sigh. "It could be tomorrow. Hell, it could be a couple of days. I work, you know, and when he's coming in at three, four in the morning and then sleeping the whole day~"

Dale had moved away from the house and looked down the street. She'd had enough of lousy dads to last a lifetime in the past few weeks and had no interest in listening to this one. She almost overlooked the man on the sidewalk at the other end of the block. It was the bicycle that made her look twice and, even though he was too far away to see his face, she was positive it was Philip. He was under the shade of a tree, shoulders hunched, not riding but staring in their direction.

"Diana..."

Philip seemed to realize he had been spotted. He picked up his bicycle and turned it around, climbing back onto it and shoving off with one foot.

"Diana! It's him!"

She was already running down the driveway, and Dale hurried to catch up. William came out onto the porch.

"I thought you just wanted to talk with him!"

"Stay in the house, sir!" Diana called without looking back.

Dale had barely gotten in the car before Diana pulled away from the curb. She yelped a curse as she groped for her seatbelt.

"He went around the corner," Dale said, "to the north."

Diana grunted her response, focusing on the road. She took the turn and spotted Philip up ahead. The red light on her dashboard strobed as she maneuvered around parked cars. Dale kept her eyes peeled for pedestrians as Philip continued increasing the distance between them. He took another turn, east this time. Diana was about to follow when a truck pulled out of a driveway in front of them. She slammed on her brakes to avoid crashing into his back bumper and tried to angle around him, but he was too far out into the road. He also stopped, then laid on his horn to express his irritation.

"Damn it!" Diana slapped the steering wheel, then backed up. She went around the block, hoping to cut Philip off at the next corner, but he was nowhere to be seen. As the seconds clicked by, Dale knew he could be weaving and dodging through a neighborhood he'd probably been exploring his whole life. Diana growled again as she continued to prowl from block to block, hoping to get lucky but knowing their odds were extremely grim.

"Maybe he looped around to go back home," Dale said.

Diana sighed and shook her head. "I know I told you most times, just having the restraining order is enough to make someone back off. I think we have to start talking about the other times."

CHAPTER TWENTY-TWO

PHILIP MARTELL didn't go home. Police were told to be on the lookout, but Ari was pretty sure they wouldn't find him. He seemed to have an uncanny ability to go unseen when he wanted to. She decided that she would be with Dierdre around the clock until the shows were done and she was ready to leave Seattle. It was only a week and a half until the first show, and she wasn't going to take any chances with security. Segura would be posted outside the house as often as possible, and Diana said she would increase patrols in the area.

Dierdre was so shaken when Ari reported what happened that she refused to even go out to her studio for two full days. Going to the Callahan for rehearsals was completely out of the question. With Dierdre on self-imposed lockdown, Ari was also stuck inside. She killed as much time as she could looking for bugs, cameras, or anything that might have told Philip when Dierdre would be home alone. Two days of searching came up empty. Dale helped by bringing groceries so they could cook dinner now that any restaurants were out of the question.

"The threat is actually minimized now," Ari tried to explain. "We know who has been sending the notes. We'll see him coming."

"It doesn't matter," Dale said quietly. She had been putting away the groceries while Dierdre stayed close to the window, staring out at the backyard. Since she didn't seem willing to join the conversation, Dale explained. "Before, he was the boogeyman. He was some invisible monster. She could put him out of her mind. Now he has a face and a name. It makes him real."

"She's right," Dierdre said quietly without looking at them.

Ari said, "Well, a face makes him easier to punch. And tackle. In the meantime, Dale has spent the past few days digging into all his online stuff. She probably knows more about this kid than his own parents probably do."

"Oh. About that," Dale said. "There's something a little awkward I wanted to bring up. I guess now is as good a time as any."

Dierdre turned to look at her. "What's wrong? What did you find?"

Dale rested her hands on the kitchen island, her shoulders hunched. She looked at Ari, then sighed. "The police have Philip's laptop, but I was able to get into his personal account to explore his history."

"How did you do that?"

Ari shook her head. "We don't ask Dale that question. We just trust that she can do it and look the other way."

"Anyway," Dale said, "I was mainly trying to find his contacts. I wanted to see if there was anyone he might be hiding out with, but I came up empty. He doesn't seem to talk with anyone much, and the people he does interact with live all across the country. Too far to be hiding him now. But, um, I was looking at his most visited sites. I found a site called HotChat."

Dierdre tensed. "Oh no."

"The site kept a history of his chats, including three with a user named BoardChik10."

"No, no..." Dierdre put a trembling hand over her mouth. Her eyes were shining with tears. "What... wh-what was his name on the site?"

"Touch-Me-Elmo," Dale said.

"I remember." Dierdre's voice was tiny, smaller than Ari had ever heard it. "I remember talking to her. H-him. He said he was a woman online when we first started chatting. He told me the truth the second time we talked. He seemed sweet. He was so nice." Her voice broke and she fought back a sob. "Why would he do this to me?"

"I don't know," Ari said. "You said Nellie checked out everyone you talked to on the site. Do you remember what she found for Elmo?"

Dierdre shook her head. "She never told me specifics. If someone had red flags, she told me to block their user name and stay away from them. She didn't do that with Elmo."

Ari said, "He may not have been an obvious threat at the time she looked into him. Normal kid, living with his parents, delivering pizzas. I probably wouldn't have flagged him if he hadn't been caught red-handed. I'll go over the chats to see if I can find anything that might have set him off." She realized what she was suggesting, that she meticulously read through Dierdre's private sex chats, and looked over at her. "Are you going to be okay with that?"

Dierdre shrugged, resigned. "Might as well. Don't expect high erotica."

Ari said, "For now, what we know for certain is that he bought a ticket to your first show. At least we know where and when he plans to show up."

Dierdre said, "Unless he knows you and the police will be watching for him, skips the first night, and buys scalped tickets to one of the other shows."

"You can always cancel," Ari said, even though the suggestion had been shot down before.

"I won't do that to the fans. Just promise me you'll be there."

Ari nodded. "Every night, every show."

Dierdre said, "Okay. Good. Thank you." She tucked her hair behind her ears. "Dale, please stay and have dinner with us. I've kept you away from your girlfriend way too many nights since I hired her. I'll even be your server. Sit, relax."

"That would be lovely."

Dale took a seat next to Ari at the table. Dierdre, seemingly more awake now that she had a task, went into the kitchen and gathered the things she would need to prepare their meal.

"The problem is that he's right."

Ari and Dale both looked at Dierdre, then at each other.

"Philip. In the notes. He calls me a coward? He's right." She threw a measuring cup into the sink. "My songs are about being true to yourself and not being ashamed. Then I get up and sing them wearing a mask."

"You do that to protect your privacy," Dale said.

"That's just a bonus," Dierdre said. "The real reason is because the first time I got up to perform all those years ago, I almost threw up on myself backstage. The manager had already paid me upfront and I needed the cash, so there was a mask hanging on the green room wall. I took it down, tied it onto my head using a scarf, and I was able to go out and sing. I've never had the courage to be myself."

Ari said, "What about when you're recording?"

"You mean out in that shed, with the door locked? Did you see anyone in there with me? Ever? Renata Morning has offered me an obscene amount of money to do a collaboration but I can't bear the thought of anyone being in the room when I sing."

Dale shrugged. "Okay, so what if he has a point? Maybe you're a hypocrite, maybe you're not. It doesn't change the meaning of the songs. And it doesn't give him the right to terrorize you."

Ari pushed her chair back and stood up. "You know, I don't think you're in the mood to cook right now. Why don't we go grab something greasy and fattening?"

"I'm not going out there," Dierdre said.

"Well, I am. And Dale is. So unless you want to be here alone, you better get your shoes on."

Dale eyed Ari suspiciously, aware she was planning something but unable to decipher the clues. "Puppy, what are you doing?"

"Going to get dinner. With you. And Dierdre. I know just the place. Come on."

Dierdre remained in the kitchen, eyes wide, lips pressed together. Ari backed toward the door and held her hands out to either side.

"We're going," she said. "You don't have to come with us, but we're gone."

Dale stood up, clearly ready to support Ari even without the full picture. "I could do with something greasy and fattening."

"Look at it this way," Ari said, "where will you feel safer? A bar with us that Philip Martell has probably never even heard of, or a place where he knows he can find you?"

Dierdre surrendered by slumping her shoulders. "Fine. But let me change first."

"We'll give you fifteen minutes," Ari said.

Dale waited until Dierdre was upstairs before she raised an eyebrow at Ari. "Wanna fill me in?"

Ari smiled and rubbed Dale's shoulder. "You'll see when we get there. Just promise you'll still respect me in the morning."

Dale narrowed her eyes.

John Joiner's was a hole in the wall in Capitol Hill near the college, an ugly green building with its sign mostly obscured by trees. It was easy to find parking and, while the bar seemed to be doing good business, it wasn't by any means crowded. There were about a dozen people at the bar and another seven or eight at tables throughout the room. She saw a pool table and a stage with various instruments displayed in case a band magically appeared.

Dale was the last one in the door, right behind Dierdre. She wasn't sure if she and Ari had purposefully blocked her in so she couldn't run, but she put a hand on Dierdre's shoulder to let her know things would be okay, no matter what Ari had planned. Ari went to the bar and immediately attracted the attention of the bartender. He was huge, both wide and tall, and it seemed like the bar had to have been built around him. He smiled and held out one baseball mitt hand when he recognized Ari.

"Willow-girl!" he said. "Been about a million years. Looking like you got your feet under you."

Ari let him crush her hand. "Yeah, been working hard lately." She twisted and gestured at Dale with her free hand. "Dale, this is Braun. Braun, that's my partner, Dale."

His face softened, becoming childlike. "Partner like 'partner'? Ah, hell! Willow-girl, she's gorgeous! No wonder you didn't have time for us. Who's your other friend?"

"This is Dierdre. We're helping her out. Listen, do you still make those charred burgers with a mountain of fries?"

"Absolutely. And for you, on the house. Three orders?"

Ari nodded. "Yeah. You still do open mics?"

He looked confused. "Yeah..."

"Excellent." She turned to Dale and Dierdre. "Have a seat. I'll be with you in a second."

Dale said, "Ari, what are you doing?" Ari's smile only widened and she winked. "I'm starting to get very anxious about what those winks mean."

"Go. Sit. Wait for the food." She kissed Dale and headed across the room.

Dierdre moved closer to Dale. "What is she doing?"

"I don't know. But we might as well see it through."

Dale guided Dierdre to one of the booths and they sat down on the same side so they could both watch Ari, who had ended up on the stage. Braun flipped a switch behind the bar and a spotlight snapped on. The microphone whined briefly as it was also turned on. A few of the other patrons turned to look, but the majority were focused on their beers, their phones, or their companions. Ari cleared her throat and held the microphone with both hands.

"Good evening, Seattle," she said. "I used to come here to JJ's a lot back in the day, before I had a job or a house or... well, before I had much of anything, really. And one thing I always remembered is the karaoke. I never once heard anyone good, and yet, everyone I heard was amazing. I never had the guts to get up on the stage myself, but tonight is kind of a special occasion. So I hope, uh, I hope you don't mind what's about to happen."

She crouched and touched a small monitor next to the screen.

Dale put a hand over her mouth. "Oh no."

"Ari sings?" Dierdre said.

"No," Dale said without hesitation. "No, she does not sing even a little bit."

The music started, a Pink song called "Raise Your Glass." Ari stood, gripped the microphone, and proceeded to confirm what Dale had just said. She shouted the lyrics with little to no rhythm, stomped her foot to the beat, and punched the air with her free hand to punctuate every word of the title when she reached it. A few of the customers bobbed their heads to the music, and one or two shouted out the chorus along with her, although Dale assumed they were just trying to drown her out.

An interminable three minutes passed before the music came to a merciful end. She stepped to one side and gave a theatrical bow, which received a few scattered claps. She jumped off the stage and made her way over to the booth, where Dale was red-faced from trying to contain her laughter. She got up, put a hand on either side of Ari's face, and kissed her hard.

"Brava, puppy. That was... that was something else."

"Thanks, but I think I'm retiring from the music business."

"Music and fans of the art form will thank you," Dale said.

Ari dumped herself into the other side of the booth. "So," she said to Dierdre, then gestured at the room. "What do you think?"

"What?" Dierdre said.

"I just got up there and made an ass of myself. Maybe some of these people are laughing at me. My girlfriend, for instance." Dale snorted and covered her mouth. Ari ignored her. "But it was exhilarating. And it was fun. I had fun. And so did these people. I don't know why you're scared to get on-stage and sing when you're legitimately talented, when you have hordes of people who love what you're doing, but whatever it is, whatever makes you want to wear the mask, I'm telling you... it doesn't matter. The audience only cares about one thing: having a good time. You can give them that whether you're wearing a mask or not."

Braun appeared with a tray displaying three burgers that were almost too big for their plates, the excess space filled with fat fries. He deposited them on the table along with three bottles of a local brew.

"Should've had you on that stage more often, Willow-girl. I might have even paid you a little."

"You'd actually *pay* her to sing?" Dale said.

Braun said, "Doubt it. Never heard her sing, but I'd pay for more of that comedy routine I just saw." He winked at Ari and waved the tray at them as he left the booth. "Let me know if you need anything else, ladies."

Dierdre chewed her bottom lip, then tapped Dale on the arm. "Can I get up, please?"

Ari said, "If you want to leave, I can ask Braun to~"

"I'm not leaving."

Dale got up to let her out, and Dierdre smoothed down her skirt. She looked at the stage like it was Everest, as if she was taking her life in her hands just by getting close. Ari and Dale both watched her with their breath held, afraid to even move for fear of startling her. Finally, Dierdre started moving. She weaved around the tables and stepped up onto the stage. She eyed the karaoke machine, then turned to look at the instruments at the back of the stage. She picked up the guitar and carried it to the microphone.

"Hi." She wet her lips, her raspy voice sounding awkward through the speakers. "Uh. Hi. I'm Sss... I'm... Dierdre. M-my name is Dierdre Macrae." She kept her head down, her hair over her eyes. "My friend subjected you all to that because she wanted to encourage me to get up here. So... uh, so here I am. I hope you... I hope... it's, uh, worth all that."

She cleared her throat and started playing. Ari got up and moved to sit on the other side of the booth with Dale. Dierdre found the tune and leaned closer to the mic.

"We are precious,
I'm not going to throw us away
But I'm done being quiet
I have something to say
I hear your name in my heart
I feel broken when we're apart
You came into my life as a friend
Please don't let this be the end.
I want to be your shoulder
I want to stay in your heart
Your warmth when the nights get colder
Turn on the light when your world is dark."

Dale risked a look around and saw that the other patrons were paying attention. Conversations stopped and heads turned toward the stage. The song started out slow, with Dierdre speak-singing the lyrics until she became comfortable enough to give herself over to the melody. Dale thought the song was beautiful, and nothing like anything else she'd heard on any other Saint Artemis albums. She wondered how long Dierdre had been holding onto it, and if anyone else thought the voice sounded vaguely familiar.

"If I'm nothing more than your friend
Then that's everything to me
I don't need to be the one in the end
I don't need you to love me
As much as I'm in love with you
I'm not asking anything from you
There's nothing I need you to do
You just need to hear it, and I needed to tell
I was so afraid you heard the sound when I fell."

She stepped back and played the bridge, her head bowed and her fingers moving over the strings with no hesitation or error. By now, everyone in the bar was watching. Even Braun stood still behind the bar and watched, rapt, as she finished and stepped forward again to repeat the chorus.

"If I'm nothing more than your friend
Then that's everything to me
I don't need to be the one in the end

I don't need you to love me
As much as I'm in love with you."

She repeated it twice more, bringing the song to a quiet conclusion. She lowered the guitar like she was putting away a tool, averting her gaze and scanning the stage for the quickest escape route. Dale wanted to start the applause, but a pair of men at the next table beat her to it. A second later, the entire room joined in. Dierdre blushed and tucked her hair behind her ear.

"Thank-thanks. Thank you." She put the guitar back on its stand, hurrying back to her booth. A few of the other patrons stopped her to shake her hand and tell her how much they liked the song, giving Braun time to come out from behind the bar so he arrived right behind her.

"Did you write that?"

"Oh, no. No, that's a Radiation Canary song. I could never perform something I wrote in public."

Braun said, "Well, still. What did you say your name was?"

"Dierdre. Um, Macrae."

He handed her a card. "We have live music every Friday. It pays a hundred bucks and a meal. We're booked this week, but if you ever want to swing by, you've got a standing invitation."

"A hundred bucks?" Dierdre said.

Ari bumped her foot under the table. "That's a lot, very generous."

"Oh. Yeah, okay. Yes. Thank you. You liked it...?"

Braun said, "Liked it? Miss, I'm crossing my fingers that one day you let me tell people this is where the famous Dierdre Macrae got her start." He looked at Ari. "You, never sing here again. Never sing anywhere. Ever."

Ari laughed. "You have my word."

"But hell, if it inspired her to get up there, I guess it was worth it." He winked at Dierdre and then went back to his station.

Dale had been watching Dierdre as Braun praised her. She was flushed, which brought out her freckles, and her eyes were slightly glazed.

"So?"

"So," Dierdre said. "I don't know. It felt... good. It really felt like the first time I'd ever performed live. I'm still buzzing a little." She laughed nervously and tucked her hair behind her ears, and pressed her hand to her forehead.

Ari said, "It helps that you actually have talent. Boatloads of it. But audiences don't really care as long as the heart is there. They had fun with me, but they loved you. Just have a good time, let them enjoy themselves, and you're not going to disappoint anyone. Once you've figured that out, you can take any stage and face a crowd of any size."

"I don't know if I'm ready for that," Dierdre said. "But it's definitely something to think about."

"That's all I ask. And maybe if you get the courage to lose the mask, Philip will lose any leverage he has on you. Maybe he'll just go away on his own."

Dale crossed her fingers, but she didn't hold out hope. Going from emails to leaving notes on someone's front door with a hammer and nail was the kind of escalation that wouldn't just go away. Ari knew that, but clearly wasn't going to say as much to Dierdre. All they could do was keep an eye out for Philip, hope that the shows over the weekend went smoothly, and be ready to move when things went bad.

CHAPTER TWENTY-THREE

DIERDRE WAS exhausted by the time they got back to the house. The adrenaline of performing without a mask had faded, and now she was running on fumes. She went directly to the stairs but stopped long enough to invite Dale to spend the night. "Ari's been around long enough that I know she can still be on guard even if you're here. Just try to keep it down, girls. The walls are thick, but they're not that thick."

When Dale agreed to squeeze onto the couch with Ari rather than going home to their big, comfortable bed, Ari smiled and kissed her. There wasn't much room, but they managed to make it work. "Well, if I doubted your love before, consider me convinced after this sacrifice."

"And the fact I was willing to be seen with you after that debacle at the bar."

Ari laughed. "Shut up, I'm great."

Dale rested her head against Ari's chest, and Ari used the arm of the couch as a pillow so she could see the back door and front windows.

"This reminds me of that time we fell asleep together on the office couch," Ari said.

"Which time?"

"Before we were dating. You'd given me a massage and we just passed out. You were dating someone else, and it was... awkward."

Dale said, "Oh right. This is much nicer." She kissed Ari's collarbone through her shirt. "Can I ask you something? It might be uncomfortable and you can tell me to wait for a more opportune moment, but I wanted to ask while I'm thinking of it."

"Go ahead."

"You seemed like a regular at JJ's. I mean, it had been years but Braun still recognized you immediately. That place is practically down the street from our office, and yet we've never been there. I've never even heard you mention the name. It seems like a nice enough place."

Ari kept her voice low. "Yeah. It's great. I used to go in there when I was... after I left Mom's house, when I was living on the street. Braun figured out I didn't have anywhere to go. He'd give me free meals and let me sleep in the back room in exchange for sweeping up and watching out for break-ins. It was a life saver. Literally. Once I got a job and an apartment... once I had a life, going back felt like risking fate. Like if I went back to JJ's, I would somehow be that lost person again."

Dale said, "I think I understand that. It's the same reason I'm terrified at the thought of going back to Pennsylvania with Dad. I lived there when I was scared, lonely, confused. Seattle's the only place I've felt like I had a home. With you."

Ari cupped the back of Dale's head. "Me too."

They kissed. Dale scooted closer to Ari as Ari pressed her against the back of the couch. "How thick are the walls...?"

Ari laughed and slipped her hand down Dale's flank to the curve of her hips. "I can be very quiet."

"You're not the one I'm worried about."

Fifteen mostly quiet minutes later, their strategically removed clothes put back into position, Dale was close to sleep when Ari's phone vibrated against her hip.

"Ah-ahh," Dale half-moaned. "Did you have that there the whole time...?"

"Shush." Ari squinted at the screen and saw it was a text from Segura. "PM didn't know when you weren't here... he's casing the street looking for your car. Just saw SOB."

She'd read the text out loud, so Dale wasn't surprised when Ari suddenly jumped up and reached for her pants. She handed the phone back to Dale.

"Ask her where."

Dale typed the text and read the response. "I'm on foot, approaching Thirty-First." She looked up and watched Ari hastily button her shirt. "You're not going to wolf out?"

"I'm taking the car. If I catch up with him, I want to have a chat." She took her phone back. "Stay here and watch Dierdre. Do not wake her up unless you have to. With any luck she can sleep right through this."

"Be safe, puppy."

"You too." She kissed Dale and hurried out, taking the stairs three at a time and running to her car. Segura sent another text - "North on 32" - as Ari backed out of the driveway.

Two minutes later she passed Segura running down the street. She hit the voice-transcription button on her phone. "Go back to Dierdre's. Stand watch outside." She saw the bicycle up ahead, Philip hunched over the handlebars, pedaling as if he knew he was being chased. Ari increased her speed and pulled up alongside him, wary of the cars parked on either side of the street as she rolled down the passenger side window.

"Philip Martell!"

He swerved but didn't look over. He was wearing a black baseball cap pulled low over his eyes, his chin thrust out with determination as he pedaled faster.

"We know who you are. We know your parents. It's only a matter of time before this is over, so why don't you pull over so we can have a talk?"

"Go to hell!"

He slammed on the brakes, turned the bike on the sidewalk, and started pedaling the way they'd just come. Ari cursed under her breath and put her car in reverse. By the time she caught up, he was already around the corner and lost in the shadows. Ari growled and turned on her brights, flooding the street with an unnatural daylight which reflected off the parked cars and rendered the extra visibility almost useless. But she could still see movement, and she spotted Philip as he took another turn.

"Little bastard is out here playing life-sized Pac-Man..."

She managed to keep up for three turns, but each time he put a little more distance between them until eventually she lost sight of him. She pulled to the curb and slammed the heel of her hand against the steering wheel. When she calmed down enough to talk, she took out her phone and called Dale.

"Any luck?" Dale was whispering, obviously trying not to wake Dierdre.

"I lost him," Ari growled, angry at herself. "He has to be sleeping on the streets. I know a few places he might go, so I'm going to check those out."

Dale said, "Puppy, no, come back here…"

"It's fine, I'm not too tired…"

"Ariadne." Dale's voice was firm. "The first Saint Artemis show is in two days. You've had a lot of sleepless nights, or nights where you barely got any sleep. You need to be on top of your game during the concert and it won't happen if you keep running around all night."

Ari cleared her throat, intending to argue, but she knew Dale was right. More than that, she knew she was starting to notice the long nights. She looked out the window hoping that by some miracle Philip would zip past. She really did feel tired. And damn, was the first show really in two days? She pinched the bridge of her nose.

"Puppy?"

"You're right," Ari said. "I'm exhausted. I'm on my way back now. Is Segura there?"

Dale said, "She's keeping watch outside. Dierdre is still asleep as far as I know."

"Okay. We can decide in the morning whether or not we want to tell her that he came back. See you soon."

"Drive safe, puppy."

Ari hung up, looked around again for the bicycle, then sighed and pulled away from the curb. The only bright side was that Dierdre was leaving Seattle after the shows were finished. One way or another, the case would be closed by this time next week.

"You can't be serious," Ari said. "I can't come with you for the rest of the tour."

Dierdre paused pouring the milk into her oatmeal pan, looking up with surprise. "Of course I'm serious. This man is still out there. Last night, he proved he's still trying to leave notes on my door. He's not going to stop just because I leave Seattle. You'll be paid appropriately."

"It's not about the pay." Ari was grateful Dale had already left before this conversation started. She was pretty sure they'd be on the same side, and she didn't want Dierdre to think they were ganging up on her. "I doubt Philip will follow you…"

"But the notes will continue. I can't take it, Ari. I can't just sit here and wait for the next note to show up, knowing it could appear at any time."

"Philip doesn't have his support system now. It's only a matter of time before a patrol car spots him or he goes back home to face the music. I'm confident the notes will stop once you're out of Seattle."

Dierdre chewed her bottom lip and slowly stirred her oatmeal. "I still want you to come with me when I leave."

Ari closed her eyes. "Dierdre~"

"I'm alone, okay? For the first time, when the car arrives from the record company, I'm going to pack up all my own shit and move on to the next city. Where I'll set up in another house just like this one. Alone. Philip found me here and now he has nothing to lose. What if he does follow me? What if he decides to skip the shows? He waited until you left to put notes on my door. What if he knows he just has to wait until I'm in Portland to make his move?"

"And if nothing happens there, I follow you to Chicago? Boston?"

"Whatever it takes until you catch him!" Dierdre snapped. She caught her anger and pulled it back, lowering her head and letting out a series of slow breaths. "I feel safe with you, Ariadne. You convinced me to sing without a mask, which no one has ever been able to do. I slept so soundly that I had no idea you and Shae were on high alert. That's what I need."

"I'm sorry, Dierdre, but my life is here. My… my family." Her mind briefly stuck on thoughts of her mother and Milo, still missing, and with no further word from Henrik Bayer. "I can't leave."

Dierdre pressed her lips together and angrily transferred her oatmeal to a bowl. "Then I suggest you find this asshole before my last show. I'm going to go eat in my room."

Ari sighed and watched her go, then went to the front window so she could look out over the street. Everything she'd said was true. She didn't think Philip would follow Dierdre to another city. But she also didn't think he would let the upcoming shows go off without a hitch.

They would be his last opportunity to make good on his threat, whatever it was, and it terrified Ari that she couldn't even decide if it would be violence or an unmasking.

She needed to call in some help.

CHAPTER TWENTY-FOUR

ARI HAD always expected the shows to be a minefield of potential risks, but she was unprepared for how much work was involved in preparing Saint Artemis to take the stage. The day was laid out like a military maneuver, beginning with a car arriving at noon to take them to the venue. Dierdre confirmed the people in the car were from the label and knew her identity, but she still wore dark sunglasses, a scarf, and a hoodie for the ride. Ari examined the car and checked everyone's credentials, even with Dierdre vouching for them, and kept watch the entire way through the tinted windows for signs of Philip Martell.

Dale and Segura were in a car behind them. Diana and her partner were already at Callahan checking security and making sure Philip hadn't already snuck in to hide in some nook or cranny. There was a heightened police presence around the hall, and the record label insisted on hiring special security to watch the entrances for signs of anyone acting suspicious. Everyone had seen Philip's picture, they had him memorized, and Ari was confident they'd done everything in their power to secure the building.

But she couldn't stop wondering what they might have missed.

The bright side was that she had plenty of time to speculate, since Dierdre had barely spoken two words to her the past few days. Dale had obviously sided with Ari, but she sympathized with Dierdre. If they didn't catch Philip by the last show, could they really leave her defenseless? Segura offered to go, but even if her parole officer granted permission, it wasn't a permanent solution by any means. Eventually she would have to come back, and then what would Dierdre do?

Ari had spent her free time reading the chats between Dierdre and "Elmo." There was sex, obviously, but they also had long conversations about Saint Artemis' music. The kid seemed sweet. Sad. She tried to imagine this kid also writing the mean, angry notes, but she couldn't. Something had to have pushed him over the edge. Losing his job, dropping out of school... something big happened, and for some reason, Saint Artemis was the target for all his rage.

The car entered Callahan Hall through a parking garage on the north side of the building. The driver showed two forms of ID to the guard before the crossbar was lifted. Dierdre remained in the car once it was parked, and Ari checked to make sure the path to the elevator was clear before letting her get out. The label's four-man security team formed a phalanx around her and moved as a single entity to deposit her into the car. One of the men radioed ahead to confirm the path to the dressing room was also clear before he allowed the doors to close.

"You could always hire a couple of these guys to follow you to Portland," Ari said.

Dierdre remained still, eyes cast down, arms crossed over her chest. "I don't know them," she finally said. The scarf pulled up over her nose muffled her voice. "I know you. I trust you."

"They seem fine."

"We're talking about them like they're not standing right here," Dierdre pointed out. "Like they're furniture or something."

One of the men said, "It's our job, ma'am."

Dierdre sighed and hunched her shoulders. "I don't want to be a job. I don't want to be someone's client. I thought we were becoming friends, Ariadne. But I guess I was just another client to you."

Ari bit the inside of her cheek and said nothing.

The elevator arrived and they were met by a trio of men indistinguishable from the group which had ridden with them in the car. Dierdre and Ari were surrounded, and she could hear the brushing cloth as the men's sleeves rubbed against the walls on either side. Once Dierdre was in the dressing room, one of the men put his hand on Ari's shoulder.

"We'll have two men on the door, two at the elevator, and two more at the emergency stair access. The last man will be a floater, going wherever he's needed so none of the locations is ever compromised. Will you need anything else, Miss Willow?"

"I think we're good for right now. Thanks."

He nodded and turned to hand out the assignments to his men. Ari went into the dressing room and closed the door behind her, twisting both locks. When she turned around, Dierdre had already removed her disguise and left the hoodie and scarf tangled together on the couch. They were in what she would have described as a massive hotel suite, with a seating area and another area separated by a half-wall where Ari could see a bed and a writing desk. There were no windows, and only the one entrance, so Ari pushed down a surge of claustrophobia as Dierdre finished peeling off her outer layers.

"I hate that shit," Dierdre said. "But it's what I would have to wear every single time I left the house if people knew what I looked like."

"The lesser of two evils," Ari said.

"I guess so." She went to the mirror and looked at herself, then turned to face Ari. "I know I'm being a brat. It's selfish to ask you to uproot your whole life and follow me around. But I'm scared."

"Can I be blunt?" Dierdre shrugged and motioned for her to proceed. "The whole point of the mask is to keep you from being scared, to let you live your life. But you're not doing anything with that freedom. Yes, you don't have to worry about people recognizing you in clubs, but you never go out. You said you want a love like I have with Dale, but you're not opening up to anyone."

Dierdre held her hands out to either side. "How am I supposed to open up with people? By the time I trust someone enough to tell her who I am, I'll be destroying whatever trust she may have in me."

Ari remembered having the same fear. She couldn't have told every woman she dated she was *canidae*, but at what point was she supposed to bring it up?

"I told you before that there's something about me, something pretty major, something that any partner of mine would have to deal with. I worried about the same thing. When do I tell, how do I tell. I didn't have to tell Dale because we started out as friends. She knew all about it by the time we became lovers. People knowing who you are will change your life, yes, but it might also give you an opportunity to start living it. It's something to at least consider."

Dierdre hugged herself and looked down at her feet. "I'll... I'll mull that over. For now, though, I need to get ready. The seven men out in the hall should probably be enough protection if you need to go do something else."

Ari said, "I'll make the rounds. If you're sure..."

"I'll be fine. I need space to get into the whole Saint Artemis mindset."

"I understand." She held up her cell phone. "If you need me."

Dierdre nodded. "Thank you, Ariadne."

"Sure. See you soon."

She stepped out of the room and found herself flanked by two men who were at least a foot taller than her, and maybe a foot wider as well. They both looked at her, and she returned their stares.

"Hi, fellas."

"Ma'am." The one on her left started to look away, then looked at her again. "You really been watchin' Saint Artemis this whole time by yourself?"

Ari said, "Yeah. But I have faith that the seven of you will be almost as good." She patted him on the arm and smiled as she walked away.

"For the record," Leftguard said, "that wasn't a sexist thing. I trained with an Israeli lady who once hit me so hard my jaw still clicks when it gets cold. I just wanted to know how scared of you we should be."

She laughed and didn't look back. "Terrified, my man. Absolutely terrified."

Ari took the elevator down to the lobby, which was spacious and almost entirely vacant other than a few employees preparing for the barrage of fans they were about to face. Tall banners bearing the image of Saint Artemis lined the front of the hall, blocking the people waiting on the sidewalk outside from seeing in. Security was doing the last checks, ushers were doing a walk-through of the auditorium, and a few people in suits that she assumed were from the press stood around in clusters and talked amongst themselves.

"Puppy."

Dale's voice echoed off the tile and glass of the lobby but Ari pinpointed its origin without hesitation. She was coming from the main stairs, dressed in a brown suit over a black blouse. Behind her was Melissa Vogel, Segura's partner and a guard at the jail. She was in a concert T-shirt and blue jeans. Her hair was down, and Ari tried to remember if she'd ever seen her so casual.

"Everything okay with the Saint?" Dale asked. They'd agreed not to use Dierdre's real name if there was any chance of being overheard.

"She's tucked away, all snug," Ari said. "Anything to report?"

Dale shook her head. "Segura is outside going up and down the line to see if Philip is trying to sneak in wearing a disguise. I don't think it's very likely he would try coming in through the front door, but it's worth checking out."

"Definitely." Ari wished her mother or Milo had been there to try picking up his scent. She would have done it herself, but she needed to be present for Dierdre. She nodded to Vogel. "Thanks for using your night off for this."

Vogel said, "Hey, I get to see a concert and act like a spy. I know there are very real stakes here, but I'd be lying if I said I wasn't having a great time." She looked back at the security checkpoints, which everyone coming into the concert would have to pass through. "Do you really think he's going to try something tonight? If I wanted to hurt someone and saw all of this, not to mention those redwood trees the Saint came in with, I think I would postpone for another day."

Ari said, "He doesn't have much of a choice. It will happen here, either tonight or during one of the other shows. Philip has been planning this for a long time, waiting for the Saint to show up, and he's only been escalating. He isn't going to let this opportunity pass him by."

"Then he's probably not expecting to get out. Look at all this. If these measures don't stop him from getting in, there's no way he'll get past it all once he pulls whatever he has planned."

Ari said, "Small comfort when the damage has already been done. We'll have to deal with that when the time comes. If he pushes us, and if he succeeds in hurting the Saint, then we'll do whatever is necessary to stop him from getting away with it. If he's not here already, he has to get here soon. Everyone keep your eyes peeled and be safe. We don't know how far he'll go to finish this."

She squeezed Dale's hand before they all split up. Ari went to a backstage access door which led her down a dark corridor which curved alongside the auditorium with a series of closed doors along one side. She tested each door as she passed, poking her head inside the unlocked ones and taking a quick look around before she moved on to the next.

The locked doors bugged her. It was conceivable that Philip had gotten into the building days ago, maybe he'd been camping out in one of these dressing rooms ever since their chase the other night, but she didn't think it was likely. Security had been on high alert, and too many people had been in the building multiple times since then. She assumed whoever had the keys had already searched these areas, but she would confirm the next time she saw someone.

She wished she could figure out his goal. She agreed with Dierdre that he didn't seem interested in inflicting harm. Maybe terrorizing her was the whole point. Maybe he just wanted her to be scared. But what did he get out of that? Why had he targeted her specifically? Was it because of their chats? She hadn't seen anything in the transcripts that she considered incriminating, but who knows what might have set him off?

One of the rooms held a half dozen racks of costumes, props, and miscellaneous gear. Ari searched it carefully for anyone who might be hiding among them, but came up empty.

Her search led her through a crowd of dancers performing some pre-show ritual. The men and women were all tall, lithe creatures in matching costumes. They were surrounded by a cloud of perfume and the powdery smell of makeup, and Ari held her breath as she passed through it. Every person who would appear on-stage had been thoroughly vetted by the label's security company but she still scanned every face.

She walked onto the stage and looked out over the sprawl of empty red seats. She went to center stage where Dierdre would be spending most of the concert. She would also dance, moving from stage left to right and occasionally strutting down a long spit extending out into the crowd. The whole point of this set-up was for every seat in the house to have an unobstructed view of the performer. In this case, line of sight had a distinctly ominous context.

Out in the lobby, she heard a loud clicking noise. Someone shouted, and then the clicking repeated a half-dozen more times. Then she heard what sounded like a wave crashing up onto the shore. Ari had a good idea what it was, but she still looked at her phone for confirmation.

A text had just come in from Dale. "They're opening the doors."

Ari put the phone back in her pocket and walked offstage.

It was showtime.

CHAPTER TWENTY-FIVE

THE SHOW was sold out, and the venue had three thousand seats. Even if some of the tickets weren't redeemed, with security, stagehands, dancers, and various crew, Ari estimated there were still probably at least thirty-five hundred people in the building. She returned to the lobby and watched the mass of humanity as they snapped pictures with their phones, crowded around merchandise tables, and drifted inside to find their seats. There were more girls than boys, more teenagers than twenty-somethings, but looking for someone who matched Philip's description was still a daunting task.

She was also bombarded by a million various scents as she weaved through the crowd. Every kind of perfume, cologne, aftershave, hairspray, bodywash, and of course the ever-present reek of teenage body odor. It formed a single cloud which seemed to press on her sinuses, blurring her vision. The wolf's heightened senses were rarely such a disadvantage, but she definitely wished she could turn them off at this particular moment.

The lobby cleared out faster than she would have thought possible. The show was set to begin at eight, and a glance at her phone revealed it was almost time. She also saw a string of text messages.

Dale: "Nothing."

Mel: "No sign."

Diana: "All clear."

Segura: thumbs-down emoji

Ari pressed her lips together. A security guard approached her, obviously intent on shepherding her inside to take her seat, but she held up her lanyard.

"Oh, are you the private eye?"

"Yeah. Have you seen anything suspicious?"

He said, "I assume you don't mean kids trying to sneak in vape pens or beer, stuff like that?" She shook her head. "Nah, just the usual stuff."

She thanked him and he moved on, leaving her alone. She went to the door and looked out into the auditorium. This was the show for which Philip had bought tickets. Row FF, Seat 13, Stage Right. They'd never been able to search his room, so there was a chance he still had the ticket and could use it to get in. Mel was currently occupying that seat in case he showed up, but Ari believed he would just buy a new ticket from a second-hand seller to get in undetected.

The lights dimmed and the crowd hushed before exploding in applause. The curtain rose. Purple-pink smoke flooded out across the stage and spilled into the first few rows as a steady drumbeat began to echo through the room like a pounding heart. The music faded into a song Ari recognized but couldn't name, the crowd's cheers rose to a deafening level.

And Saint Artemis appeared.

She strolled through the smoke in the flame-inspired mask Ari had last seen at the house, sitting on Dierdre's coffee table. She wore a form-fitting purple jumpsuit with a white belt loosely slung around her waist. She held her arms out to either side, revealing feathered wings attached at her wrists and swooping down to meet behind her back. She bowed slightly forward as she walked down the extended stage like a model on a catwalk, swinging her hips to the beat of the song.

"Hello, you stunning Seattle souls!"

Dierdre's voice was amplified by a microphone in her mask. Ari recognized it, but there was definitely something artificial in her tone. She was speaking as the Saint, not as herself, and even her movements seemed alien and unfamiliar. The woman she knew was definitely there, but she was channeling something Ari had never seen.

"My time in your beautiful city has been a bit tumultuous, I must admit. But every time I felt scared or worried, I saw something beautiful or I met someone with the biggest heart, and I knew what makes this city special. Thank you for being here tonight, loves, and I hope you enjoy our time together as much as I plan to."

As the music swelled and the fog cleared, Dierdre backed up down the catwalk to be surrounded by dancers dressed similarly to her, save for the mask. The lights moved over the stage in waves rather than strobing, making it look as if every solid surface was covered with a thin layer of water. Everyone in the audience was reduced to a silhouette, making any type of identification impossible.

Ari stepped back out into the lobby to clear her head and think of another angle. She reached for her phone and caught motion from the corner of her eye. A woman in a leather jacket and jeans had just come around the corner, moving quickly but not running. Ari looked up and the woman stopped short with a deer-in-the-headlights look, then turned and hurried away with her head ducked down. Ari started following her out of instinct, uncertain why she was doing it other than the woman's clearly suspicious behavior. When the woman began moving faster, Ari recognized the way she was holding herself.

She moved like Philip Martell.

"Philip?" Ari said.

The woman started to run. Ari pursued. She pulled her phone out as she ran, lifting it to her mouth and holding down a button to dictate a text.

"I'm chasing Philip Martell through the west corridor, heading north toward the backstage area! He's in disguise as a~" Several things clicked in her mind and she realized something important about the person she was chasing. There were no threats in the notes, no promise of exposure, and there was no way out once Philip did whatever he had planned. "Suspect is dressed in a leather jacket, jeans, long black hair. Send."

They were approaching the backstage entrance. Seconds after Ari sent the text, the doors flew open and a burly man in a tight black T-shirt stepped out. Philip slammed into the man, knocked him out of the way, and disappeared into the darkness.

"Watch it, lady!"

Ari said, "Damn it, that was him! That was the guy!"

"What?"

Ari ignored him and continued the chase, immediately blinded when she ran through the doors. She slammed into something and hurt her shoulder, but managed to keep herself from falling over. The music was even louder here, a hollow pounding that seemed to start inside her head and drum against the inside of her skull. She could see the vague outline of Philip moving through the darkness and kept on him. She didn't know where the others were, but she couldn't let Philip get onto the stage.

It turned out that wasn't his destination. He stopped, his feet skittering on the concrete floor as he spotted something to his left. He stretched out for it, grabbed hold, and swung out of sight. Ari caught up before he could climb the ladder out of reach. She wrapped her arms around his waist and pulled, but he held tight. He flailed and kicked, long legs wildly swinging and his sneakers making contact with Ari's hip and stomach. She refused to let go.

Suddenly there were huge bodies on either side of her, two huge security guards who reached up and peeled Philip off the ladder. All of his weight went into her arms and she grunted as she fell backward. She heard Philip cry out and wail, his attempts to escape more desperate now. Ari repositioned her arms so she had him in a full-nelson, arms pinned and her head next to his ear.

"I know what's happening." She had to shout due to the music, which made it as intimate as a whisper.

"You don't know shit!"

"I do. I just figured it out. I know. I know you're not wearing a disguise, I know your name isn't Philip. I know you don't want to hurt the Saint."

Philip's movements slowed down. One of the security men put a hand on Ari's shoulders. "We'll hold 'im here, you go call the cops."

"No cops," Ari said. "I have this under control. We just need to go somewhere quiet to talk."

The security men didn't look happy about it, but the biggest one motioned for Ari to follow him. Philip also stopped struggling, although she couldn't tell if that was from surrender or conserving energy for a better opening. Ari awkwardly walked Philip through a claustrophobic corridor that ran behind the stage. She saw a dozen people dressed in black with balaclavas over their faces so they would blend into the shadows as they made the spectacle on-stage happen.

One of the men opened the door to a dressing room littered with duffle bags, shoes, and cubby holes filled with street clothes. Ari took Philip inside and finally released him once she confirmed there were no other exits. She looked at the security men and nodded her thanks to them.

"Stay outside the door."

"You sure you're okay alone in here?"

Ari nodded. "Yeah. Just stand guard. I'll be fine."

She took out her phone and sent a group text: "Got Martell. Stand down." She slipped the phone back in her pocket and faced her quarry, who had taken a seat on one of the benches that ringed the space. Head down, shoulders slumped, a posture of total defeat. Ari approached cautiously.

"What's your name?"

"You know my name. You went to my damn house, ran me out of it, thanks a lot."

Ari said, "I know the name your parents gave you. What's your real name?"

Philip looked up. He was surprised, wary of the kindness in her tone, suspicious that this was a trap. Ari stared back without blinking, patient.

"Jane. I go... I'm Jane."

"Hi, Jane, I'm Ariadne. I was hoping you could answer some questions for me."

"What does it matter?"

Ari shrugged. "It doesn't, really. I just don't like loose ends. We figured out that you were riding your bike past the house every night looking for my car so you'd know if the Saint was alone. That's one mystery solved. But I have so many more. How did you find out who she really is?"

Jane sniffled and looked down at her feet. "We used to chat. In a... th-there's a, um, chat room. Fantasy chat room. She said she would roleplay as Saint Artemis for me. We hit it off. I didn't figure it out until a few months later when she released a new song. The chorus was 'I'm a hollow shape of myself, and you're tapping the edges to see if I'll break.' I knew I'd heard that somewhere, so I went back into the chats and found it. She said it six months before the song came out. It was *her*. It was really her."

"How'd you find her real identity from that?"

"It was kind of easy. The site doesn't have the best security. I found the email she used to sign up, and from there I just kept digging. I found her manager's email. Nellie. She wasn't as careful about covering her tracks. Once I had access to her email, I just lurked there."

Ari nodded slowly. "That answers my next question, about how you knew where she would be staying."

"Nellie set it all up. She got the confirmation emails and I just opened them, and marked them as unread before I left." She sniffled and wiped a hand over her eyes. "I wasn't going to hurt her. I know how it looked, but I–"

"Oh, I know," Ari said.

"You didn't know."

Ari gestured at the door. "Yeah, I put it all together when you went up instead of out onto the stage. You never threatened the Saint, either with violence or exposure. The notes were a threat, but not against her. They were your suicide note. You were going to kill yourself in the middle of this show."

Jane's lower lip trembled. She refused to look at Ari, her eyes obscured by her hair. "She says she's like us. We're all together, we're standing together, we're strong when we're together. But she's not brave. She's a liar and, and–"

"A coward."

"A *coward!*" Jane spit. She stood up and began pacing. "She wears a mask. She doesn't have to… face anything. She can hide. She has no idea what it's like to be out here exposed all the time. I want to tell people who I am. I want that every single day, but I'm terrified. My best friends. My parents. She tells us that we need to be true to ourselves but she won't even tell anyone her real name."

Ari sat down on one of the benches. "And what would jumping onto the stage during her concert prove?"

"I don't know! But… but it's s-something, and I can't do nothing anymore. I want her to see me. I want her to see what happens when a coward tells people they need to be brave."

"Dierdre *is* scared," Ari said. "She's scared like you are. She wants to be herself, to live, and move through the world without the baggage of celebrity. That's why she wears the mask. And… also… I think the mask allows the audience to see her as extensions of themselves. She's not a person, she's the embodiment of their true selves. She's their courage."

"She's not my courage," Jane murmured, head still bowed.

"I'm sure there are a lot of people like you out there who feel the same way. They heard the lyrics and felt like they were complete horseshit. Dierdre is one of them, I think. She puts on her mask and she becomes someone new. Someone who can believe what she's saying. Without the mask, she's just another person who is hoping for answers."

"That's not very comforting."

Ari shrugged. "I'm not here to comfort you, Jane, I'm here to make sure you're around to hear the encore."

Jane gave a quick, startled laugh.

"What?"

"You're the first person who has ever called me Jane."

"How'd it feel?"

"Good," Jane said quietly. "Real good."

Ari said, "Be a shame if it was also the last time." She stood up and put her hands on Jane's shoulders. "I know you're hurting. You're scared, and confused, and you feel completely alone. I wish I had any kind of answers for you, but I don't. I'm not the right person to help you through this. But there are people out there who can help you. They've been through this. They know how you feel because they felt it, too. I can help you find them. I know there have been a lot of unbearable days, and a lot of pain, and tears. There's probably going to be more down the road. But I think admitting who you are, as painful as that is right now, is the first step of getting out of that rut."

Jane wiped her eyes again. "I guess you should call the cops."

Ari sighed and squeezed Jane's shoulder. "I'm going to leave that up to Dierdre. But I think when she knows the whole story, she's going to agree with me that it's not the right thing to do. We're going to get you help. Find someone you can talk to. And if she doesn't agree that's the right course of action, then I'll convince her. Now... I assume you got in here with a second-hand ticket?"

"Yeah."

"Right. So why don't we sit here until you feel up to going out and actually watching the show you paid twice for?"

Jane laughed weakly. Then she hung her head and Ari put a hand on her shoulder. After a few minutes of sniffling in silence, she glanced at Ari. "You don't have to sit here with me all night..."

"I know. But I'll sit here as long as you need me to. And if you want to talk, I'll listen. If you want to just listen to the music, that's fine. Whatever you need."

Jane wiped her eyes. "I like your name, by the way. Ariadne. It's mythological. It's cool."

"Thanks, Jane," Ari said. "I like your name, too."

CHAPTER TWENTY-SIX

ARI AND Jane eventually left the dressing room to watch a few songs from the wings. When the Saint indicated it was time for an intermission, Ari asked Jane to go back into the dressing room with security standing guard. "For your safety more than anything else," Ari said, but Jane was already nodding. Ari went into Dierdre's dressing room, arriving less than a minute before the woman herself swept in and pushed the door shut behind her. She looked completely alien out of context, her hair feathered out around the mask and her human eyes staring out from the openings of the mask. Her chin was painted a sparkling yellow, and her lips were fire engine red.

"Well?" she said. "Did you find anything?"

"We found her."

"Her...?"

Ari gestured at the couch and they both sat. "Philip Martell is trans. The chat rooms were the only place where she could be herself, and she felt you pretending to be someone else was... ah... a violation of the trust. The song lyrics about being true to yourself and finding your strength grated on her because she thought you were essentially hiding."

"Being a coward," Dierdre muttered.

"Right." Ari rubbed her hands together to dispel some of her nervous energy. "Jane felt like she had to wear a mask just to get by."

Dierdre said, "So she was... going to run onstage and rip off my mask?"

Ari swallowed. "No. That wasn't her plan..."

"I'm confused."

"She... she was going to get above the stage. And jump."

Dierdre shot to her feet. "God!"

"I talked to her." Ari held Dierdre's hand. "She's fine. She's in the dancers' dressing room. Security is keeping an eye on her, just in case. We're going to figure out what to do after the show, but I thought you'd want to know we'd taken care of the threat."

"Wow." Dierdre sat down again. "This is a huge relief. And of course I'm not going to press charges on the poor dear now that we know everything that she's been going through. She didn't really do anything wrong."

Ari said, "Well... she hacked private emails, accessed personal information, trespassed-"

Dierdre waved her off. "In retrospect, nothing I feel she needs to be punished for. Like you said, we can discuss it later."

"Yeah."

"Thank you." She hugged Ari, the plaster of the mask pressing coldly against her cheek. "This is such a huge weight off my shoulders."

"You're welcome. I'm going to let you get ready for the second half. Do you need anything from me?"

"You've done more than enough, Ari, truly. I'll see you after the show."

Ari left the dressing room and went back to where she'd left Jane. Diana was waiting with the security men and excused herself to meet Ari halfway.

"I talked to Jane. Diedre's not pressing charges?"

"No, she doesn't think it's necessary given the information we have now."

Diana nodded. "I don't think she's going to walk away scot-free, but no one will probably want to spend too much time on this. In the meantime, I can babysit her back here if you want to go out and enjoy the rest of the show with your girl."

"Are you sure?"

"You've earned it. So has she. Go on, enjoy."

Ari kissed Diana on the cheek and found her way through the labyrinth of backstage corridors until she found the auditorium. The lights had come up a bit and the room was filled with the dull hum of hundreds of conversations. The dancers were still onstage, moving to a pre-recorded piece that sounded like a lullaby. Dierdre had gotten tickets for the whole team, and Ari found Dale seated between two empty chairs, her head slowly pivoting back and forth as she watched the crowd. Ari approached her from behind and leaned down.

"Anyone who would let a pretty woman like you sit by all alone should be locked up."

"We tried locking her up once," Dale said, twisting to look up at her, "but the bitch got out."

"Female dogs will do that." Ari pecked Dale's lips. "Is that seat taken?"

Dale patted the cushion and Ari stepped over the back to drop down into it. Dale rolled her eyes. "Who do you think you are, Johnny... um... Danny... Danny... John Travolta's character in Grease."

Ari grinned. "Where's everyone else?"

"Segura and Mel are stretching their legs. I don't think this is really Mel's kind of music. And I assume you saw Diana." Ari nodded. "Is it really over?"

Ari squeezed Dale's knee. "Yeah. I think it is. We're going to get Jane some help. Dierdre will most likely insist on paying for it, now that she has the whole story. For Jane, it's just beginning, but as far as we're concerned... yeah, I think it's done."

Dale put her head down on Ari's shoulder. "You did good, puppy."

Ari kissed Dale's hair and put an arm around her.

A few minutes later, the lights flashed and dimmed. People returned to their seats as the dancers assumed a new formation. The crowd applauded, some cheered, and the Saint strutted back out onto the stage. Once again Ari was struck by how different she seemed. A few minutes ago, this woman had sat next to her on the couch, and it seemed like Dierdre playing dress-up. Now she would have sworn the Saint was a completely different person. No mask, no costume, just someone who burst into existence when she walked onto the stage.

"Thank you for waiting on me, lovelies. I hope your intermission was as insightful and illuminating as mine was. I want everyone out there to take a moment and look at the people around you. Maybe they're the people you came with. Maybe they're strangers. But they're you. They're me. Everyone in this room is here because we found something in this music, some message that resonated with us enough to spend your money, spend your evening, to come out here and share this one moment in time with people like us. Thank you. Thank you."

The band played the intro to a song and the Saint bowed her head, swinging her hips from side to side. The audience moved in time to the beat. Ari reached for Dale's hand, found it searching for her, and she clutched it tightly as the Saint moved down the catwalk in long, confident strides. She recognized the song as "My Worst Sin," one of her earliest songs and an unusual choice for such a big night. She didn't think it had ever been enough of a fan favorite to include it.

> "You live unchanged in my memory,
> In that red sweatshirt I bought for you
> Promises were easy and love was true
> You swore you'd always be there for me
>
> Until I fell off a tightrope I couldn't even see
> Promises are simple
> Keeping them, impossible
> We try and we fail
> Swear we'll try harder
> It's a fairy tale
>
> I tried so damn hard to keep you
> Dug my nails in 'til I bled you
> Said every word that came to me
> Except the ones that said I'm sorry
>
> So I'm standing here now, just me
> Defenses down, I hope you see
> What I'll do to let you know
> My worst sin was letting you go."

When she hit the last word of the verse, she pressed her palm against her mask so suddenly that Ari was momentarily afraid she'd just gotten shot. But her other hand came up and went under her hair, tugging on something at the base of her skull. She sensed Dale sitting up straighter next to her but it took her an extra second to understand what was about to happen. Someone in the audience shouted, "Oh my god!" and it became a banshee wail as Dierdre dropped her hands and brought the mask down with it.

The Saint was gone; Dierdre Macrae stood exposed in the spotlight.

Her eyes were wide and wild, sweeping over the silhouettes of the audience as they erupted in stunned applause and cheers. Pulling off the mask had left her bangs standing out in wild spikes. Only the lower half of her face and a space around her eyes had been painted, leaving her looking a bit like a harlequin. The band was still playing, but Ari could see them exchanging confused looks. She was breathing so heavily that Ari thought she might hyperventilate. But she took the microphone which had been threaded through her mask and brought it up to her mouth.

"Hello," she said, her voice almost breaking on the second syllable. Phones were raised now, at least two dozen people recording the unmasking of the century. "Hello," she said again, and an uncountable number of voices shouted *Hello!* in response. Dierdre smiled nervously. The mic trembled in her fingers.

"My name is Dierdre Macrae," she said, tears cutting through her makeup, "and I'm Saint Artemis. It's *fucking wonderful* to meet you all."

The cheering got even louder. Ari winced at the sound but she was too transfixed by Dierdre to care about the pain.

"I want to thank..." She waved her hands to get the crowd to quiet down, but it barely made a dent. "I want to thank Ariadne... and Jane... for giving me the strength to do this. Thank you so much, ladies. And if it's okay with all of you, I think I want to do a little of the show just like this. Maybe just the next few songs. What do you say?"

The crowd roared. Dierdre beamed. Dale pressed tightly against Ari's side. When she looked down, she saw Dale was also crying. She didn't touch her own cheeks because she was fairly sure she knew what she would find if she did.

"Well... okay, then, let's get this thing started..."

She turned to the band, signaling for them to go back to the beginning of the song she'd chosen for her grand unmasking.

"From the top, everyone..."

CHAPTER TWENTY-SEVEN

THE SAINT performed the rest of the concert unmasked. Ari could see the nervous anxiety in her smile and the manic wideness of her eyes, but she knew that was only because she'd spent so much time with her. Everyone else in the audience seemed too stunned to pay attention to the details. People were still taking photos, shooting videos, and hunching over their phones to send a flurry of text messages. By the encore, Ari assumed the whole country knew the name Dierdre Macrae.

It was close to midnight when the show finally ended. Jane agreed to let Diana take her to talk to a counselor about her plan to commit suicide. Ari thought she seemed fine, but Diana insisted given that Jane had apparently been planning to kill herself for months. Jane hugged Ari and thanked her for the talk and willingly left with Diana, who slipped out through a service exit to avoid the crowds leaving through the front of the building.

Once they were gone, Ari went to Dierdre's dressing room. Four security men were standing in front of the door, and two of them stepped forward with the clear intention of removing her without bothering to have a conversation.

"I just want to make sure she's all right."

"The Saint says no one gets in."

Ari said, "Can you just promise me she's okay?"

Before he could answer, the door opened a crack. "Ari? Is that..." The door opened wider. "She can come in. She's okay."

The men stepped aside and Ari entered, shutting the door behind her. Dierdre wrapped her up in a hug, trembling and breathing had as if she'd just finished a marathon.

"What did I do? Ari, what did I do?"

"You did something very brave. Are you okay?"

Dierdre stepped back and pressed both hands against her cheeks as she stepped back. "I don't know. Maybe. Yes? I think so. Yes. God, it's going to be insane the next few days."

Ari said, "If you'd like me to stay with you until you leave town~"

"Yes. Definitely. Please. Especially now. We don't know that Philip is the only person out there who has issues with me."

"Jane."

"What?"

"Her name~"

"Right, yes. Jane. Jane." She took a deep breath and let it out slowly. "Where is she?"

"Detective Macallan is taking her to talk with a counselor."

Dierdre nodded. "Good. Good, yes, okay." She paced in a wide circle and then shook her hands out as if drying them. "God, I'm manic. I feel like I could run to New York."

"You might need that energy to get out of here. Security said press has set up camp outside. We may need to get creative about how we leave."

"Oh."

"Don't worry," Ari said with a wink. "I have a plan. But I'm going to need your mask."

Dale stood behind Mel, Segura, and three muscular men whose names she hadn't caught. She reached up and adjusted the mask so it wasn't smashing her nose. They were waiting for the security leader to receive a message that Ari and Dierdre were ready before they moved. Segura looked back at her and smiled, then reached up to adjust her bangs. "I'd be fooled if I didn't know you," she said.

Mel looked back and nodded. "Yeah, it's pretty convincing. We won't let anyone get close enough for a good look. We're going to move quick, out the door, wave to the crowd, across the lobby, then backstage again. Nice and easy."

"Yep," Dale said. "But I really wish one of you had red hair so I wouldn't be stuck playing decoy. God, this mask is hot. I don't know how Dierdre does it with a spotlight shining on her."

The security man turned. "Ready, ladies?"

"Ready, Dale?" Segura asked.

"Let's get this over with," Dale said. "People are supposed to get fifteen minutes of fame. I think I can handle it for fifteen seconds."

Mr. Security touched his ear and then spoke into his lapel. "We're go in ten." He silently counted off, then planted his hand on the push bar of the door. It swung open with an echoing click and he led them out into the lobby. Segura and Mel followed, then Dale, and the other two security men brought up the rear. Across the lobby, separated from them by a velvet rope, a crowd of fans were waiting. Several people seemed to see Dale at the same time, and a shriek went up.

"There she is! Saint Artemis! Look!"

Cameras flashed. Reporters elbowed their way to the front of the crowd for the best view. Dale stood up straight and bowed a little, then blew kisses to the left, right, and center. Below them, in the parking garage, she knew Ari and Dierdre were in a car. Not the same car they'd arrived in, just in case someone had been watching. They were waiting for word to spread that Saint Artemis was in the lobby so everyone waiting by the garage exits would relocate. Seconds stretched out, and her face got even hotter under the mask.

"They're moving now," Mr. Security said quietly, his lips barely moving. "We'll let them get to the next block."

"No rush," Dale whispered.

"We love you, Saint Artemis!" someone shouted, which prompted a cheer, and then someone began chanting "Dier-dre! Dier-dre! Dier-dre!"

Mel beamed. "Hopefully that makes it on the news so she can see it later."

"If she even watches the news anytime this year," Segura said. "I'd throw out my phone and never look at the internet again."

Dale felt like she'd been waving to the crowd for a full half hour before Mr. Security motioned for her to start walking. The crowd kept shouting and Dale kept waving and blowing kisses as she was ushered to the other entrance. She didn't slow down until she was in the dark hallway and heard the click of the door shutting behind her. She stopped and bowed her head, reaching back to unbuckle the straps holding the mask in place. Mel stepped closer to help her.

"Thanks," Dale said. "Seems strange to regain my anonymity by taking a mask *off*."

Segura said, "It's only fair that you get to play superhero once in a while. Why let Ari have all the fun with a secret identity?"

Dale grinned. "Believe me, I'm glad to be the mild-mannered reporter once again. Now can we please go find my real clothes so we can get out of here?"

They took extra precautions for the ride home. Some might have called it overkill, but Ari wasn't going to risk anyone following them back to Dierdre's place. She was more vulnerable than she'd been in years and spending a little more time driving aimlessly was worth it for peace of mind. They were in Ari's car, non-descript and not the sort of thing anyone would have expected Saint Artemis to be in, and Dale was distracting the press so they'd all be looking at the front of the building while Dierdre snuck out the back.

After twenty minutes of driving in the wrong direction, Ari declared them safe and turned around. She looked over at Dierdre in the passenger seat. Her face was now scrubbed clean of makeup, her hair pinned back but falling loose at the temples, and she wore a pair of Dale's sunglasses. Lights from passing buildings flickered over her face, but they weren't bright enough to read her expression.

"How do you feel?" Ari finally asked. "Any regrets?"

"Even if had some, I can't put the milk back in the jug. It's out there, it's made a mess, and I have to decide if I'm ready to live with it." She was silent for close to a mile. "And I am. I really am. I can't wait to see what happens next."

"I'm really happy for you," Ari said.

Ari parked in front of the house and spotted their guest before shutting off the engine. Nellie sat halfway up the stairs, leaning forward with her elbows resting on her knees. She sat up straighter when she saw the car but remained seated. Ari looked at Dierdre, who was pressing her lips tightly together.

"I can make her leave."

"That might be fun to watch," Dierdre said, "but no. I think this is a good thing."

Ari said, "Sure?"

"Sure enough."

Ari got out of the car. Nellie stood, but didn't come down the stairs until Dierdre started walking toward her. She held up her hands, fingers spread wide.

"I'll leave. I promise." Her voice was quiet, smaller than Ari had ever heard it. "But I saw what happened and I needed to know you were okay. Are you? Okay?"

Dierdre nodded. "I'm okay. And I think in the morning I'll be even better. I think tonight was a really good thing."

Nellie looked relieved. "Good. That's very good." She touched the collar of her blouse and averted her eyes. "That's all I came for. I just wanted to hear it from you in person. I apologize if I overstepped my boundaries. I'll leave you alone now. Sleep well, Dierdre."

She stepped around them and started down the driveway.

"Ari caught the person who was sending me notes. It's all taken care of."

Nellie said, "Ah," and the relief in the single syllable was impossible to miss. "That is wonderful news. Well done, Miss Willow. I'm grateful Dierdre had you watching over her during this difficult time."

"It would be easier if you were here. Tomorrow. The usual time." Dierdre had said this without turning to look at Nellie. "Everything always is. You know. Easier. When you're there. If you're still willing to put up with me."

Nellie also wasn't looking at Dierdre, but Ari looked between them both. Finally Nellie nodded and said, "I'll come in at ten. Give you a chance to sleep in a little. I'll bring you breakfast."

"Okay. Thank you, Nellie."

"Always, Dierdre."

They stayed on the lawn until Nellie had driven off. Ari watched Dierdre and finally nudged her. "You okay?"

"Mm-hmm."

"Big night for you."

Dierdre laughed hollowly. "Yeah." She started up the stairs, moving as if the entire night had just caught up with her. "Big nights aren't really the same when you go home and enjoy the aftermath by yourself. No one there to celebrate with you. Or be proud of you. I don't know. It takes some of the pep out of it, you know? I stood on that stage and had hundreds of people cheering for me." She turned and looked up at the empty house. "Now...?

Nothing. No one."

Ari said, "I think you took a big step in finding that tonight. You're not hiding anymore. You can open up your heart a little more."

"Yeah. But now I'll have to wonder if they want me or the Saint." She pushed her hair out of her face and looked down at her shoes. "It's never easy, I suppose."

"No, not really," Ari said.

Dierdre sighed and stretched. "Okay. Thank you for getting me out of there, but your work here is done for the night. You have someone to celebrate. Go home, let her treat you like the hero you are."

"Are you sure?"

"I'm positive. Thank you, Ariadne. You were perfect in every way."

Ari smiled. "You weren't so bad yourself, Dierdre. Sweet dreams."

She started to walk away, but Dierdre called out to her from the top of the stairs. "You said you had a secret of your own. Something that you were always worried about telling your partners. I don't suppose you'd be willing to tell me what it was. You don't have to. I've just been going crazy trying to figure it out."

Ari chuckled under her breath, ducking her chin as she considered her answer. Finally, she looked up and met Dierdre's gaze.

"I'm a werewolf."

Dierdre laughed and nodded. "You know... given everything I've seen you do over the past few weeks, I could almost believe that. Give my love to Dale."

"Will do. She sends her love back, I'm sure."

Dierdre pointed at Ari. "Next time I'm in Seattle. VIP tickets and dinner. Promise."

"I'm holding you to that."

She went back to her car and looked back at the house one more time. Dierdre had already gone inside. No lights were visible from the street. She knew she would be back the following day to take Dierdre back to Callahan, but with Jane getting help, the case was essentially over. She'd spent so much time at the house that she felt a little melancholy about leaving it behind. She was going to miss the place, but she knew Dierdre was who she would really miss.

Ari finally got into her car and drove home. The lights were off inside, and Dale was sitting at the dinner table with her head down on folded arms. She sat up when she heard the door open. She linked her fingers together and stretched her arms, smiling sleepily at Ari as she tilted her head for a kiss. Ari bent down to oblige her.

"My hero," Dale said. "Another case closed, no violence required. The woman I love is safe and sound."

"And we get a nice big paycheck for all the nights I left you alone."

Dale said, "No paycheck is worth that. But it's a nice consolation." She wrapped her arms around Ari's neck and leaned against her.

Ari looked down at Dale's arms. "What are you doing?"

"Carry me to bed."

"I'm tired. I had to chase Jane down. You should be carrying *me* to bed."

Dale wrinkled her nose. "But you're so tall and lanky. Nothing but knees and elbows."

Ari pulled Dale to her, and Dale wrapped her legs around Ari's waist. Ari grunted as she pivoted to carry Dale into the bedroom.

"You're going to pay for that knees and elbows crack," Ari informed her.

Dale chuckled. "Punish me, puppy."

Ari dropped Dale onto their bed and settled her lanky knees and elbows down on top of her. She received no complaints in the aftermath.

CHAPTER TWENTY-EIGHT

THE LAST two Saint Artemis shows were absolute insanity. Pictures of Dierdre were all over the internet and #TheSaintUnmaked was the number on trend on Twitter for most of the day. The demand for scalped tickets skyrocketed, people online offering to pay several thousand dollars for the chance to be in the audience for another unmasking. Streets around Callahan were impassable due to the crowd of fans, hopefuls looking to get tickets, and the media covering the furor. Nellie convinced the Seattle Police Department to provide an official escort, and on both nights, Dierdre was delivered to her performance in the backseat of a squad car while an empty limo with tinted windows acted as a decoy.

Diana reported that Jane was going to start counseling and, in the meantime, she was staying with a family friend. Apparently her parents reacted just as she'd feared, and she was no longer welcome in their home. Jane insisted she didn't care, which Ari didn't quite believe. Jane also said that she was no longer suicidal, which Ari did believe, although she was glad she had someone she could talk to if the bad thoughts came back.

Dierdre offered to meet Jane after her last show so they could talk through what had happened between them. Ari facilitated the meeting in Dierdre's dressing room. Jane apologized, Dierdre accepted, and they had a long talk about courage and cowardice. Ari wasn't aware of what was said between them, since she respected their privacy, but she did note that there were tears when the women hugged goodbye. Dierdre asked Jane to stay in touch, and Jane promised she would.

"I already have your email address, right?"

"Maybe you can start signing your messages when you send them," Dierdre said.

Jane also hugged Ari, whispering a painfully sincere "Thank you so much" in her ear before letting her go.

Ari said, "I'm sorry it took me so long to realize this case had two clients."

When the last show had been played, Dierdre stayed in Seattle one more day to clear out the house. Nellie arranged everything, renting their next house and scheduling the movers to come and take the personal belongings on ahead. Dierdre stopped by the Bitches office to say goodbye and deliver the final check for Ari's services. Dale had sent the invoice and even she was a little taken aback by the size of it, but Dierdre insisted she considered it a bargain.

"I guess this is it," Dierdre said. "I really hope I never need your help ever again, but if anyone I know ever has an issue, I'm giving them your number."

When Saint Artemis finally left Seattle, Ari took a few days off to unwind. Segura took the opportunity to invite her and Dale to dinner at Mel's apartment. It was a casual evening until the food was done and Ari caught a loaded glance between their hosts.

"Everything okay?"

Mel nodded. "Everything is fine. But there's something we need to talk with you about." She folded her arms in front of her on the table. "Michael Terrence. Shae's parole officer."

Dale said, "We met him. He seemed like a good guy."

"He is. Solid, upstanding, by-the-book. He believes Shae is genuinely reformed and starting a new life on the straight and narrow. He even called her his prized parolee."

Segura shifted in her seat. "I feel like a kid who brought home straight-As."

Mel reached over and squeezed Segura's shoulder. "But he does have a concern. We had to give up the story we told about how we didn't do anything while she was a prisoner. He never truly believed it, and I could tell it might cause issues down the road. So we told him the whole truth just so we wouldn't have anything between us."

Dale bristled. "He can't make you break up…"

"No, no," Mel said. "He never suggested that. He never actually suggested anything. He just told us that he thought it might be an issue if people found out. He thought that was the big secret you were hiding, Ari. I thought it was easier to let him believe that than explain about *canidae*. He said it could become an issue with guards or other prisoners, lawyers, basically anyone who might want to make trouble for me. I have to agree. So Shae and I discussed it, and I decided I shouldn't stay in my job at the prison."

Ari said, "Are you sure?"

"Yeah. To be honest, sleeping with Shae wasn't the most ethical thing in the world." She looked at Segura and her eyes softened. "Worth it, definitely, but regardless. I applied for a job with a police department in a tiny little town up north. I gave them full disclosure about my relationship with Shae and the lines that were crossed, and they offered me the job anyway. Mr. Terrence agreed to let Shae move out of Seattle with me as long as we keep up with regular check-ins."

"That's amazing!" Dale said, but her smile immediately wavered. "But… when you say north…"

"Too far to commute," Segura said, with real remorse. "I have to resign from Bitches. I'll never be able to thank you enough for finding out what happened to my sister, and being a lifeboat when I got out. Whatever I might have done to help you in prison, you've paid me back in full. In fact, I might be in your debt. You're my hero, Ariadne Willow."

Ari got up and stepped around the table to hug Segura. Dale hugged Mel, and then they swapped. Segura said she would stick around until the actual move, which would happen in two or three weeks.

On the drive home, Dale reached over and scratched the back of Ari's neck. Dale drove while Ari lapsed into silence, watching the stores drift by outside.

"Looks like it's just you and me again, puppy. At least until Mom and Milo show up again."

Ari looked over at her. "What?"

Dale said, "Mom and Milo… you know, whenever we figure

out where they are and bring them home."

"Hon…" Ari stopped herself and looked out the windshield. "What?"

"Dale, Mom and Milo are dead."

Dale tightened her grip on the steering wheel. She wanted to say 'what are you talking about,' but it only came out as "Whuh…"

"It's been months, Dale. The last time we spoke with Henrik, he said their pack was as stumped as before. No sign of them. They disappeared looking for hunters. What part of that gives you any hope that they might still be out there?"

Dale blinked the tears out of her eyes. "Hell of a way to break the news to me…"

"I'm sorry. I thought we… I just… thought… we weren't talking about it. I'm sorry, baby. Pull over up here." Dale managed to get into a parking lot before she started crying. Ari leaned across the seat and hugged her. "We should have talked about it."

"How long have you… how…?"

"I don't know. I didn't wake up one day and give up hope. But I can't keep holding out for a miracle. We might never know what happened to them." Ari closed her eyes and started to cry as well. "Thank you for making me give her another chance. You gave my mother back to me, Dale. You helped us heal before she…" She didn't finish the thought. "Thank you."

"I love her," Dale said. "I love you."

"I love you, too."

Ari kissed the tears off Dale's cheeks, then kissed her lips. She put her hands in Dale's hair, holding it tightly, their foreheads pressed together. Dale sobbed quietly and moved her head down to rest it on Ari's shoulder, and Ari rocked her as best she could, given their awkward positions.

"Just the two of us again," Ari said. "You and me, beautiful girl. It's all we ever needed anyway."

Dale nodded but didn't say anything, burrowing her face deeper into Ari's shirt.

Ari held her and let her cry.

INTERLUDE

VAL DIDN'T know if her experience with Ariadne Willow and Dale Frye made her a better doctor, but she knew it changed how she saw her patients. She'd known about *canidae* her entire life. Most of her education had come from a hunter father who wanted her to "know thy enemy." She eventually grew up and made her own decisions about the creatures she'd been raised to hunt and decided to put her skills to good use. Part of her had always thought of wolves as an abstract concept. She knew the women in her care could transform, there was no doubt about that in her mind, but to actually witness the transformation had changed something in her as well. It was beauty. It was magic. It was something that should have been impossible, and she couldn't stop seeing it when she closed her eyes.

The only problem was the other things she saw when she closed her eyes. Ariadne and Dale kissing, their naked bodies, a hand sliding over a thigh. It was definitely becoming a problem. She'd never had a threesome before, always thought they were overrated, but damn, holy hell, and shit, she was a convert. Being with two women was definitely worth the hype. She didn't know quite how this sort of thing worked, but unfortunately, she had a feeling that calling for an encore was probably up to the couple. The third wheel couldn't just show up with a bottle of wine and ask if they wanted to party.

Unless...

No. She couldn't. It wasn't her place.

But boy, did she want an encore.

After that night, she'd asked one of her patients about *canidae* night spots that might be amenable to a human patron. The woman had looked at her and said, "You lookin' for a little doggy style, doc?" Val had blushed, but she'd gotten the name of a club where she wouldn't be shunned because of her inability to transform. She went, she danced, she had a great time. The first time she went to the club, she went home with a woman named Mona who was a very lively companion but, in the end, not quite what Val was hoping for. The second time, she was on the lookout for couples. She was upfront about the fact she was human, since it appealed to as many women as it repelled. She wanted another threesome. She had gotten a thrill out of the knowledge Ari and Dale were in love but she was just there for lust. It made her feel completely sexual, and now she craved that tingle.

She was leaving one of the clubs alone, wondering if she was at risk of fetishizing *canidae* or if she was just expressing a preference. She wanted to be with someone like Ariadne, someone who was powerful and wild. The *canidae* she knew had a presence that human women couldn't match. They were closer to nature, calmer, more peaceful. That was what she was drawn to. That, and being with a couple. She sighed at herself, worried she was looking for something it would be impossible to find.

"Valerie Byrne?"

She turned toward the voice and saw a man hurrying toward her from the direction of the club. She thought she must have dropped her ID or something and faced him fully.

This gave the man behind her a chance to drop a black bag over her head. His hand covered her mouth before she could release a scream. His other arm went around her waist, her arm pinned to her side, and he lifted her feet off the ground. The other man caught up to them, grabbed her legs, and they both carried her a short distance before dumping her into what she assumed as a van. Her legs and ankles were bound with unbelievable speed, the ropes cinched tight enough to hurt.

Everything she thought to say, every question that came to

mind, seemed ridiculous and pointless. She focused on her breathing. She wouldn't panic. She refused to let fear overtake her. The bag was musty and smelled awful, which made her want to hold her breath, but she forced herself to inhale and exhale slowly as the van rocked under her. She felt like there were three, maybe four people in the van.

"What's happening?" she asked.

"Relax, Doc," the man who'd called her name said. "Everything is going to be just fine."

"Who are you?"

A woman from somewhere near Val's feet said, "We're friends, Dr. Byrne. And for the foreseeable future, you're going to be working for us."

EPILOGUE

THE NEXT few months were a return to normalcy for Bitches. Ari took cases from people in need and waived her fee when necessary. Dierdre's check still provided a healthy cushion in their bank account so she could be charitable for those who couldn't afford them. She tracked down deadbeats for mothers in desperate need of child support and only charged for a tank of gas. She tracked down the person who had been catfishing a senior at U-Dub, which required her and Dale to take a class about how to navigate social media. She checked up on Jane, who was living on her own and seeing a therapist twice a week. "No more anger," she reported, "and no more thoughts of hurting myself."

And through it all, the wolf ran. Ari spent long nights exploring the wooded corners of Seattle, trekking up toward Ravenna again because of all the Interesting New Smells she'd discovered the last time she was there.

They kept in contact with the Bayer pack, just in case. No reported sightings of Gwen or Milo. No updates. Ari could declare they were dead as much as she wanted, but Dale didn't want to give up hope until they knew for certain. She couldn't.

Gwen had taken care of the rent on her house before she left, but Ari had to assume the money would run out eventually. The house was just sitting empty, waiting for someone who was never going to come back, but even six months after they disappeared, she couldn't bring herself to suggest selling it. Dale would consider it the last confirmation that Gwen and Milo were really never coming back, and it would crush her.

Time rolled on. Ari was hired for more cases, investigated, got paid. She took Dale out on dates. They had dinner with Diana and Lucy. They argued and made up. Dale, who had found it so awkward to make room in the office when Segura started working for them, now had to get used to her absence. They discussed the possibility of hiring part-time help, but there was no one they trusted enough.

On the first truly cold morning in September, Ari slipped out of bed just before six. Dale protested her departure until Ari bundled the blankets from her side of the bed and dumped them onto her. Dale burrowed in and fell back to sleep as Ari snuck out of the house. She was only gone twenty minutes, taking the car instead of transforming, and returned home to find Dale was still fast asleep. She climbed up onto the bed and straddled the lump of Dale's body under the pile of blankets.

"Hey," she said to the tuft of red hair on the pillow. "Wake up."

"Mpph."

Ari pulled down the blanket to reveal Dale's face. Dale squeezed her eyes tighter shut. Ari bent down and kissed three spots on Dale's temple.

"Stop. Why. Don't."

"Happy birthday."

Dale opened one eye and twisted to look up at her. "Hm? We don't celebrate birthdays..."

"I know, not usually. But with everything that's happened this year... your dad, Mom and Milo, everything with Isaac Hayden. I thought it would be nice to celebrate the fact you're here. And you're with me. And we never really figured out if our anniversary is when we met, when you started at Bitches, or when we started sleeping together, so this seems like the best option."

"That's so sweet, puppy." She sat up and kissed Ari's lips. She brushed the hair out of Ari's eyes and smiled sleepily. "It would have still been sweet at eight or nine o'clock, but still... sweet."

"I also got you an ice cream cake and thought you would want time to enjoy it before you had to shower and get ready for work."

Dale's eyes widened. "Ice cream cake...?"

Ari smiled and kissed the corner of Dale's mouth. "Get up and dress. I'll cut you a slice."

They were at the dining room table sharing the slice when Ari saw movement outside. It was early for a guest, but she understood when she saw it was Diana. She got up and went to the door before Diana could knock, trying to read her expression through the glass. Worry, fear, upset... she assumed it was a troubling case that she needed help with.

Ari opened the door and smiled warily. "Hey, Diana. What's wrong?"

"Hey. I'm glad you're already up. I..." She had glanced at Dale, who was still in her pajamas. "Is that cake for breakfast?"

"It's Dale's birthday," Ari said.

"Oh." Diana seemed to snap awake. "Oh, shit..."

"It's okay. We never make a big deal about it."

Diana looked down. Ari could almost hear her train of thought get derailed. "Ari, can we talk outside?"

Ari looked at Dale, then back at Diana. "No."

"Ariadne..."

"It's *Dale*. I'm just going to tell her what you say anyway."

"And maybe it'll be better coming from you," Diana said sharply. "Please, Ari, just come outside with me."

Ari was confused. She looked at Dale, who gave a worried nod.

"Okay," Ari said.

Diana led the way outside and back up the steps to the lawn. Ari closed the door and joined her. The sky was dark even though the sun had risen on the other side of the thick clouds, and Ari shivered as a slow wind pushed across the yard. She hugged herself and watched Diana.

"What's going on?"

"We found Milo. She's alive."

Ari shivered again, this time from a mental chill. She had a thousand questions and was fairly certain she didn't want to know any of the answers. She squeezed her hands into fists until her fingernails dug into her palms. Diana gave her time. She swallowed the lump in her throat, blamed the moisture in her eyes on the wind, and finally managed to speak.

"*You* found her? Seattle PD? She's here?"

"She's at Interbay Urgent Care. A couple of uniforms found

her wandering on Alaskan Way, down by the stadium. She was in shorts and a T-shirt, her hands and feet were filthy, she looked like she'd been dragged behind a truck. Basically the way you sometimes looked when I would pick you up after a transformation back in the day."

Ari remembered those days well. "They thought she was a junkie?"

"They didn't know what to think. She refused to speak and fought them when they tried to get her into the car. She..." Diana pressed her teeth together and turned her head, squinting into the wind. "She tried to bite one of the cops."

"Fuck." Under ordinary circumstances, someone trying to bite a cop is bad news. But when the biter is *canidae,* it could be a death sentence. "Did she break the skin?"

"She bit his arm. Just got the sleeve. I wasn't on duty so I couldn't take over and make sure she got sent to a proper doctor. But I don't think it will be a problem. Right now they're treating her as a victim who escaped from a bad situation, but it's only a matter of time before they start asking hard questions."

Ari said, "Right. What can we do?"

"I can get you into the medical center where they're holding her. I know the cops who are watching her. I think I can convince them to give you some time alone."

"Thank you. And... a-and..."

"No word on your mother. I'm sorry."

Ari shook her head. "You've done enough." She squeezed Diana's arm. "Let me go get dressed and break the news to Dale."

"Apologize to her for me. This isn't exactly news anyone would want to get on their birthday."

"No," Ari said. "But it's a reminder of why we don't really celebrate."

Interbay Urgent Care was a squat, unassuming building of grey stone with a row of green windows running along the top of its walls. Ari was grateful Diana was there to drive since she spent the entire trip trying to figure out how Milo had gotten to Seattle from Germany, where she'd been for the majority of the past year, why she wouldn't - couldn't...? - speak... where was Mom? She chewed on her thumbnail and looked out the window. The sky looked like it wanted to storm, but only a handful of raindrops hit the car.

Dale had almost been sick when Ari broke the news to her.

She cried, Ari held her, and promised she would find out everything as soon as she could. Dale wanted to come but waved Ari off when she started to explain why it wasn't possible. "No, never mind. It's probably hard enough for Diana to get you in. But please, *please* keep me in the loop." Ari promised and kissed Dale before changing clothes so she would look more professional.

When they got into the building, Diana showed her badge to a doctor named Kalwar, a petite Pakistani woman who barely looked up from her tablet as she escorted them down the hall.

"No signs of sexual assault," she said, something Ari hadn't let herself think about before that moment, "but the woman has been through hell. Trauma on her shoulders, knees, hips, and bruises on every extremity. I believe she was held in some sort of restraining device for a very long period of time."

"Thank you, Dr. Kalwar."

They had arrived at a room with one police officer sitting outside the door, with another standing across the hall from him.

"This woman needs to be treated as a victim, Detective," Kalwar said firmly.

"She is, I promise," Diana said.

Kalwar nodded to her, glanced at Ari, and then moved off to deal with someone else's crisis. The officers recognized Diana but she showed them her badge anyway.

"Miss Willow needs a few minutes with the patient." The cop by the door reached for his radio, and Diana said, "No need for that. It's just to see if she can make the lady talk."

The cops exchanged a look. Door Cop shrugged and waved her in. Diana nodded to Ari and stayed in the hallway.

Milo lay on top of the blankets in a hospital gown, curled on her side with her back to the door, knees tucked up by her chest. She didn't lift her head when Ari came in but, when she walked around the bed, she saw that her eyes were open. They snapped toward the movement and Ari held up her hands.

"Hey, pup," Ari whispered. "You're looking pretty rough, here. You had us really worried."

Milo shuddered and stared. Ari crouched down next to the bed.

"Where have you been, Millicent? Where's Mom?"

Gwen.

Ari started to respond before she realized the word had appeared in her mind, like a memory of Milo's voice than actual speech. It was the same way she conversed with dogs and other *canidae*, but only when she was in wolf form. She risked taking Milo's hand, squeezing the fingers. Milo looked down as if she didn't understand the touch, but she didn't pull away.

"Milo? Are you in there?"

Confused, 'Ri. Scaredhurt.

"Milo, can you speak?"

Not like this.

Ari furrowed her brow and then realized what was happening. Milo's brain thought she was in wolf form. She'd never heard of it happening before. Hell, as far as she knew, it shouldn't have been possible. But if she could maintain a certain amount of control over herself as the wolf, then maybe the wolf could take over while in human form. She didn't want to think about what kind of trauma that might require.

"We're going to get you some help. I'm going to go see if we can get you to a proper doctor. Sit tight."

She started to stand, but Milo tightened her grip on Ari's hand hard enough to hurt. She pushed herself up on her elbow and stared hard at Ari with wide, terrified eyes.

Hunters. Here. Have Gwen.

Ari tensed. "I'll get you out of here."

Milo released her and sank back down onto the mattress. Ari reluctantly left her and went out to find Diana leaning against the wall. She straightened when the door opened, and both officers glanced up, clearly curious about their mystery patient. Ari mentally worked through how to say what needed to be said without giving away too much.

"She's been hurt bad. We need to get her to Dr. Snow."

"She spoke to you?" one of the cops asked.

Ari said, "She... made it clear enough. This place isn't going to give her the help she needs, and we need her to get better to find out exactly what's going on."

Diana nodded. "I'll see who we should talk to about getting her released."

Over Diana's shoulder, Ari saw Dr. Kalwar round the corner, eyes still glued to her tablet. She was walking with a trio of men, all of them in suits and a full head taller than her. Ari didn't give a second thought to the men until she started walking toward them and saw one of them jerk in surprise. She looked at him then and recognized him. His hair was shorter with a bit more silver in it than the last time she'd seen him, but he was otherwise unchanged.

Isaac Hayden.

"Take that woman into custody, now!"

Dr. Kalwar was frozen in surprise, looking at Hayden before she tried to figure out who he was talking about. Both of the uniformed cops rose, their hands instinctively moving to their holsters. Only Hayden wasn't frozen in place, and he ran toward Ari. She recovered from her shock just before he was in arm's reach. She shot her right foot out, kicking his leg out from under him. When he fell forward, she brought her left knee up and caught him on the chin. He went limp and hit the floor hard enough that his hands slapped the tile like dead fish.

"He wants to hurt Milo," Ari explained. "He's probably involved in whatever happened to her in the first place."

The officers drew their guns. She was relieved to see they were aiming at the other two men and not her. Diana also drew her weapon and looked at Ari.

"We'll cover you. Get her the hell out of here."

Ari ran back into the room. Milo was still curled on her side, but this time she sat up when she heard the door.

"Come on, Milo. We have to get out of here. Hayden's here."

Milo's eyes flashed and she bared her teeth. Milo patted her shoulder. A man shouted in the hallway. "Later. He has hunters with him. Diana is covering for us, but we have to go. Now. Come on."

Milo got off the bed and dropped into a crouch, her hands flat on the tile.

"Oh, come on," Ari muttered. "Seriously? You were walking upright when the cops..." There was another shout from the hall, followed by something heavy falling. "Never mind. Let's get the hell out of here."

They were almost to the door when Ari heard what sounded like cellophane wrapper being wrinkled. Diana called out, "Ariad~" but the word was disturbingly cut off before she could finish. Ari opened the door in time to watch her friend hit the floor. The two hunters were standing in the center of the hallway holding small black boxes like guns. Diana, the uniformed officers, and Dr. Kalwar were all lying on the ground. Hayden was on his knees, holding his nose with a bloody hand. He glared at Ariadne.

"I'm going to fucking kill you this time," he said.

"You want the gloves off, that's fine by me," Ari said.

Hayden jabbed a finger at Ari and shouted at the other hunters, "Take this mutt down!"

Milo launched past Ari, an arrow aimed at the nearest hunter. He fired his taser but missed, and Milo slammed him into the wall with enough force that it shook like an earthquake. His partner turned to help, and Ari took advantage of his distraction to jump on his back and cover his eyes with one hand. She reached down with her free arm to dig her fingernails into the back of his hand. He dropped the taser but managed to throw her off, spun on her, and shoved her hard against the wall. He pulled back to punch her but his body went rigid before he could follow through.

Ari looked down to see Diana, still lying on the floor and looking dazed, had recovered the fallen taser and fired it at her attacker. He collapsed like an axed tree, his head cracking against the drywall on his way down. Diana looked at Ari.

"Get her the hell out of here, Ariadne."

"You..."

"I'm a *cop*," Diana said, tossing her keys to Ari. "Take my car. Go."

Ari didn't fight her. Milo had her hunter pinned and was pummeling him, but Ari pulled her off. "Run, wolfie, run," Ari said. "We have to run."

Milo understood. She turned and dropped onto all fours before she darted off down the hall. It was hardly ideal, but Ari didn't have time to complain. Besides, she was moving faster than Ari would have thought possible given the awkward shape she had to bend her body into. Doctors and nurses came out into the hall to see what the commotion was, but they were too distracted by Milo to stop Ari as she shoved past them.

She unlocked Diana's car and Milo leapt into the backseat. It was disconcerting to see her move like a wolf while in human form, but she didn't have time to be freaked out by that. She started the car as Hayden came out of the building and ran at her. She was sorely tempted to run him over, but she didn't get the opportunity. He ran at the car but only managed to slap his hands against the door as she sped past him. She let go of the wheel long enough to show him her middle finger before she pulled out onto the road and turned right, tires screeching as she narrowly avoided a collision with another car.

Milo was on her knees to look out the back window. *Bad man. Bad dude Hayden. Has Gwen.*

"So Mom's alive?"

Alive. Gwen. Hurt. Alive.

Ari exhaled and felt the relief like an ice pack pressed between her shoulders. "Okay. That's... okay, I can work with that."

Milo stuck her head between the front seats and stared out the windshield. *What now?*

"Now I'm going to take you to Dr. Snow. I'll call Dale and have her meet us there." She grimaced and tightened her hands on the steering wheel. "And then, I guess we're going to restart the war with the hunters."

ABOUT THE AUTHOR

Geonn Cannon is the author of over fifty novels, including the Riley Parra series which was adapted into an Emmy-nominated webseries by Tello Films. He's also written two tie-in novels for the television series Stargate SG-1. He was the first male author to win a Golden Crown Literary Society Award for his novel Gemini, and he won a second for Dogs of War. Information about his other works and an archive of free stories can be found online at geonncannon.com.

Prize Fighter

Six years ago, professional boxer Max "Wrecker" Reszke lost control in the ring. One moment of blind rage puts her opponent into a coma from which she never woke. Though cleared of any criminal charges, Max hangs up her gloves and swears that she'll never risk losing control like that again.

Until one night, a chance encounter in an alley, a damsel in distress. Max leaps into action and saves the stranger. She soon learns that the woman she saved is actress Renee Lamar. Renee, anxious and paranoid about security, offers to reward Max's chivalry with a job as her bodyguard.

Max has nothing to lose by agreeing, but soon discovers Renee might be her own worst enemy. Half a decade after leaving the ring, Max faces a new fight that can't be won with fists.

The Claire Lance Series

If you are in the mood for a suspense filled action packed book that is sexually charged with strong female characters, and a captivating story, this one is worth it. - JL Good

Claire Lance is on the run.

For the past year, she has kept on the move, keeping her head down, keeping out of trouble. Until she reaches a tiny town in Texas and trouble finally corners her. Forced to take action to save another woman's life, she suddenly finds herself over her head.

Blood on her hands, forced to go on the run with the woman she was protecting or end up in prison, Lance finds herself forced to revisit the life she thought she had left behind and reopen painful old wounds.

2010 Rainbow Award Runner-Up: Best Lesbian Contemporary
2011 Golden Crown Literary Society Finalist: Mystery/Thriller

www.ingramcontent.com/pod-product-compliance
Lightning Source LLC
Chambersburg PA
CBHW070941190726
48292CB00004B/1290